Before Beltane

A Prequel to the
Celtic Fervour Series

Book Zero

Nancy Jardine

Ocelot Press

First Edition Nancy Jardine with Ocelot Press 2022

"The entire series is set firmly among the very best of early Romano British novels."
Helen Hollick Discovering Diamond Reviews.

Find Nancy Jardine online:
http://www.nancyjardineauthor.com/
Join Nancy Jardine on Facebook:
https://www.facebook.com/NancyJardinewrites
Follow Nancy Jardine's blog:
https://nancyjardine.blogspot.com/
Follow Nancy on Twitter: @nansjar

Nancy loves to hear from her readers and can be contacted at nan_jar@btinternet.com or via her blog and website.

Dedication

I dedicate this novel to reader/reviewers of my Celtic Fervour Series, some of whom commented that they would have liked more historical references to the late first century Roman Britain era in Book 1. I partially addressed this during the writing of the following books of the series, adding historical contexts within the stories, and in the additional matter added to the end of the books.

When different readers commented that they would have liked to know more about Lorcan and Nara before they meet in Book 1 of the series, I decided that a prequel to the whole series would whet their appetites.

Acknowledgements

I send an enormous thank you to my fellow authors in the Ocelot Press co-operative: especially to Sue Barnard; Vanessa Couchman; Cathie Dunn and Jennifer C Wilson. They give me endless help and encouragement throughout the whole writing process. They assist with beta reading and editing which is invaluable. Lending their expertise and advice comes so naturally to all of my Ocelot colleagues, and it's very much appreciated by me. It's so wonderful to have them with me along the publishing journey.

I also give thanks to my cover designer Laurence Patterson for designing the wonderful cover for *Before Beltane* which matches the other five books of the series. From my vague ideas, he has produced the perfect cover image for the story.

My thanks also to Bramble Graphics for the Celtic symbol that appears on the cover.

Contents

*In **Before Beltane**, the reader will find that the separate stories of Lorcan of Garrigill, and Nara of Tarras, are presented consecutively an episode at a time. Each separate event is titled with the name of the character involved in that episode. Both stories take place in early AD 71, beginning before the Festival of Imbolc (Feb 1ˢᵗ) and ending a half-moon before the Festival of Beltane (May 1ˢᵗ).*

Characters

Please note that I have attempted to add the pronunciation within ( ) and the meanings of the words within [ ], though different sources may vary across the internet.

Characters – Lorcan's Story:

Ailin *(aye-a-leen)* – Brigante chief [a rock]

Alaw *(ah-low)* – woman of Cynwrig's village [melodious after the river of same name near Anglesey]

Berwyn *(beh-oo-win)* – guide from Ailin's village [fair haired]

Bradwr *(bra-oo)* – warrior at Nudd's village [traitor]

Carn *(car-win)* – Tully's helper at Garrigill [fair and loved]

Cleuch *(cl-oo-ch the ch as in Scottish loch)* – farmer, on Garrigill territorial border [ravine]

Creik *(crake as in bake)* – chief [influencer; stony]

Cuinn *(kw-in)* – Venutius' warrior [wise]

Cynwrig *(sin-rig)* – Carvetii chief [high hill; friendly, charismatic]

Efan *(eff-fan)* – young lad at Stanwick [rock]

Hedrek *(head-rek)* – Carvetii warrior [tawny-headed]

Irala *(ee-ra-la)* – Chief Druid at the Sacred Groves

Kesar *(kess-ar)* – Venutius' warrior [small black one]

Lorcan *(law-r-kan)* – warrior from Garrigill Hillfort [fierce one; small fierce one]

Maran *(ma-r-an)* – druid at Stanwick [man of the sea; also warrior/knight]

Nudd *(nud as in mud)* – Brigante chief [warrior/knight]

Orlagh *(or-la)* – Ailin's wife [golden queen]

Thoft *(toff-t)* –Brigante chief at Stanwick [reliable]

Tully *(tul-ly as in dull)* – Chief of Garrigill, Lorcan's father [quiet or peaceable which he is not/ ironical use]

Venutius *(ven-yew-tee-us)* – King of the Brigantes: authentic name; [adventure; emotional; highly attractive]

Names of those mentioned but with little, or no, dialogue in Lorcan's story:

Arian *(are-ay-an)* – Lorcan's older brother, 1st born son of Tully [noble/superior/high-born]

Brennus *(brenn-us)* – Lorcan's younger brother, 4th born son of Tully [strong]

Cartimandua *(car-ti-man-dew-a)* – Queen of the Brigantes: authentic historical name [carti: chase; mandu: pony ?]

Delyth *(dell-ith)* – woman molested at Ailin's village [neat; pretty]

Eurwyn *(yew-uh-win)* – druid mentioned at Cynwrig's village [white/blessed gold]

Gabrond *(gab-rond)* – Lorcan's younger brother, 3rd born son of Tully [invented/ cheery]

Gweirmyl *(G-weir-mill)* – Lorcan's first hearth-wife [shy; modest]

Marsali *(mar-valley)* – Cynwrig's hearth-wife [pearl]

Mearna *(mer-na)* – Lorcan's young sister

Rhyss *(ree-s)* – Lorcan's young brother

Rigg *(rig)* – Chief of Raeden, Selgovae hillfort

Characters – Nara's Story:

Afagddu *(ah-vag-th-e)* – Hydref's abusive hearth-husband at Tarras [darkness]

Branwen *(brand-wen)* – acolyte [possibly raven]

Callan *(ca-lan as in car)* – Nara's father Chief of Tarras Hillfort [battle/rock]

Cearnach *(kerr-noch as in a Scottish loch)* – warrior at Tarras Hillfort [victorious]

Derw *(der-oo)* – farmer from Selgovae farm [oak]

Eilir *(ale-i-er)* – Hydref's daughter [alluring or spontaneous]

Fergal *(fer-gal)* – young guide at Tarras [valorous]

Hydref *(heed-rev)* –abused Tarras tribeswoman [autumn]

Iola (eye-oh-la) – Cearnach's hearth-wife

Meinir *(may-n-r)* – woman of Selgovae farm [tall/slender]

Nara *(nah-rah)* – acolyte; princess daughter of Callan of Tarras [happy]

Niall *(n-eye-al)* – Nara's brother [cloud/champion]

Owaina *(ah-wine-e-a)* – newest recruit at the nemeton [unknown/perhaps god name]

Rhawn *(rah-oo)* – acolyte [course long hair]

Swatrega *(swat-ray-ga)* – High Priestess of the nemeton on the Islet of the Priestesses [invented name]

Wynne *(win)* – priestess [white-haired]

Gaenna *(ga-en-na)* – Nara's young sister, mentioned only [fair and smooth]

Eachna *(ach-na)* – Nara's filly [horse/steed]

LOCATIONS
IN
BEFORE
BELTANE

SELGOVAE FARM

LOCHAN
OF THE
PRIESTESSES

TARRAS

NOVANTAE
BORDER

RAEDEN

SACRED
GROVES

GARRIGILL

NUDD

BLENNERHASSET

CYNWRIG

BRIGANTIA

STANWICK

MONA

EBORACUM

VIROCONIUM CORNOVIORUM

TRIBES
IN
BEFORE BELTANE

VOTADINI

SELGOVAE

NOVANTAE

CARVETII
SETANTII

BRIGANTES

PARISI

CORNOVII

ORDOVICES

CORITANI

ICENI

DOBUNNI

CATUVELLAUNI

Lorcan

An Avenging Warrior
Brigante and Carvetii Territorial Border

Lorcan of Garrigill mulled over the events of the previous evening as his horse plodded on towards the river-crossing. The path they travelled was frost-laden. It was brittle and sparkling in places where puddles in the dips had iced over, though a nippy spell around the time of the Festival of Imbolc was fairly predictable.

The visit he had just made to Chief Creik had not been as successful as he had hoped for. The chief had been reasonably hospitable and open-minded, but some of the village tribesmen had shown continued resistance to the latest circumstances that people, the length and breadth of Brigantia, had found themselves in.

"Lorcan of Garrigill! Is this not the finest of mornings?"

Startled by the call, Lorcan whipped up his chin and looked around him, acknowledging that his surveying of the area had been dire. The hailing had come from the line of alders and gnarled willows that lay ahead, close to the ford. Deep suspicion knotted in his gut when he recognised the speaker who stepped free of the trunk and other winter-spindly growth that had conveniently concealed him.

It was one of the more outspoken men around chief Creik's hearth.

The warrior pointed his spear aloft and shouted again.

"Look above! *Ambisagrus* smiles upon us. Our weather god is in a playful mood this morning. May the deities grant you a favourable visit at the next roundhouse you journey to."

In contrast to the scowls and barbs of the night before, the man's greeting seemed affable, the wide smile appreciative of the pleasant scene around them. Perhaps the tribesman had wakened thinking differently?

Giving the warrior the benefit of the doubt, Lorcan likewise addressed him.

"Aye, indeed, I am looking forward to that." He indicated the empty sack strapped around the man's back. "The day is good and clear for spying your prey."

When Lorcan's horse drew closer, the warrior's initial toothy-smile faded and was replaced by a single raised brow.

"You mean that my quarry will be easily seen?" The warrior's jaw tightened. Pure malice flashed, and the next words spat free of clenched teeth. "You are right about that!"

Lorcan only just glimpsed the man's handgrip flipping, before the spear hurtled towards him, like a thunderbolt from the god *Taranis*.

Pure instinct made him force his upper body sidewards, his arm flying up to protect his face. Almost sliding off the horse, it was impossible to avoid the spear completely. The sharpened point sliced along the edge of his palm before the spear careened on to thump the ground behind him. Urging Dubh Srànnal to leap ahead using knee pressure alone, Lorcan grabbed the mane and righted himself.

His attacker had turned tail and was sprinting away. Lorcan yanked his sword free of the metal scabbard that hung from his belt, but in a blink tossed the weapon across to his left hand, the sheer agony of his wound belatedly making its presence felt. His palm felt as slick as tallow torch brand, blood now flowing freely from it.

In a few horse-strides, he was upon the fleeing figure and with one wide sweep of his blade, he whacked the warrior to the ground. Though not intended to behead, the slice at the shoulder was forceful enough to make the man's flesh ooze free, and a deep-red stain spread onto the ground.

Leaping off Dubh Srànnal, Lorcan used the flat of his foot to roll his assailant over.

The warrior's furious glare berated him.

"My spear should have sung more sweetly than that, Lorcan of Garrigill." Huge gasps came Lorcan's way as the downed man persisted, attempting to scuttle himself backwards and out of reach using his heels. "The gods must favour you…because my aim is usually known to be infallible."

The warrior tried to raise himself on his uninjured side, his rant not nearly over. Lorcan kicked hard at the thighs below him, to keep his assailant prone.

More agonised grunts spat Lorcan's way.

"All supporters of that useless supplanter – Venutius – must be wiped from Brigantia," the warrior gasped. "Queen Cartimandua is still our ruler."

"Venutius is useless? You still think this even after all of the explanations that you heard last night about Cartimandua's duplicity with the usurping Roman Empire?"

Lorcan willed his temper to recede. The man below would not have the pleasure of riling him.

The warrior used his elbow to gain height, though managed to lift his body only a tiny bit before an eruption of frustration forced another collapse. The breath almost knocked out of the warrior, Lorcan was surprised when the man's harangue continued, the facial expressions still venomous under the agony.

"Your…persuasive visits to the hamlets around here… must be stopped!"

Thumping his left foot onto the man's stomach completely stifled a renewed attempt to rise. The resulting noises and pathetic squirms beneath him pleased Lorcan greatly, though the continuing conflict of opinions over who now ruled Brigantia created a deep disappointment in him, too.

The flash of the warrior's small knife, fumbled free from its belt sheath and thrust upwards, was a last frantic attempt from the downed man.

The spear attack was bad enough, but for the warrior to attempt a second wounding? That was beyond reason for Lorcan. The raising of his sword hilt-high above the man's neck was deliberate, and his words were equally unhurried.

"My death will surely come, warrior of Creik. Nonetheless, it will not be by your hand," he declared. "Of that, you can be certain."

He watched the eyes below turn from a ferocious glare to glazed over when he drove the sword-tip down into the most vulnerable part of the throat and all the way into the ground. A few frothy bright-red gurgles escaped, and then Lorcan heard nothing. A reedy blood-trail leaked from the warrior's mouth and slid down past his ear, to join the pool that slicked under his neck.

Lifting his fist free of the hilt, Lorcan was glad that those who did not know him had no knowledge that he could use his blade equally effectively with his right hand or his left.

Heaving with the exertion of the attack, he removed his foot and stood back, his newest injury smarting and stinging like a multitude of tiny burns from a sparking fire. He bent down to remove the sharp little blade from the front of his leg, but found his fingers were too slick with the blood flow from his wounded palm to get a proper leverage. Yanking it out with his left hand, he brandished it in front of him.

The wooden grip was crudely made, though the thin blade shone brutishly. Keeping the weapons of a dead warrior was the practical thing to do, yet a tumultuous loathing flooded Lorcan. Possessing the knife would be too much of a reminder of the deadly tensions amongst tribes he regarded as his fellow Brigantes.

Limping to the ford, he padded down into the knee-deep water. The eddying flow around him took on an even darker stain when he bent down and wafted his wounded hand in it. Tucking the warrior's knife into his waist belt to keep it out of the way, he fumbled with the rolling up of the leg of his woollen braccae.

On inspection, the incision near the bone just below his knee was quite deep considering the spent man who had wielded the blade; however, it was clean enough and he did not think it would not hamper his progress too much. He paused for a moment to allow the freezing water to swirl around his legs.

His palm wound was more debilitating. It was a long ragged gouge, and from experience he knew it would take longer to staunch the blood. He held it under the icy water till the feelings in his fingers almost disappeared. Stepping back to the riverbank, he grasped the strongest ferns and hauled himself out of the water.

Fumbling a painful fist-hold at the bottom of his checked woollen lèine, to hold the tunic material taut, he drew out the warrior's knife. After slicing off a couple of strips, he threw the blade down and wrapped one piece of cloth around his thumb and palm, tucking the ends in as best he could. The other strip was used to bind his leg. They were poor jobs, nevertheless, they would have to do.

Inhaling deeply, he raked around the ferns to find the knife that had all but disappeared. Raising his gaze to the blue above, he held the thin blade aloft.

"*Belisima* of the ford?" he cried. "This weapon did little damage to me, though, because it belonged to one who lived nearby, I return it to your folds."

Dropping the blade into the water might have been more reverent, and much easier to do, but the disenchantment and frustrated anger at what had just occurred had not yet dissipated. Turning up-river, he hurled the weapon as far as he could. The resulting plop when it landed beyond the tumbles and burbles of the low waterfall was a definite relief. He had no desire to see it any more.

He trudged back to the corpse and gave the warrior's leg one last kick, sending embittered curses to those Brigantes who were still inclined to cling to the past. He rocked his sword back and forth a few times to loosen it. When it plopped free of the ground beneath the warrior's neck bones, he raised the blade upwards, his gaze following.

"*Andraste*, my goddess, I thank you for protecting me and giving me the stronger arm. Believe that I did not seek to begin this particular fight, nevertheless I have ended it."

Looking back down at the inert warrior, he bemoaned such losses of men all over Brigantia. He did not know this person who had tried to kill him, not even his name, though doubtless it had been mentioned the previous evening by Chief Creik. The man was, most likely, well-loved and respected by his hearth-wife and his immediate family.

Remorse for what he had just done flooded Lorcan. There had been too much aggravation over ruler loyalties for many, many seasons and it had to be resolved. Frustration tore at him. He really had thought he had made some progress, however a corpse at his feet could never be termed a sign of success.

He swore to *Andraste* that he would never allow a similar incident to occur again.

For the briefest moment he debated whether to go back to Chief Creik's village, to inform the chief about the unwarranted attack and the state of the warrior at his feet, but he reasoned that was probably not wise. The warrior would eventually be missed and would be found – probably even sooner if someone else used the ford to cross the river.

His vow to help make Brigantia a realm at peace with itself had been made before Venutius, his king, though he needed to remain alive to fulfil it.

The persistent throb of his hand wound reminded him of the spear that caused it. As with the knife, his instinct was to leave the weapon where it lay, yet his practical nature nagged at him.

Grabbing a hold of Dubh Srànnal's reins, he plodded back along the pathway, seeking the glint of the spear-tip. It took him little time at all to root it out in the undergrowth, and grasping it up with his good hand, he felt the balance of it. It was a well-made spear. He had no need to check how sharp the blade-edge was: he knew that already. After another deep sigh and a shake of the head, he tucked the spear into the leather holder that was strapped around Dubh Srànnal's belly, alongside his own.

The vault back up onto the horse was a lot more difficult than his dismount. The life-force that had beat inside him, caused by the suddenness of the attack, had returned to normal. Nonetheless, once he was astride, he thanked the goddess *Epona* that his horse was well-trained and had not wandered away.

Grasping the reins in his left fist, he urged Dubh Srànnal on towards the ford. Unfortunately, the current was not strong enough to demand all of his attention as his horse paced slowly over the worn stones of the river-bed. A distraction would have been good to take his mind off the recent event.

He did not consider himself a violent man, but when his life was threatened he had no option over retaliation. Another profound groan whiffed over Dubh Srànnal's mane. The warrior who had just attacked him had not been his only assailant since he had begun his task for King Venutius.

Many of the tribes of Brigantia had changed allegiances during the previous winter, having eventually accepted that Queen Cartimandua was gone for good. Even Chief Creik had resigned himself to laying more of his trust in King Venutius, and had turned his attention to their common threat of Rome, rather than continue any antagonism against King Venutius.

Creik's avenging warrior had clearly not been of the same mind.

Having urged his horse up the far banking, Lorcan paused to properly scan all around him.

Something akin to a droplet of water slid down his backbone. He could see no-one around. However, the sensation that he was not alone was pervasive – though the unseen presence continued to puzzle him rather than cause him to be fearful. During the moons he had been moving from hamlet to hamlet on his undertaking, there had been similar occurrences. He was convinced it was not an unworldly presence that observed him, however, as before, he felt it did no harm to seek support from his most-revered goddess.

Raising his head, his plea was no louder than the merest whisper. "*Andraste*. Your command is greater even than that of King Venutius. Make me worthy of my task. I am not nearly done, though I have already faced many trials."

He was not sure that any of the gods or goddesses held him in high esteem when no signs appeared to show that they were listening.

Feeling successful was eluding him, so why should his deities think differently?

Nara

A Tricky Birth
Tarras Territory, Selgovae and Novantae Borderlands

Nara drew aside the tattered woollen draught-cloth, and then bent her head before she stepped out from the inadequate wattled entryway of the roundhouse.

The whole dwelling was becoming dilapidated. Though, when time was limited for maintenance, she knew that the hearth-husband had no choice but to tend to the livestock, and to turning over the ground when *Ambisagrus* – the weather god – gave him favour. She made plans to return sometime soon with some of the younger acolyte priestesses, to give help wherever they could with the basic upkeep of the house.

She raised her chin to appreciate the weak-warmth from the blinding orb above her which was getting closer to being directly overhead, where only a few scudding white tufts of sheep's fleece marred the immeasurable blue. It was so peaceful and serene.

Widening her arms and raising her palms to shoulder height, she intoned, "Blessed *Bel*, as your golden light rises every new day, may you always shine upon this place and shed warmth on all who dwell here, especially on the newest life within."

Allowing a smile of sheer satisfaction to break the tension that had been at her cheeks for a long while, she snatched a few deep and cleansing breaths, lowered her arms and just stood there doing nothing.

Late-winter winds nipped around her, tugging and tussling her thick woollen dress and her cloak, both of which hung to below mid-shin level. Despite that the gusts almost knocked her off her feet, they were a very welcome bother after the stuffy confines of the roundhouse that she had rarely left since her arrival the previous day. Grasping a curl of errant dark-red tresses, that tickled at her nose and chin, she stuffed them back behind her ear. Her hair had not been loosened and combed out for days, and more of it was escaping her long braids than usual.

Yielding to indulgence, she spent a few more moments reflecting on the support she had given at the recent birth process.

She decided that her manipulation of Meinir's belly and back probably helped, especially when the woman had been bearing weight on her hands and knees. When she had gently rubbed her hands over the mound many times, to help ease Meinir's pains, it had slowly shifted, though only the fertility goddess *Arianrhod* knew what was actually happening. Nara did not; however, it meant that eventually the head came out first.

The relief of that had been immense.

She swivelled back towards the roundhouse, lifted her hands again in supplication, though this time she bent her head.

"Please receive my heartfelt thanks, *Arianrhod*. I vow to use my newly-gained knowledge, should you allow me to witness similar circumstances on another occasion."

She remembered the time when, a few seasons past, she had stared helplessly when the blue-black feet of a babe were the first to slip free. Both mother and child had died, the blood loss worse than the famed battlefields that she had heard of in stories told by the druid bards. All she could do was to give her help wherever she could, and however she could. It was *Arianrhod* who gave some babes the ability to live and took it from others.

Her prayer ended, she turned around and smiled at the contented pastoral scene before her.

Nara had long ago recognised, and accepted, that birthing her own baby was not an experience she would ever endure. Promised to the priestesshood of the goddess *Dôn* from a young age, maintaining celibacy was never a problem. Yet, in all honesty, when her blood courses had begun signalling the onset of her womanhood, it had taken her a long time to learn to suppress the natural desires that had sometimes beset her.

But now she had the next best thing.

The goddess *Arianrhod* had granted her the privilege of witnessing a healthy babe being born to a woman of Tarras Territory. Though it would never be her own child, it was a moment of incredible joy that she looked forward to sharing in many more times in the future. The expectation of seeing new life appearing to swell the number of inhabitants at Tarras was something she was sure would never fail to uplift her spirits – whether she was still an acolyte, or a fully-initiated priestess.

The sounds of chatter in the roundhouse behind her interrupted her contemplations. The chirpy words of the lad near the door amused her since he had been almost silent for so long that morning.

"Nay, the priestess never did. She never stopped to eat, or drink, or even rest since she arrived. I do not even think she knew I was there. She spent the whole time tending to my mother."

Nara heard chuckles of soft laughter follow his protestations.

"Did you know that she is not a proper priestess?" asked the boy's aunt.

The lad's answer was vehement. "Nay! But my father said…"

"Your father is almost correct. Nara is a good as any of the priestesses at the nemeton, probably even better than most of them, but she still has to learn a little more before she is allowed to conduct all of the priestess rites."

Nara cocked her head, wondering what more was to come.

The boy's tone continued to be adamant.

"Well, I am sure that she is the best priestess that I know."

Nara squelched the chuckles that rippled her lips. The boy had probably never met any of the other priestesses from the nemeton.

A small sigh escaped. She could not deny that what the aunt said was true.

She had expected to take the final priestess rites in the sacred nemeton home of the priestesses when she was seventeen winters. Yet, for various, almost credible reasons given by the High Priestess, Swatrega, it had not happened, even though she was now twenty-one. Swatrega had claimed she was spending too much time conducting her duties as a healer which did not leave her enough time to properly worship the goddess. She had then tried harder every day to devote time to all of her tasks, though it had made no difference to her status. Another excuse was that she spent too much of her day away from the nemeton home, yet it was impossible to do all of her duties if she did not cross the linking bridge.

Nara had been bitterly disappointed at the time, but was now much more relaxed about it.

Taking those final rites would happen, when the goddess *Dôn* willed it.

Becoming a fully-initiated priestess would give her the authority to conduct the most important ceremonies; however, there were enough older priestesses who regularly did that. Her time was already well-spent doing what she was trained for, and she adored the variety of tasks that she performed every day. Being confined to the Islet of the Priestesses, as some of the higher-order priestesses usually were, was not a welcome prospect. She loved to be out there across Tarras Territory, helping in all sorts of ways.

Acolyte priestesses were taught how to observe and maintain the druid faith amongst the tribespeople. They learned many practical skills, and some of them had been trained in the healing arts, as Nara had. However, the range of Nara's skills had always been slightly different from most other novices.

As the elder daughter of Callan – Chief of the Hillfort of Tarras – she automatically ranked, by birth, as a tribal princess. Though being of that status had almost never made any difference to how she was treated at the home of the priestesses. In fact, from the moment she had entered the sacred nemeton, her title of princess had been laid aside, was rarely mentioned, and being Callan's daughter had only once made any difference to her priestess training. The children of a chief were instructed in sword-skills and warrior-training, but Nara had not expected that to happen to her.

At the age of thirteen winters, she had been summoned to the roundhouse of Swatrega, the High Priestess, where a small group of tribal elders awaited her. They had informed her that she should prepare to attend the training grounds the following day.

"Why does my father allow this to happen?" she had asked, stunned, and yet extremely excited about the news.

"Callan," one of the elders had replied, "does not wish you to have the opportunity. He is very much against the idea."

A second elder had added, "We, on the other hand, do wish you to have what is due to you as a princess of our tribe."

The honour had been hard-won. Young as she still was, Nara had realised that the elders had had to exert considerable influence to get Callan to change his mind. For reasons she could never fathom, her father had always disliked her intensely, and he had rarely allowed her privileges of any kind. She was only given the warrior-training because the tribal elders were more rigid in their pursuit of maintaining traditional formalities, and had forced Callan to give his agreement.

Once her warrior-training had been undertaken, it had then been a natural progression for her to take on the role of overseer of the defences of the Islet of the Priestesses. Being a healer, a trained-warrior, and a representative of the goddess *Dôn* was a strange mix of accomplishments. Nevertheless, Nara liked being different. She enjoyed using all of her skills as a priestess-in-training when she went among the folk of Tarras.

Whether it was a fully-initiated priestess or an older acolyte, the tribespeople of Tarras gave due respect to their druid leaders. They feared the power and the wrath of the goddess *Dôn* and, as such, her priestesses were not considered normal people. That was how it had always been and, Nara imagined, always would be.

Her future at the sacred nemeton was a life she relished. She looked forward to every new dawn and the challenges of every new busy day.

The sounds of someone exiting from the roundhouse behind her ended Nara's final moments of solitude and reflection.

"Oh, you are still here? I am just fetching some water. For my aunt."

Meinir's eldest son sounded apologetic, as though leaving the dwelling was an abandonment of everyone inside.

Nara's smile aimed to reassure. The little lad of not much more than six winters was exhausted but had struggled on.

"You have been very helpful to your mother," she praised. "Breathe deeply, and enjoy this wonderful fresh breeze provided by the god *Ambisagrus* while you fill the bucket from the stream."

14

She watched the young lad's worn-out nod. He sent her a weak smirk before he trudged off with the wooden bucket banging against his calf.

Up ahead of Nara, a handful of horses ambled around in the closest strip-field. A couple of others dipped their heads to the feed that was set out next to the wattled panels which enclosed a few snuffling pigs. Hens clucked and pecked their way around the muddy space between the animal pens and the roundhouse eagerly seeking and claiming anything worth swallowing. All of the creatures went about their daily business in a normal fashion.

Nara adjusted the hide sack that hung cross-wise over her chest and headed towards the open-sided stall where her horse, Eachna, was tethered.

The birth she had just attended had not been an easy one, even though Meinir had already delivered three bairns, stepping stones born less than two winters apart. The woman had experience of what to do, yet one thing that Nara had learned about childbirth – during the last seven winters – was that there was rarely any consistency about the process.

Generally, her presence as a healer was not required at a childbirth. Most women at the Hillfort of Tarras relied on a sufficiently-old-enough daughter, a female relative who shared the same dwelling, or a neighbour.

Meinir had none of those to hand when the birth pains had come upon her earlier than the woman had expected. The roundhouse behind Nara was an isolated outlying one close to the territorial border between the Selgovae tribe and the Novantae, and the nearest dwelling was some distance away.

Derw, the woman's distraught hearth-mate, had sought Nara's help when the regular agony had lingered from dusk till dawn on the first night of pains, with nothing to show for it. The three sons of the roundhouse were too young to be messengers, so, at the first hints of daylight the man had bundled the youngest two astride his horse. Dreading the worst outcome, he had left his eldest son to tend to his mother, and had ridden off to summon assistance.

"Derw?" Nara called, seeing nobody around. "Where are you?"

"Down here," came a soft reply. A tousled tawny-haired head slowly appeared, over the drystane dyke that enclosed the crop field, as the man unravelled himself. "I have been sitting here enjoying *Bel*'s heat and encouraging this little mite of ours to give me some peace." The youngest of his sons was struggling to remain awake in his arms, the little one's eyelids reflexively opening to stare wildly every time his chin drooped.

Almost immediately, the crown of another orange-brown head popped up shakily over the wall, the finger grips on the stones precarious as the rest of the upper body was revealed. The middle son's chin was well on the way to being scraped to shreds before he managed to get himself astride the wide stone wall.

Nara looked at the boy's anxious, pinched face and tearful expression. Having just passed four winters she knew him to be a talkative little lad from the previous day, yet he was presently too scared to ask the question that now came from his father.

"Is all well?" Derw asked. "With…both?"

"Aye, they live." Nara's simple words drew huge smiles of relief from father and son as she approached them. "This time the goddess *Arianrhod* has blessed you with a girl-child who may be very small, but she is as lusty as any healthy babe I have ever seen."

"I knew that being a daughter must be the reason," Derw said, "when the straining continued for so long."

Nara laughed, even though she was bone-tired. "Do not blame the timing on the fact of it being a new daughter. I have seen male babies take just as tortuous a route to entering our roundhouses."

"Aye, indeed. Some of my foals are not easily coaxed to show themselves either, however, they do not usually tax the mares as long as that new girl-babe has exhausted her mother." Derw joined in with her mirth, shushing the restless son in his arms into sleep, then sobered a little. "How fares my Meinir?"

Nara maintained a happy expression. In truth, it would be the goddess who determined how the mother and the babe progressed in the coming days. Women died during the process of childbirth, and some also succumbed in the days following.

"Both she and the babe sleep just now. Meinir is exhausted, though she will regain strength quickly now that her sister has arrived to help. Your hearth-wife may be tall and slender, as her name indicates, but she summoned the strength needed to eventually slip the babe out – even though the little one was facing the opposite way from the usual."

Nara chuckled at the memory, yet at the time it had been a fraught moment since the babe had taken so long to appear. She had not told Derw earlier that she had feared the breath would have been stolen from the child before its head appeared.

"You may think on that when you name your daughter," she suggested.

"I shall not be likely to name her the speedy one." Derw's mirth continued. "Still, I do take heed of your advice. Your presence has been invaluable, and none more so than during that desperate ride back here."

Nara untied the tethers before she vaulted up onto Eachna, acknowledging his comments with a nod. The poor man had been riddled with guilt, and had been panicked about leaving Meinir with only his oldest son's assistance for the time it had taken to fetch help. She sought to reassure him again that his options had been limited, and that she had enjoyed the frantic ride with his middle son in front of her.

"Your Meinir is a determined woman. She knew very well what she was doing when she sent you to fetch me. Her faith in *Arianrhod* remained strong even though she was being thoroughly tested. She was more resolute than you know about not leaving you to raise all four bairns on your own, and you can be very proud of your eldest son. He gave her good assistance, even if the responsibility was terrifying for him."

"Aye, he learns well." Derw's grin faded and his tone grew solemn. "I have already given my special thanks to the goddess *Dôn* and will do so regularly, of that you can be sure."

Nara sought to lighten the mood. Meinir was lucky in her hearth-husband. He not only provided the best he could for her and the children, but it was easy to see that his love for his woman was sincere. It was unfortunate that not all dwellings on Tarras Territory were similarly blessed.

"I have left some potions with Meinir's sister. They should help Meinir gain her strength back in the coming days and that, in turn, will benefit your guzzling daughter."

"If she resembles her mother then I will be best pleased." Derw's good humour was returned, his smile more relaxed. "Though I do not mean that Meinir is a greedy woman, except maybe when it comes to my attentions."

"In the name of *Arianrhod*, daughter of *Dôn!*" Nara raised her hand in caution, yet continued to grin. "Meinir will need your support, and will welcome it, however, not much more than that from you till at least a full moon and some more has passed. She has come through an ordeal that would have been far too much for many of our women."

"The god *Taranis* may strike me down with his thunderbolts should I do anything to harm Meinir. I know very well how *Arianrhod* allows new life to spring from the mating process."

Derw's words sounded humorous, yet Nara knew he had been unnerved by this latest birthing.

18

His three sons had come to Meinir so easily.

The man continued to speak. "The next foal bred from the dam – the one that you admired in the far field – will be sent to the sacred nemeton home of the priestesses. Eachna is as fine a filly as I have ever seen, but the one to come soon has a good sire and should make a prime horse. And, before you say it, Chief Callan of Tarras will still get the amount I agreed on for his horse pens, when summer comes."

"*Tapadh leat*!" Nara's words of thanks were sincere. "We will look forward to its arrival. You will have the heartfelt gratitude of all of us at our sacred home, since our horse stock is low just now."

She acknowledged that Derw could ill-afford to send a new horse to the priestesses. However, the man ran a competent farm, and if the gods willed it, all of his horses already in foal would deliver safely. Derw would probably have to work even harder than usual to raise even more new stock come the next spring season, yet Nara knew that giving such a gift was necessary to maintain the man's self-respect.

Derw's oldest son, though still a little lad, was already helping to tend the horses and the other livestock which gave them milk and eggs. And, the goddess willing, the other boys would soon be helping with some of the more basic chores.

"Can I go and see my new sister?" the middle son asked, looking a lot less worried than before.

Nara looked down at the eager little face. Derw had taken his younger sons from the roundhouse just after dawn, and had kept them outside, to allow Meinir to concentrate only on getting the babe born.

"Aye, you can." Nara bent down to him, hard put to suppress a grin. "Though you need to be quiet about it. Your mother needs her sleep, and if you wake the new baby then sleep won't happen because she'll howl so fiercely it will

19

rouse the people at Tarras Hillfort, never mind your mother."

"A girl can wail that loud?" The look of horror, mixed with a touch of admiration on the boy's face when he looked askance at his little brother, was worth the jest.

Nara chuckled again.

"Time will tell, but go quietly and do not pester your aunt when you enter the roundhouse. She is busy preparing you all some food."

"We will go together, my impatient son. I know where your priority will lie!" Drew's cupped hand at the boy's shoulder meant no further words were needed.

"Let the light of the goddess *Dôn* be with you," Nara chanted and then bid Derw and his sons farewell. She felt assured that Meinir's sister would take on the duties of looking after the bairns, leaving the man more time to tend to the farm.

She turned her horse in the direction of her home, the sacred nemeton on the Islet of the Priestesses of the goddess *Dôn*.

By the time Nara had crossed the desolate moorlands and had reached the shores of the small Lochan of the Priestesses, the god *Bel's* vast golden orb was slipping out of sight. It bathed the water in even paler gilt hues, with tendrils of light sparkling across the gently rippling water. The surrounding foothills were darkly-dappled, a myriad of browns and deep rust-reds highlighting the winter-burned shorelines. In amongst the brittle brackens, the denuded saplings and reedy tree trunks were light-filtered shadowy spaces.

"Home." She drew in an elongated, satisfied inhalation.

Though she was exhausted, the journey had been pleasant enough since the day had continued to be fresh and clear. Subtle knee grips halted her mare's plodding gait along the alder-bordered path close to the water's edge.

"Rest a while, Eachna." She gently patted the withers of her filly. "I would spend a few moments here."

If asked about a favourite place to be in all of Selgovae Tarras Territory, then this was definitely it.

The downy water's edge alders were sparse at this particular spot, allowing for the best place to view the priestess nemeton out there on the islet. Withered brackens and smaller dried-up ferns were still abundant in the undergrowth, the winter not having been bitter enough to shred them completely, and all too soon there would be a carpet of tiny blue blooms underfoot, though it was not quite yet that time.

A deep sense of satisfaction rippled through Nara as she peered through the purple aura of the catkins. Over the undulating, twinkling lochan water lay her home, and no matter how much time she spent in the dwellings of the tribespeople at the Hillfort of Tarras, or its surrounding territory, she loved returning to the priestess community in the sacred nemeton.

"*Rhianna*, my favourite goddess, I thank you for the scene before me. It never fails in making me feel so blessed."

A sudden, strident, and harsh wailing to her left drew Nara's attention as an impressive yellow-beaked bird, dark-streaked from its eye to the end of its long crest, fluttered up from the lochside. The grey bird hovered for a moment, as though waiting for her gaze to alight upon it. More of the *Cailleach* old-hag screeches were emitted before it wheeled away.

She watched the crone of winter glide gracefully over the shadowy waters before it flew off towards the hills. Nara's breath hitched, and held, when in the distance two more of the birds rose up from different hidings to join the first in a graceful circular dance. Swooping and swirling, their raucous moans eventually faded as their dark outlines twirled farther and farther away.

21

A frisson of satisfaction rippled down Nara's back. The signs were favourable. The guardians of the Otherworld had shown her that they had other places to be, and that the circle of life was continuing. It must mean a good future for the new-born babe that she had just left? Perhaps continued success for her fellow-inhabitants of the nearby cluster of priestess dwellings? Or some other auspicious beginning was being feted?

The creation of the nemeton, a tale of deep wonder, popped into her thoughts. The very first High Priestess of long ago had chosen the site of the lochan as being of sacred importance.

Nara giggled, her only audience being Eachna under her thighs and the chirruping river birds as they prepared to settle in for the coming cold night. The name Lochan of the Priestesses was deceptive, since it was not a small loch at all. Surrounded by four hills, the river that coursed along the valley floor was mainly fed from the north west. However, water from the many burns that cascaded down the hills had joined the river flow to nestle in an extensive deep hollow in the land. It had created a body of water that was large enough, and just deep enough, to make it seem like a sizeable lochan, even though a minor continuation of the river carried on southwards to the firth that made the sea boundary of Selgovae lands.

The original High Priestess had declared the small islet that had risen out of the swollen waters to be sacred land, and extra special. Flat-bottomed coracles had been used many times over to transport sufficient rocks and soil to make it artificially larger. It was a crannog island that had become big enough to construct a village of roundhouses at its centre. The crannog was truly blessed indeed. Since the initiation of the nemeton home, the supreme goddess *Dôn* had continued to ensure that the lochan waters never dried up, and flooding at the waters-edge was extremely rare.

Nara adored looking at the wonder of it.

Lorcan

Lorcan had been aware of the silent company since Dubh Srànnal had padded from the open moorlands and into the sparse woodland that bordered Carvetii territory.

Sometimes the beast appeared to his left and sometimes it was on the other side. So far, it had not come close enough to endanger him and he wished that to continue. He had no patience for confronting yet another enemy on the same day and no desire to unnecessarily kill the creature who shared the dwellings of the forest-god *Cernunnos* with him.

The cheery blue of the earlier post-dawn had been gradually replaced by a darkening, snow-laden heaviness above as he had journeyed westwards.

Presently, he allowed the light flakes to melt on his eyelashes, since to wipe them off – however slowly he may do it – might encourage the animal to come closer. More importantly, it would take his free hand off the leather reins.

If it was indeed a real wolf? He had not heard a single sound from it. Not a howl, nor the swish of a tail, and not even the tiniest pop of a hidden twig under the light-white blanket that was only just beginning to form and settle all around him.

But then, nothing else around the area made any noise, either.

It was not quite as bone-chillingly cold as it had been earlier while crossing the higher heaths. Yet, a dull ache at his nose lingered on from the prolonged biting conditions which almost rivalled the spasms of agony throbbing at his palm.

Perhaps *Cernunnos* of the forest had sent him a protector? In spite of his frigid cheeks, a derisive smirk widened Lorcan's lips.

"My thanks to you, *Cernunnos*, though a wolf shade would have been a lot more useful this morning at the ford."

His sarcastic huff broke the deadening silence that comes with snowfall. Not a breath of wind was to be felt, just a light fluff that fell from above through the well-dispersed trees directly down onto the rough track his horse tramped along.

Looking askance he realised the beast had, in fact, come closer. Now it half-crawled on its back legs, its mouth agape, though he had yet to see it properly bare its fangs. He knew from the first sighting that it was an old dark-grey, but enough snow was now clinging to its matted fur to make it seem like a mottled white one. In the weird-dim, with the feeble yellow light of the god *Bel* in a gradual wane high up above him, the wolf was the only creature around doing anything – apart from Dubh Srànnal who picked his way forward, every step anxious, head straining and alert to the potential danger.

Under his cloak, Lorcan shifted his injured palm against the soothing warmth of his middle. Nestling it just above his belt, he winced when his horse snorted again, the wound jarring against the hilt of his knife.

"Easy, Dubh Srànnal."

He awkwardly gentled his mount, his left hand rigid around the clutch of reins. He had suffered from much worse wounds in the past, but every movement brought fresh blood-flow to this latest one, the flimsy wrap he had twisted around it completely useless.

With careful movements of the finger-tips of his right hand, he plucked aside the leather loop on his belt that held his knife-sheath in place, to make more space at his front, all the while cursing his stupidity. He should have trusted his instincts, should have been more cautious but, while he had ridden along the riverside that morning, he had been concentrating on plans he needed to put into action as soon as possible.

"How could I have been duped by that sociable greeting?" The comment that barely whispered free of his frozen lips was enough to start another set of agitated splutters below him. This time he was less patient.

"Enough, Dubh Srànnal! You do not always have to live up to your black-snorter name. As soon as I can contrive it, you will be replaced."

He looked around for the wolf, though it had disappeared. It was still out there but was now so snow-encrusted it was no longer a visible antagonist, unlike the tribespeople who still felt such ill-will against fellow Brigantes.

For most of his four and twenty summers, the clashes between Queen Cartimandua and her divorced husband Venutius had been ongoing. Habits and allegiances had become so ingrained it was in the hands of the gods when the whole of Brigantia would be truly at peace. Unfortunately, the ending of Queen Cartimandua's dealings with the occupying Romans had brought new lethal threats to Brigantia.

One source of war was being supplanted by a different one. There were still chiefs among the Brigantes that he needed to persuade, needed to convince that the danger from Rome was far greater than a dislike of accepting Venutius as their Brigante king.

As his horse continued along the track, he looked all around again knowing that a wolf which was determined to trail its prey tended to keep abreast alongside. A lone wolf was not so unusual a sight. Its pack would be reachable if it chose to re-join them. However, if for some reason it had been banished from the group, it could be a very desperate beast.

This time it was Lorcan who snorted.

"At least the wolf probably has a band to go back to, unlike many of our druid leaders."

In days gone past, his current task would have been undertaken by a druid priest on a regular visit to a village. But since the legions of Rome had decimated the druid community when he was a small boy, the priests who still lived could no longer cover the huge expanses of Britannia in the old way. For that reason, King Venutius had provided helpers in the north. When recruited to the new band, Lorcan had vowed that he would not fail.

Right now, as he looked up through the tree tops at the waning daylight, he was in great doubt.

"*Bel*? Where has my reputed good judgement fled to? Do you play tricks with me?"

As on many occasions before, the gods kept their own counsel.

When his horse approached a gradual descent, into the shallow dip that led from the wood out onto the meadowlands, he heard the first low growls from somewhere close by.

So...the wolf had not given up on him?

The tiniest drips of snowfall sliding off a warm coat were enough to snag his attention. Though almost completely white-covered, Lorcan could see where the wolf crouched.

He drew in his knees urging Dubh Srànnal to halt, and sliding his cloth-wrapped hand free of his cosseting cloak, he dismounted. Hooking the reins over the withers, he freed his own spear knowing his wound would make using more than one impossible.

Repeated snarls from even nearer told him that the wolf's strategy had definitely changed. The stronger smell of his own fresh blood was perhaps more tantalising than the dead bird flesh that was stored in the pouches that were slung around the horse. Or, perhaps it was a last chance for the wolf to attack before the sparse woodland cover was lost?

Bared teeth now faced Lorcan from no more than the length of two horses, far too close for a successful spear throw. The half-crawl towards him was filled with intent to pounce, the eyes a ferocious gleam.

When he grasped his spear with two hands the pain of his injured palm was excruciating, yet one fist alone would not hold the irate creature at bay. He thrust the spear forward and pressed the blunt end against his middle, to strengthen the shaft.

The wolf held still. So did he while he sustained his stare of the beast. Anger was easy to produce, but the beast would not know who he was most angry with.

"*Andraste*! Lend me your strength again for this different test of foe!"

He was ready when the creature sprang up into the air. Propelling himself forward, his spear tip embedded itself under the beast's chin, in deep enough to dangle it at bay. The distance between them gave Lorcan just enough leverage to whirl the wolf's weight to the ground before the fangs could do any of their nasty tearing. One vicious kick, as the beast attempted to rise, was sufficient time for Lorcan to yank free his long knife. Too soon though: the creature's frenzied shaking loosened the spear and the animal prepared to pounce yet again, the howls and furious gleaming eyes mirroring his own.

The old beast was a determined adversary. Its teeth, though able to create many ripping tears, were no match for Lorcan's well-honed blade. He slashed and sliced, and eventually plunged the weapon into the beast's chest when it made another lunge at him. Both man and beast fell back onto the snow. Dark spatters flew all around them in the deepening gloom, but the wolf was the loser of the resulting, frantic tussle on the ground.

Lorcan struggled for breath. He was pinned down by the wolf's dead weight, and the hilt of his long knife digging in to his midriff was no help at all.

He stared at the wolf's muzzle. Its fangs were wrapped around his right arm, having made contact through his two tunic layers and thick cloak. Grunting and heaving, praying for sufficient strength, he used his shoulders and heels to force the beast aside, just enough for him to release his fist from the knife hilt.

"My thanks, *Andraste*!" he panted, easing himself free to squirm into a crouch, since only from that position was he able to prise himself away from the teeth that trapped him.

Struggling to his feet, he grappled around for his spear and summoning enough power, he launched it upwards. "I salute you all – *Andraste*, *Bel* and the mighty *Taranis*!"

The effort being too great to do anything more, he slumped to the ground. If the snow had not still been falling, he knew he might well have succumbed into a dead faint. All around him was totally silent again, as though the incident with the beast had never happened.

Apart from his success in triumphing over the fearless old wolf, he just wished that the gods would give him some other sign that he truly was following the correct path.

Dubh Srànnal's harrumphing and hoof stamping eventually stirred him to rise and find his spear.

Nara

The Goddess Will Provide
On the Islet of the Priestesses of Dôn

"Nara? Where are you? You are needed."

"There is no need to holler." Nara grinned as she popped her head out of the entrance tunnel of the tiny weapon and tools hut, a partially-sharpened adze in her hand. "You have found me."

Owaina, the latest of the new young recruits to the nemeton who had arrived only days before, was inclined to be over-excitable when charged with a task.

"Take a deep breath, then tell me," Nara cautioned. "Who sent you?"

Nara watched Owaina's upper body lifting from the crouch she had been in, the girl's chest still heaving from her scamper.

"There is a problem with the stored food. Something has gone rotten, and we will all starve."

"Nay, we will not. Have you not yet been told that the goddess will see that does not happen to us?" Nara's chuckles sobered. "Exaggerating will do none of us any good. What are your instructions after you deliver the message to me?"

Nara wanted to be sure that Owaina knew what to do next.

The blank expression that faced her was significant. She had already learned that Owaina tended to rush away after hearing only part of a conversation. Why the goddess *Dôn* had decreed that the young girl should be brought to the home of the priestesses was not yet clear to her. She could only hope it was understood by the High Priestess and was not a mystery for too long.

Nara calmly repeated her question. "Who gave you the order to find me?"

"I think her name is Wynne, the old white one."

Owaina's response did not fill Nara with confidence. There were not so many priestesses and acolytes at the nemeton to make learning their names difficult.

"Go back to Wynne and tell her I will be there in a moment. The message you bring me is important, but there is no need for you to create a flurry of leaves in your wake as though a fierce gale blows across the islet. You will knock someone over in your haste, and that will not do – especially if it is one of the elders like Wynne, whose old bones will not withstand your mistreatment."

A chastened demeanour dulled Owaina's expressive eyes, the girl's lips wobbling.

To avert another sobbing breakdown, like the one she had witnessed the previous day, Nara gently patted the girl's shoulder. "There are many lessons to learn here, Owaina. The first is that times when anyone needs to run around our sacred village are extremely rare."

A gulped nod and pursed lips showed that Owaina was trying to heed her words. Nara watched the girl wheel around before setting off with deliberately slow steps.

"Maintain that pace, Owaina," Nara shouted at the girl's rear. "All the way!"

Retreating back into the hut, she grinned anew. She had been at the nemeton so long it was difficult to recall how it had felt to be a new recruit, yet she truly believed she had not been as impetuous as Owaina. At the age of seven summers, she had come to the village of the priestesses. She was sure she had been a quiet and biddable creature, always willing to listen and learn.

She looked down at the still-blunt tool in her hand and smirked again, her words muffled as she bent down to pop the adze in the iron basket by the door which held the weapons and ironwork still to be sharpened.

"Though, maybe that is what I want to remember and not how I appeared to my mentors!"

Knowing that her overseeing of the sharpening of everything in the weapon store would need to wait, she set off in the direction of the small roundhouse that held the food stocks. Making checks of the smoked meats, the herbs for food consumption, and the grain storage was not her responsibility; consequently, being called to deal with an issue regarding nourishment was unusual.

Owaina was already out of sight, which meant the slow pace she had been set had likely not been maintained. The sacred village of the priestesses had one large central roundhouse which was the dwelling of the High Priestess Swatrega, though it was also their main indoor meeting place. Clusters of much smaller dwellings were dotted around within the perimeter wooden ramparts. Some of them were sleeping quarters, some were storage areas, and there were also some unoccupied buildings.

The current number of acolytes-in-training was much fewer than in former days when the nemeton had been created, and the number of priestesses was likewise reduced. Nara had learned that – around the time of her own birth – the druid base on the Isle of Mona had been overwhelmed by rampaging Roman legionaries who had left alive only a smattering of druids and priestesses to continue the work of the druid system. Now, most of the newly-initiated priestesses of the goddess *Dôn*, from the Islet of the Priestesses, went away to live in other tribal communities after their final rites were taken, leaving only a few to maintain the daily life of the nemeton.

As Nara passed one of the dwellings of the initiated priestesses, not yet the place she laid down her head at night, a voice grunted above a quern stone. The sound of the upper stone disc grating against the lower one halted.

"What is that unruly girl doing now?"

The oldest resident of the nemeton tutted loudly as she shifted her bottom, and splayed her knees into a better position for cradling the grain that she let loose to sift through her fingers into the hole on the upper grind stone. With the wattled wall of the roundhouse entryway supporting her back, the older woman grinned a mouthful of over-worn yellowed teeth.

"Why can that girl not realise we revere our sacred ground and do not pound it like a herd of terrified horses?"

Nara snickered. "Owaina surely is the terrified one. She fears that our food is so rotten that she will die of starvation."

The cackle that came Nara's way was one of great wisdom. "When that little girl has been here as long as I have, she will have learned that there are ways to survive a severe lack of food. I am not yet lifeless, though that young one may think I am well on the way to the Otherworld."

"Aye, and the goddess always provides for us, as well," Nara agreed. She had already been at the nemeton for two-thirds of her life. There had been times when food had been scarce, but the priestesses had always found ways to resolve a lack.

"I have difficulty believing that young lass has seen nine summers." The old priestess' expression was sceptical.

Nara sighed. "Then you will not like to know that she has already passed her tenth summer."

"So many?" The response from the old one was even more dubious. "In that case, you should tell the horrified Owaina how well your spear sings when you go on the hunt, Princess Nara of the bold blue eyes. Even better, take her with you on your next one. There can be no better time than the present. Do not wait! Teach her how you accomplish a successful hunt, princess, and get her trained early. I feel the urge coming upon me to taste some deer meat before my time is claimed by the goddess."

The old priestess' words surprised Nara. Had the goddess truly warned the old woman that death awaited her? Sooner, rather than later? And what was the rest of the conversation all about?

"The *Imbolc* festival is almost upon us. Will that be timely enough for you?" Nara asked, struggling to keep shock from her tone.

The resigned sound that followed was a mixture of a deep sigh and a huff.

"Aye, it will have to do. And, till you provide me with some succulent and well-fired deer flesh, I will produce sufficient milled grain at my quern stone for someone to make me small breads."

Nara watched the wrinkled hands, awkwardly twisted at the knuckle bones, begin the grinding once more. The old one's head dipped back to her allotted task, her conversation over.

After promising once again that venison would be the main fare at their forthcoming festival, Nara continued on her way, pondering on that one particular word used twice by the old one, and about the need for hurrying with hunt-training. The old priestess had never referred to her being a princess before, so why repeat it twice? And why now, given that she was also being urged to hurry Owaina's training? It would be many seasons before Owaina was ready to lift a spear.

Did the priestess truly know something that Nara did not?

Her princess status was so rarely mentioned at the home of the priestesses that it was a bit unnerving to hear it coming from the lips of the old one. Being the daughter of Callan was unimportant to Nara. Her life as a future priestess of the goddess *Dôn* was her everything. Nevertheless, she could not deny that she was the daughter of the Chief of Tarras – even if he was never interested in her, or her progress.

"*Ciamar a tha thu?*" Nara asked as she approached Wynne.

"Me? I am doing very well, Nara," Wynne answered, echoing the question. "And you?"

Nara's grin was rueful. "Like you I am very well, but I fear our newest recruit does not feel too contented just now."

Wynne huffed and puffed before she located where the hapless Owaina was, to stare at her. "That girl! She learns too slowly."

Nara waited till Wynne's gaze turned back her way. She wanted to agree to the statement, but it would be unworthy of her.

"Thanks to the goddess *Rhianna* that you have come, Nara."

Though Wynne was definitely the priestess with the most abundant long white hair, she was still reasonably sprightly as she beckoned Nara towards the grain pit.

A wooden container sat beside the stone-lid of the opened storage hole. Nara bent down to look at the contents at the bottom of the pail. The barley grains were definitely mouldy. There was a light fuzz over the top like the finest of sheep's wool, and the stink of poor-fermentation wafted up her nose, making her straighten up again.

"Is this drawn from the top of the grain pile?" Nara asked.

Wynne's shoulders rose in uncertainty. "I cannot be sure. The pit is fairly empty and the bucket is dragging whatever it can reach."

Nara did not bother to ask if Wynne had ventured down into the pit. The opening was wide enough for someone of Nara's size; however, Wynne was considerably wider in the hips.

"Come over here, Owaina," Nara ordered.

The girl reluctantly unfolded herself from her place under the overhang, the shelter that was created where the roof beams of the roundhouse overlapped the low wattled wall. Looking dubiously at the dark pit-hole, Owaina's eyes stared.

"The bottom of the pit needs to be checked to see if there is any grain that still remains fresh. It is a small space but you…"

Nara got no further. A horrendous wailing blast at her ears.

"Nay!" Owaina was terrified. "I cannot."

Before Nara could say another word Owaina had bolted, as agile as the young goats at the priestesses' main farming area over on the foothills. She sighed. The girl would have to be chastised, even punished if the High Priestess declared it necessary, but that gave Wynne no help right that moment.

"Is this not the older of our two pits?" Nara asked.

Wynne's small smile was full of resignation. "It is. The other one still holds fresh supplies, though Owaina has no knowledge of that, as yet. When she arrived to help me today, she took flight when I bemoaned the fact that the pit would perhaps have to be abandoned."

Nara worked through what had not yet been said. "So, Owaina assumed that we would all starve as that bucket of grain is mouldy?"

Wynne nodded, her expression more whimsical.

"Why did you send her to me?" Nara could envisage the scene quite easily, wondering yet again why Owaina had been thought a good candidate to enter the home of the priestesses.

Wynne almost doubled over, her mirth now uncontained. "I did not. That foolish girl has made up her mind that you are the only person on this islet who can solve problems!"

"Ah. A thoughtless girl, indeed." Nara looked down at the pit hole, a deep chuckle escaping that almost echoed back to her. "Then, since I am here, I may as well do what I can to enhance that wonderful reputation that I seem to have acquired."

She reached for the pin that held her bratt in place, whipped the cloak material from her shoulders and set it down on the ground.

Wynne wiped her eyes, her tears of laughter cast aside. "It will not be before time if we have to abandon this pit. It has served us well for many, many harvests since I came here as a young girl. I do not think you will tell me anything I have not already known."

A short while later, Nara had been lowered down by a braided reed-rope and was at the bottom of the pit. She allowed herself a small smile in the dim light that filtered down. Owaina had not even waited to be told that it was much wider at the bottom, and was not as confining as the girl believed. Checking a pit was not the most pleasant maintenance task, though it did not have to happen too often. Nara chuckled, her laugh echoing up from the stone-lined base. Either Owaina had a great fear of the dark, or an extreme dislike of insects. However, on seeing the girl's reaction, Nara believed it might be both.

It was too dim down below to see the condition of the barley, but she extracted some more from the remains that lay on the bottom and let them drift through her fingers.

"Send a clean wooden pail down to me, Wynne," she called, then added, "And after that, can you wind a lit brand around a rope and lower it? I would like to check the sides of the pit."

From touch alone, Nara could feel that the encrusted stone sides of the pit were not as they should be. The pit was slightly wider than the extent of her stretched-out arms when she stood in the centre, though one step from the middle in any direction had her fingertips touching the stone blocks that lined the interior.

"Take care," Wynne shouted down to her.

Nara's visibility gradually increased when a very thin reed torch was lowered down very slowly. Reaching up to grasp the rope-end, she snared the twirling torch brand and ensured it was held far enough away to illuminate the pit-sides without damage to herself.

After a thorough inspection of the pit sides, she looked up at Wynne's worried face which almost blocked the pit-hole.

"The bottom stones are much more damp than higher up the walls. The lowest stones no longer have their original tight fit, and watery soil seems to be seeping through the cracks. The grain around the edges is useless, but some in the middle might be saved."

"I had feared that would be the case." Wynne's voice sounded strained.

"Pull up the brand, and let it remain just above my head for a few more moments," Nara instructed. "While I fill the bucket."

Nara waited while bucket and brand were hauled aloft, then took a firm grab of the rope when it descended once more. Her feet braced flat on the bottom of the pit, she jumped to grasp the rope further up, knowing that Wynne was not strong enough to pull her up without help.

Moving fist above fist, she allowed the rope to slide past the dress material she was keeping wedged at her knees, and lower down between her leather-shod feet. Levering herself up, bit by bit, she edged closer to the opening.

A head still short of the top, Nara felt the first pinging splits of the rope where it lay taut over the pit edge. It sent her into a spiralling that she could do nothing to stop. The back of her head banged against the chamber wall, and her upper arm scraped a way down when the rope completely gave way.

Before she managed to draw breath she had hurtled down to the pit-bottom. Her landing was painful, one foot awkwardly bearing the brunt.

"Nara!" Wynne's panicked voice seemed far away. "Talk to me. Tell me you are not dead."

Banishing the feelings of disorientation, Nara was acutely aware of the heaving of her chest and the ridiculous urge to laugh. Sidling her bent foot from underneath her bottom, she squirmed around to a sitting position, the bunched up material of her long dress an encumbrance she could have done without.

"I still live," she called, finding the strength to holler to the panicked priestess up above. "Though I have injured my foot. You will need to ask some of the others to help haul me out of here."

As soon as her words were uttered, Nara became aware of other stabbing sensations, at places other than her upper foot.

"Do not move till I return!" Wynne's voice was receding quickly.

Nara allowed a weak smile to escape. She did not intend to move far, but she had to get onto her knees to inspect her other injuries.

In the dimness of the hole, she ran the fingers of one hand down the scraped arm. As suspected, the material covering her arm was damp. Gingerly feeling the lump at the back of her head also produced some stickiness, though the bleed there was not as bad as she had feared. However, the swelling was not the size of an insignificant hazelnut. It felt more like a goose egg.

Nara did not have to wait long on her knees. Two strong ropes were soon lowered down, the gaggle of priestesses up above not taking any chances of one fraying again.

It was a surprise to Nara when the voice of Swatrega, the High Priestess, drifted down to her. "Are your hands injured in any way?"

"Nay, they are fine. I can grasp the ropes."

This time all Nara had to do was to hold on tight once she had slipped her good foot into the loop that had been formed at the bottom of one of the ropes. The other foot dangled uselessly.

Gradually, the ropes were pulled upwards till her hands were level with the ground, where two of the strongest priestesses grasped her wrists, then her elbows, and hauled her free. They let go of her only after she had plopped free of the edge and her length was fully sprawled onto the packed earth that surrounded the pit.

When Nara rolled over onto her back, the face bending over her was that of Swatrega.

"I see that this test of the goddess has not overstretched you," Swatrega declared, her expression serious. "Though, be aware that the goddess will have many more tests for you soon, Princess Nara of Tarras."

Nara felt Swatrega's piercing eyes glide away from her, just like her bony frame, when the High Priestess turned back to Wynne.

Back onto her knees again, Nara took some deep breaths to adjust to the pains that now stabbed at her limp foot. After she had composed herself, she looked across at Wynne whose expression showed a hearty relief that she was safely out.

"What about the grain in that last bucket?" she asked.

"It is in much better condition than you seem to be. Not edible enough for us to eat, but our pigs will appreciate it well enough," Wynne said as she tipped out a little, so that Nara could see it.

While Nara was helped to her feet, Wynne gave Swatrega the news about the grain pit.

"Then I will ask the goddess *Rhianna of the Hearth* where to build a new pit. She will guide me. As will the goddess *Dôn* guide me over other new developments to come at our nemeton home." Swatrega declared before she walked away from the small group.

The excitement of the incident now over, the priestesses went back to their chores.

"What are you doing?" Nara asked, as Owaina pulled forward one of her arms before ducking under it.

"I will help you back to your roundhouse. Your foot is very swollen."

Nara looked down. The girl was not wrong. She sighed, knowing that hobbling back on her own would be a painful process, though she unfairly wondered if that would be better than the speed that Owaina would probably want to deliver her?

"*Tapadh leat*, Owaina." Her thanks given, she smiled down at the concentration across the girl's features. "Now would be a good time to be able to fly like a bird…"

She broke off her words on seeing the girl's face light up, her chuckles rippling till they were cut off short by painful throbs. "Though, since we cannot, let us go slowly."

Lorcan

When Lorcan awkwardly stooped to make his way through the entrance tunnel of the largest roundhouse in the cluster, he could hear the sounds of excited chatter. Fumbling aside the heavy fall of sewn skins that prevented the worst draughts from entering the large room, he stepped all the way in.

Many heads swivelled towards the doorway to see who entered, however there was nothing unusual about that. Lorcan, also, surveyed the company.

Cynwrig, chief of the small Carvetii clan who lived a short distance from the western sea coast, sprang up from his seat at the far end of the fireside. Intent on knowing who entered his dwelling, his announcement bellowed around the room.

"Who comes late to my roundhouse?"

The room quietening around the fireside, Lorcan pushed back the cloak-folds that were shading his face, a drift of icy snow showering down around him.

"Lorcan of Garrigill!" Cynwrig declared as he sped down the room in an amiable welcome. "It has been a while since we spoke together…" The chief broke off his greetings.

Lorcan absorbed Cynwrig's stare of assessment, yet he also watched the man's attempt to suppress the entertainment that laced his expression.

41

"I can see your journey here has had its moments, Lorcan of Garrigill. But, since you are still standing on your own two feet, you can explain your disorder to me later," Cynwrig quipped.

Lorcan absorbed the hearty clasps at his shoulders, knowing they were genuine ones, though winced when a new bruise was inadvertently thumped. His attempt to return the easy grins of Cynwrig – a man he was more than happy to name as a good friend in addition to being a reliable contact – was stiff and awkward, his cheeks frozen with cold and other traces he did not care to acknowledge.

"Your timing is not the greatest, my friend, since we have already eaten the best of our meal, but my hearth is yours for as long as you need it to be." The chief made his declaration before he accepted the snow-clad spears that Lorcan held forth in front of him, the tips purposely pointing towards the roof timbers and displaying no threat.

"There is a story to come about one of these." Lorcan kept his volume low.

His information made Cynwrig smirk again. "I can well believe that."

Also receiving the sword in its slippery metal scabbard, Cynwrig plopped the weapons into the half-empty iron rack, at the side of the door. Lorcan then felt himself being urged towards the fireside.

"With the conditions sent to us today, by the god *Ambisagrus*, and whatever else has befallen you, I am thinking that your stay might need to be longer than you planned."

"Aye. Time will tell about that." Lorcan was slow to slide free the pin of the circular bronze brooch that held his cloak together at his shoulder, his fingers so chilled that he could feel almost nothing. "I thanked your local god *Ialonus*, many times, that he had seen fit to allow me to almost reach you before this snow started to drop down on me in earnest. It is just as well that I can recognise your local landmarks, even when a white blanket almost disguises them."

He stopped speaking to swing the ice-encrusted wool off his shoulders, taking care to keep it from showering onto his host. "Thankfully, *Ialonus* also kept at bay squally winds, otherwise my arrival might have been completely thwarted."

A raucous bellow from Cynwrig showed his agreement. "My favoured god favours you, then. Are you come to tell me that those Romans have yet another new emperor?"

"Nay." The smile that broke free was a painful one for Lorcan. "I am not at all sure that would be good news for any of us."

Cynwrig's soft fist to his shoulder was predictable. "Ah! You disappoint me, my Brigante friend. It would be amusing, though."

Lorcan stamped his sodden leather-clad feet free of the snow that was melting quickly. The heat inside the roundhouse being considerable, the drips were absorbed into the floor brackens. He had enjoyed his previous visits to Cynwrig's dwelling, but he was even more deeply grateful to be inside the home of a friend after his eventful trek. "I think, Cynwrig, that you are more likely to have important news for me."

"Take the cloak, Alaw," Cynwrig ordered.

At the chief's beckoning, a young woman came forward to shake his woollen bratt free of icy snow before she draped it over one of the wooden racks next to the iron weapon basket.

Looking at the tattered cloak she tutted a welcome, adding, "When this dries, Lorcan, I believe some hearty repairs to it might keep it from falling apart." A quick look at him had her adding, "And perhaps the rest of your clothes, too."

The humour behind her words was not lost on Lorcan. "Then, I will thank you in advance for that, Alaw."

He returned what was now a full-blown grin till she noticed his grubby blood-soaked hand wrap. Shaking her head she continued the tutting, "Tsk! It looks as though other parts of you will also need the use of a fine bone needle."

The name Alaw meant nothing to Lorcan. She seemed vaguely familiar, nonetheless he could not be sure that she was the woman he had coupled with on his last visit. Cynwrig had plied him with so much of his strong honey-brew, he could barely remember anything that had happened when he had wakened up alone the following morning.

He dropped the bag of provisions that he had removed from Dubh Srànnal after the outer guard of the settlement had verified who he was, before his horse had been led away to be tended to at the communal covered enclosure. He had been only just managing to clutch the drawstring with his injured hand. Squatting down, he rummaged through it, his fingers now tingling. Removing a cloth-wrapped package, he stood up again to formally hand it to Cynwrig.

"This seems a poor offering since I have been travelling around for more than two moons. However..." Lorcan broke off speaking to smirk again. "Your horse-handler will by now have given over a pair of *coileach-fraoich* for the cooking fires – those fat, colourful birds that I know you love to savour. I slew them on the black-slicked moors this morning, on my way to your Carvetii territory. Despite the injuries you see, my sling shots flew true."

Lorcan grinned at the disbelieving expression on Cynwrig's face.

"Then, I will give the gods full credit for your success!" Cynwrig's laugh rumbled. "I have never yet known your aim with a sling to be so fruitful, though...your sword skills?" Lorcan again felt the chief's assessment before another smirk appeared on the man's face. "They used to be impressive."

"And they still are!" Lorcan stoutly defended his reputation.

Cynwrig acknowledged the boast with a short dip of the head, his blue eyes ripe with amusement. "Mmm…allow me to doubt that till later when you tell me everything." The chief folded back a corner of the parcel of nuts, berries and herbs and nodded his thanks. "We welcome any and all additions to our stocks, and your birds will be a tasty bite when they come to us already cooked."

Cynwrig turned aside and handed the bundle over to Alaw who hovered near the doorway. "Find something warm for Lorcan to eat, and then get what you need to tend to him."

Lorcan accepted the hastily-filled crudely-fashioned wooden beaker that was pushed into his hand before he was urged to sit down on the vacated log-stool next to Cynwrig, the previous occupant now settling onto another one further along the fireside.

After a public welcome and an introduction to the tribespeople who sat around the warming flames – some of them visiting from other small Carvetii villages – he realised he already knew a few.

Lorcan drank greedily from the beaker before he set it down on the floor rushes and then reached for the wooden bowl that Alaw held out, her re-entry to the roundhouse very swift. Filled with a thick barley broth, the appetising smell called to his grumbling insides. Cradling the bowl between his thighs, the roughly-torn-off piece of bannock that she also gave him was dipped into the soup with pleasure, and the food quickly devoured while Cynwrig continued to speak.

"I hope you bring me some good news, because these surely are troubled times," Cynwrig declared. "This small settlement may no longer be a safe place for my people. Less than a winter day's walk from here the Roman usurpers are building a fort at Blennerhasset."

Lorcan swallowed the last piece of soup-laden flatbread before speaking. "This is news to me. I heard that they had set up a small encampment, but that was before the winter season was upon us." He hesitated, waiting for confirmation from the chief. When a nod followed, he continued, "I do not understand this. Roman troops usually spend the winter moons in their southern fortresses, gathering their strength for a new onslaught when spring warmth softens the ground."

Cynwrig rifled his finger-tips through the light-brown hair that covered his upper lip. "Aye. That was what I was also led to believe, however, those *Ceigan Ròmanach* pigs have returned already. Hedrek..." Cynwrig broke off to point to one of the men who sat at the opposite end of the fireside, someone Lorcan did not know from before. "Hedrek's village lies close to that camp. He saw them out chopping down trees just days ago."

Lorcan raised his voice over the sparking and crackling of the substantial fire, so that all would hear. "Are you sure they gather wood for building, Hedrek, and not for their cooking fires?"

Hedrek's laugh was scornful, though Lorcan could not quite decide if the malice was directed at him.

"During any season, would you scour the woods for tall, straight trunks of oak and birch, mark them with something light-coloured like we use to make our hair ready for battle, and then have groups of men fell only those chosen trees – just to be used for firewood?" Hedrek said.

"Nay. What they do sounds purposeful." Lorcan nodded down to Hedrek, a red-headed man who looked to be only a few summers older than he was, before he turned his attention back to Cynwrig. "What more can you tell me about this camp that will soon be a fort?"

Cynwrig beckoned the man with a curved open palm. "Sit down at this end, Hedrek, and tell Lorcan everything you know about this work."

Having made his pronouncement, Cynwrig settled back on his seat, took some long pulls from his wooden beaker before signalling to a serving girl that it needed a refill. A swift reshuffle went on while Hedrek took the vacated stool three places down from Lorcan.

A short conversation later, Lorcan realised that Hedrek was the most knowledgeable about the Roman fort-building, though a few of the other men and women at the gathering added some details, here and there, to clarify what was definitely news to him.

"This latest Roman emperor has wasted little time in instructing his troops to cross into Carvetii tribal lands," Hedrek said, his fiddling with a thin wand of dried willow between his restless fingers resulting in a loud crack.

Lorcan felt the force of the man's full attention on him before a remnant of the stick pointed his way.

Hedrek continued, "It was only a few seasons ago that we learned of the turmoil amid the Roman leaders across their empire – I mean when you Brigantes were conducting your own civil war against each other, to get rid of Cartimandua and reinstate Venutius."

The anger emanating from Hedrek was palpable, but Lorcan reined in his temper and let the man rant.

Hedrek's stare was unwavering, his words accusing. "And now legionaries, from a fortress they name Viroconium Cornoviorum, are building a fort just slingshots away from my village."

Cynwrig interrupted. "I had hoped that Romans fighting against each other would mean their legions stationed to the south of here would leave us in peace. Yet, that is not what is happening."

Lorcan knew the chief referred to the rebellions amongst the Roman legions who were stationed in Britannia. As his father's emissary, he had been at many firesides where those gathered had roared with laughter on hearing about the quick succession of hapless Roman emperors who had followed the unpopular one named Emperor Nero. Rumours had abounded about men called Galba, Otho, and then Vitellius.

None of those three had retained power for any time at all before they were killed, by supporters of the one next-in-line.

The local tribal chiefs that he had visited had fervently wished that the Roman leaders would keep on bickering so much amongst themselves that they would completely destroy their Empire, and halt the relentless invasions of Britannia.

But then came Emperor Vespasian.

Unfortunately, Vespasian had now been in command of the Roman Empire for longer than the previous three put together.

"What matters to us now is that we already know Emperor Vespasian rules with a tight grip, and is not likely to be ousted so easily as his three predecessors." Lorcan's answer for Cynwrig was tinged with the deep regret that was common to the Britannic tribes who had not yet been absorbed into the Roman Empire. "I have heard many rumours about what Emperor Vespasian proposes for our northern lands."

"You Brigantes need to settle your own differences first, because what your traitorous Queen Cartimandua did affects all of us around these shores." Hedrek's deft fingers flicked one part of the broken stick at the flames, setting up a cascade of bright orange sparks.

Lorcan decided then and there that wariness would sit on his shoulder till Hedrek proved himself as a firm ally.

Cynwrig jumped in quickly to soothe down ruffled feathers. "Hedrek. Squabbling at my fireside will not help us right now."

Lorcan felt the chief's gaze turn to him.

"Have you any more news about Cartimandua?" Cynwrig asked.

Lorcan shook his head. "The rumour that went around after the battle two summers ago gets stronger, yet there is still no proof that Queen Cartimandua was escorted southwards by Roman legionaries and was housed in the Roman fortress at Londinium, before setting sail for Rome. She is, supposedly, held as a guest rather than a prisoner, but her consort, Vellocatus, is not with her. He has also disappeared without trace."

"How you can still name Cartimandua as Queen is far beyond my comprehension." This time, Hedrek tossed the last splinters of the twig at the burning logs from an open palm, where they made almost no impact.

Lorcan had an inkling that it was only out of respect for Cynwrig that the remnants were not fired at him. He swallowed down his drink, using the back of his hand to rough away some foamy drips from his stubbly chin, the skin there kept free of the long whiskers that bordered the sides of his jaws, the beard style favoured by most men of the north.

Hedrek may have been done with the twig, though he was not finished with his gripe. "For most of my growing years – no doubt much like your own, Lorcan of Garrigill – Cartimandua's dalliance with the lure of gold made her a Roman plaything, and less of a warrior queen. It galls me to the depths of my innards to think that she may now be living freely and comfortably in Rome."

"Do you know she is definitely in Rome?" Lorcan asked Hedrek.

Hedrek tossed back the dregs in his beaker. "Nay, I do not. But if I were you, I would be seeking information from the Parisii of the eastern coast. That tribe has long been dealing with the forces of Rome, almost as much as your Cartimandua was. What I heard was that this present Roman Governor of Britannia – the man named Bolanus – bribed the Parisii to ensure she boarded a boat on their eastern shores, after that last battle with your King Venutius. The vessel may have been bound for Londinium, or perhaps directly to Gaul."

Even though Lorcan felt riled at the resentment Hedrek continued to show against him, he was also impressed with the man's persistence.

"True, or not, that last battle between Venutius and Cartimandua was close to our last *Samhain* festival, and the weather during that season is rarely favourable for sailing. Perishing in the wild seas of the god *Manaan* would have been a fitting end to her."

Lorcan was not inclined to defend Cartimandua, his allegiances for years having been given to her ex-husband King Venutius, however he felt that things still needed to be said.

"The bribes Cartimandua received from Rome, over many seasons, were undeniably substantial," he acknowledged, setting down his now empty beaker. "But if she had not made her agreements with the Romans when I was a growing lad – after they invaded and settled in the lands of the Catuvellauni – our mutual northern tribal lands would have been invaded by Roman legions well before now."

Lorcan was not surprised when Cynwrig picked up the empty beaker he had been given and indicated that the serving girl should refill it.

Cynwrig's tone was firm when he spoke. "You have to concede that is true, Hedrek. Cartimandua's status as a colluding client-ruler kept the Roman legions from despoiling our Carvetii territory, purely because we lie so close to that of the Brigantes."

Hedrek grumped.

Lorcan felt the man's penetrating light-eyed stare boring into him. He was feeling drowsy from the warmth of the room, the food and the drink. Exhaustion was creeping in, and his concentration was also hampered by a renewed throbbing of his wounds. Nevertheless, Hedrek's confrontational attitude, he decided, was just one more trial he had to conquer that day.

"What stance does your King Venutius currently take?" Hedrek pushed even more. "Does he now oppose the Roman Empire with a vehemence that will take him to war against them?"

Lorcan snorted. "Aye, he does! Venutius is done with internal warfare. I can assure you that the *Cèigan Ròmanach* turds are now his only quarry."

He felt Cynwrig nudge his elbow before his re-filled cup was given to him.

Lorcan held up his beaker before he made a heart-felt declaration. "Then, let us drink to the end of Queen Cartimandua and to the success of King Venutius, who wants to cleanse all of our northern tribal lands of the Roman usurpers."

Cynwrig seconded the announcement and then changed the topic, turning his attention back to Hedrek. "Tell Lorcan your other news, about the Roman advances near your village."

Hedrek's lips twisted to the side, his brows furrowed. "Did I mention that some horsemen from a cavalry unit arrived at that camp? The Ala Augusta Gallorum was the name passed on to me."

Lorcan swallowed down some more of the small-bere before he acknowledged Hedrek's information. "I have heard of them. That unit was originally raised with men from all over Gaul, though who knows where they get the riders from now. Recruits are scooped up from all across their empire to fill up spaces in Roman cohorts, including from tribes who used to be our southern brothers of Britannia. If the complete Ala Augusta Gallorum is intending to settle at that new fort, then there will eventually be hundreds of them."

Hedrek's head dipped, just the once, but decisively, his expression grim.

Lorcan continued. "You will be seeing them gathering wood for many days yet, especially if their progress is halted by today's poor weather. We must give our thanks to the weather god *Ambisagrus* for not making it too easy for them."

Cynwrig took another long drink, and then gulped it down. "If this Ala Augusta Gallorum is so busy building their fort, it should keep them from invading my village."

Hedrek's guffaw was derisive. "Not necessarily. The soldiers doing the tree-felling are from the Legio XX. They were sent up from their fortress in the lands of the Cornovii, the one they name Viroconium Cornoviorum. It was legionaries of that same unit who built the camp defences two seasons ago, not the newly-arrived Augusta Gallorum cavalry who are the ones now patrolling all over Carvetii territory, every single day. And an informer from the south tells me there are even more foot soldiers of that Legio XX making ready to march up here!"

Nara

Sensitive Solutions
Hillfort of Tarras

A few days later, Nara limped her way along the path near the inner perimeter wall of Tarras Hillfort. She drew her calf-length woollen bratt tighter around her middle, keeping her fingers tucked inside the material's folds, for more warmth. Chilling gusts blew fiercely, buffeting her almost off her unsteady feet. They whipped up tufts of reeds and brackens newly-blown from the roundhouse roofs and dusty earth from the pathways.

She did not know what was worse – the wind bitter at her cheeks, or the fine grit that got under her eyelids and made her eyes stream.

She had just been to visit one of the older members of the tribe whose incessant and rattling cough was disturbing the other kin who shared the roundhouse. The thick mixture she had prepared, made with honey and the little blue plant that she named all heal, would be a temporary measure to soothe the irritated throat, though she knew it would not solve the old woman's main problem. Taking her last breaths seemed not far off for the tribal elder. Yet, that would only happen when the goddess willed it.

Till then, Nara considered it her task to ease the situation, in any way that she could. The family being profusely thankful for her help made her limited efforts so very worthwhile.

"Do you come to see my mother?"

The expression on the face of the young girl who ran towards her, Nara thought to be a very anxious one. The flimsy piece of material wrapped around the little one's head and shoulders fell far short of being good enough to give proper protection.

She bent down to be at eye-level with the child, to put the little one at ease.

"Nay, but I can if you wish me to."

"Will you?"

Nara felt her insides roil. It was not the first time that she had visited Eilir's roundhouse, and it appeared that the situation there had not improved. "Has your mother sent you to lead me to her?"

The lips of the child wobbled. "Nay. I am to tell nobody about her new bumps and bruises. But I remember who you are. You helped her before."

Nara willed her rising temper to cool. It was clear that the mother was trying to keep her condition unknown to her neighbours. Since Eilir was already uncomfortable, she did not want to do anything that would make the child more uneasy.

"Is anyone with your mother just now?" She kept her question casual.

"Nay. If you do not count the bairn."

Nara suppressed a smirk. The girl she was talking to had barely passed four summers, though was well able to maintain an easy conversation about her little brother. She allowed Eilir to lead her.

"Did you fall off your horse?" The little girl made her point by hobbling alongside.

Nara chuckled, she had thought her riding prowess was known by all. "I definitely fell, but not from my horse. But you can help me to walk better, if you tuck yourself in under my cloak."

Scrawny little arms snuggled around Nara's waist and although it was more of an agony to get into a walking rhythm, she suffered it gladly in order to give Eilir some shielding as the first raindrops fell to accompany the squally wind.

She gave an abbreviated version of what had happened to her as they took a different pathway, aware that the child was taking a long route to her house.

"The point to learn from my story is that you must never take it for granted that a rope is a good one. Always make sure that everything that you use is checked very thoroughly, and do it yourself."

Nara chortled even more when Eilir launched into a long tale about having to do far too many things for her brother, the story lasting all the way to the roundhouse while they tripped more often than walked.

"You know a lot about how to look after the baby. Perhaps the next time I visit you can show me what you do for him? *Tapadh leat,* Eilir!" Nara's thank you was rewarded with a beaming smile from the little girl when they reached the doorway. "I will not need your help any more, but if you think your mother does not need you to do other chores just now, then perhaps you could go and find a friend to play with?"

"I will!"

Needing the child to be out of the roundhouse for only a short while, she undid the pin at her shoulder and pulled off her cloak. Bending slightly she doubled up the material before draping it across the girl's shoulders.

"But come back very soon. I will need my cloak when I go home."

Eilir's smile was infectious before she darted away, her words soon lost to the windy gusts. "I will not stray too far, and will not be lo…"

"I know," Nara agreed.

She knew well how much the little one liked to wander around the hillfort, but she also knew that the responsibility of wearing an acolyte's cloak would have the child return quickly. Perhaps even sooner, since the children of Tarras would likely not linger outside, if the chilling rain turned to sleet.

As she bent her head to enter the roundhouse through the wattled entryway, Nara made her presence known.

"Hydref?" she called. "I was visiting nearby and wondered if I could rest a while with you?"

The reply to enter was muffled.

Nara smiled as she hobbled in to the interior, making more of her foot injury than it really deserved.

"What happened to you? And why have you no cloak on? The day is a bitter one," Hydref asked, after she turned around, attempting a welcoming smile that Nara could immediately see must be a very painful one.

Hydref had untied her braids, her thick and curly brown hair hanging loose at her cheeks. The attempt to cover her condition was a failure, since the chin-bruising was too extensive to hide.

Nara answered the second question. "Young Eilir needed the bratt more than I do just now."

"That one is always running outside to evade her chores."

The pursing of Hydref's lips indicated that the woman knew very well that the excuses for the child being outside and poorly clothed were feeble.

Nara flipped her hide pouch round to her side before she gingerly sat down on the wooden stool indicated to her, then told the tale of her foray in the grain pit.

Hydref's smile this time was a genuine one, though excruciatingly brief before her head dipped. She used one hand to shush the baby back to sleep, the little boy having roused at the sound of voices.

"I thought that priestesses of the goddess were immune to the hurts that befall the rest of us," Hydref said, her expression somewhere between being unsure and quizzical when she looked up.

When confident that her baby – lying coddled close to the fireside heat – was back to sleep, Hydref collected and filled a beaker from a tub at the fire's end. Nara could not fail to see the awkward handling as she accepted it.

"*Tapadh leat*," she said, holding it up to acknowledge her thanks. "Not at all. I can have bruises just like you have, though mine are acquired from very different situations. Accidents do sometimes happen."

The appalled look on Hydref's face troubled Nara dearly. She kept her tone low and without judgement. "Will you let me tend to you?"

Nara waited when Hydref looked away, the poor woman's shoulders as taut as a sling string ready to fire a prepared stone. After taking a few stressed paces towards the back of her roundhouse, Hydref abruptly turned back.

"Since I am unable to hide my hurts from you, I will be grateful for your help."

Nara looked at the bruises that decorated Hydref's comely face, marks that had nothing to do with any ceremonial achievement, and the wrist that was being cradled. She gulped down the remainder of the brew before she set the beaker on the floor rushes. Standing up, she examined Hydref's visible face-bruising up close before she tenderly checked the hurt arm that the woman held out. After a little manipulation, which clearly distressed the woman, she declared, "I cannot be sure that there are no bone breaks, but you do need to cradle this wrist properly for it to heal well."

Drawing her pouch from her shoulders, she set it down on the floor and rummaged around in the full contents.

"I need a small bowl," Nara said, confident that Hydref could carry it with one hand.

The tribeswoman scurried off to the pile of utensils set at the side of the room amongst an array of iron tools.

Nara selected roots of the comfrey plant from her little bound parcels and some dried leaves of the same, sniffing them to ensure they were what she wanted. Her next venture pulled free a little cloth-wrapped bundle of dried yarrow leaves.

Accepting the bowl and a wooden grind-spoon from Hydref, she added the comfrey roots and leaves, and then rose to her feet to trickle in a tiny amount of water from the water bucket that sat near the doorway. While she pounded the mixture, she teased out the circumstances which led to the beating.

"I was spending too much time feeding the baby." Hydref's list of excuses rang hollow. "I was not available when he wanted me. I allowed the children to be too noisy."

Other feeble reasons tumbled out, but Nara knew that they were mostly unwarranted. The hearth-husband, Afagddu, was known to have a foul temper, and was a man inclined to pick a fight with anyone who looked at him the wrong way. Though the woman could not bring herself to ever call him at fault, Nara let Hydref pour forth her feelings. That was much better than the woman allowing them to fester inside.

When the mixture formed a thick paste, she pulled out some cloth strips from her copious bag and applied some of the mix to one of the strips before she used it to make a firm wrap around Hydref's wrist.

"Should I look at other bruising before I use this length to support your wrist?" Nara, again, attempted to keep judgement from her tones as she held up a wider piece of cloth.

Hydref's chin dipped down, her words a muffled embarrassment. "I cannot see it, but my back is also painful."

The skin on Hydref's back was pitiful to view after Nara lifted up the dress to shoulder height. Old and healed lacerations were crossed with new weals. The only fortunate thing that Nara could see was that they were not as deep as earlier ones, the latest having only barely-broken the skin.

The bruising, and the skin soreness, that she could see on Hydref's breasts and nipples might have been caused by the baby's strong grip...or by Afagddu.

Instinct, and experience, had guided her to prepare more of her salve than was needed for the wrist. She used most of what was left to smooth over Hydref's back, and the last traces of the paste were gently applied to the woman's jawbone and to her cheek.

The nipple cracking would take more than one solution to improve the situation.

"I will make sure it will not happen again," Hydref vowed, "And then you will not need to tend to me another time."

Nara guessed it to be a fervent hope on Hydref's part, but she feared it might be in vain. While Hydref allowed the man to share a hearth with her, it was very likely not the last beating she would receive.

Lifting the emptied beaker from the floor, Nara scooped hot water into it from the small cauldron that hung bubbling over the fire. Removing some of the dried yarrow leaf powder from her little package, she added it to the steaming water.

"Drink that when it is cooler," she instructed, pointing to the beaker.

"Aye, I will. If it is what you gave me before. it helped to dull the pain." Hydref's expression was full of gratitude...and guilt.

Nara patted the woman's shoulder, a part she knew was not bruised. "Does Afagddu like the small-bere left longer than usual to become a stronger brew?"

It was more of grunt than a huff that reached Nara's ears.

"Not really, he will drink it any way it turns out. Though too many beakers of it do not help with his tendency to be annoyed."

Nara busied about with tidying her sack, looking for a particular small cloth wrap. It was one of her most precious supplies – ground seeds from the thunder flower, the very bright red bloom that was plentiful in summer in the eastern reaches of Tarras Territory.

After locating it, she handed it to Hydref. "When you next give him a drink, add a pinch of that powder to his beaker. It has a soothing outcome and might calm his displeasure."

"Only a pinch?"

Nara smiled back.

"Aye. It has a strong effect and you need only a little, but if he is still resistant and still angry, you can try some more the next time."

"It is only for him?"

"Definitely," Nara said, ensuring a firm tone.

She knew that it might help ease some of Hydref's present pain, but the woman had the children to look after and could not afford to be drowsy at the wrong time.

"Do not add it to your brew pail: only to Afagddu's beaker."

"I will do as you say."

She was glad to see that Hydref was mellowing towards the idea of making living in the roundhouse a more pleasant experience.

"I have some other suggestions that you might like to try regarding keeping the bairn happier, which in turn will also keep your warrior happy, too."

Having been in lots of roundhouses at Tarras over the many seasons of being an older acolyte, she had learned things about how a woman might maintain a happier relationship with the man who shared the roundhouse. They were strategies that had nothing to do with any of her healing potions – and ones she would never need to use herself as a celibate priestess – but were approaches which she had been told were successfully used by other women.

"Nigh on thirteen moons, I think," Hydref answered, when questioned about the age of the baby.

"Perhaps it is time to wean him? That might help with the bruising and the soreness at your breasts?"

Hydref's cheeks reddened. An answer in itself, but the woman nodded as though resolved. "Aye, the babe has always fed well. Though he now sups some thin oat brose."

Nara had always known the baby to be healthy enough, though he had a fretful tendency, possibly due to the mother's anxiety. She was pleased when Hydref agreed that an early weaning might be beneficial, though only the goddess *Arianrhod* knew if it would make Hydref's breasts withstand the treatment meted out by her man, rather than the baby.

The conversation ceased when Eilir erupted into the roundhouse, barely able to speak as she gulped in some breaths. "He is coming!"

Nara's felt the girl's panic.

"I ran really quickly, priestess. You still have time to get away." Eilir dropped the bratt at her feet and scurried towards the back of the room.

Nara's smile was a rueful one. Little Eilir had forgotten that her foot injury would not make it easy to dart away, but, on the other hand, she knew that she did not want to hurry off. It was more important to show her support of Hydref to the man who had caused the hurts. She readied herself to leave, though was in no particular hurry when she dipped her head to sling her pouch across her chest. Lifting up her pale green bratt, she draped it across her shoulders, pleased to see that it had not suffered too much from the girl's dragging it over the soil.

Nara stood her ground when Afagddu strode into the roundhouse.

The man halted on seeing her, a momentary fearful glint flaring in his eyes, but it was quickly suppressed before he turned threateningly towards Hydref.

"What is the priestess doing here?"

Suspicion dripped in his every word.

"Hydref has been very hospitable while I rested for a short time," Nara stated, unwilling to be unnerved by the glares that he threw Hydref's way.

"The priestess has a sore foot," Eilir chipped in, though Nara noticed that the little girl remained at the back of the room.

"Then you had no other reason for being here?"

Nara thought Afagddu's tone was a forced one, his attempt at being pleasant failing miserably. She also noted the man could not look at her properly when he turned towards her.

"Not quite!" Her little laugh was mirthless. "I could not fail to notice that my healing skills were required. Again." She paused and forced his attention. Fury was rumbling at Afagddu's cheeks, and she could see his arms tensing at his sides.

"Oh, you will not use them on me." Nara pointed to his fists that were readied for punching. "And neither will you use them on Hydref in my presence, and – if you have any sense at all – not after I go, either."

"You will leave now!" Afagddu bellowed.

Nara was not afraid of his intimidation.

"You can tell me to leave and not return, but that is not something you can easily say to the goddess *Dôn*. She has you in her sights and she watches every move you are making."

She watched his face pale, the tiniest tremble at his neck no longer of fury, but of fear. "You will not know when, or how, the goddess will exact her retribution, but if you mishandle Hydref again, you can expect the wrath of the goddess to befall you every time you waken in the morning."

As she limped towards the doorway she let fly another barb. "If you have trouble with your sleep, then know that the goddess will never let you rest until you properly care for those who look after you. I can, and I will, make sure that the goddess knows of your misdeeds. Know that I speak the truth!"

Nara could only hope that Hydref could gain some peace while she healed. While she made her way back to the main gates of Tarras, where Eachna was tied up, she whispered some prayers. "Heed my pleas, *Dôn*. The woman needs all the help you can give her."

Standing beside Eachna, Nara prepared herself for the piercing aches that would come when she launched herself up onto the horse. When she was astride the filly, it came as a big surprise to feel no pain at all. And while she thought about it, she realised that she had not felt any nipping at her foot all the way to the horse pens.

"Goddess *Dôn*? You work in mysterious ways, indeed." She gave even more thanks. "If I pretended earlier today that my foot was sorer than it really was, then accept my regrets. And make my salve work speedily on poor Hydref. She needs your benevolence more than I do."

By the time Eachna was in the nemeton animal pens and she was half-way along the walkway to the crannog, Nara was convinced that the goddess *Dôn* had given her quick healing for some very good reason.

Her smile wide, she entered the gates of her home.

Lorcan

Lorcan suppressed the oaths he wanted to spit out. It was not Hedrek's fault that the news carried an even greater threat.

"Is this something that can be proved and is not just hearsay?" He did not even make any attempt to soften his tone.

Hedrek once again swivelled to glare directly at him. "I would not dare to doubt the word of the person who brought me the news, but if you wish to challenge him then that is your choice."

Cynwrig soothed the Carvetii warrior's ruffled feathers, holding his hand up before Lorcan could respond. "Hedrek. This antipathy from you is unjust. I have never known you to be so offensive. You could have told Lorcan that the information came from our druid brother Eurwyn, and not have him need to ask for proof of it."

Hedrek looked at the fiery flames for an intense moment before a deep sigh escaped.

Lorcan could see that the light-blue eyes turning to face him were no longer so aggressive, but were definitely deeply troubled.

"Should the rest of the Legio XX arrive at that new fort, my people will be swamped. A whole legion of soldiers, I have been told, could number more than five thousand men." Hedrek's voice dipped despondently, as did his chin.

The rippling confrontation that Lorcan had felt brewing between himself and Hedrek lessened when Hedrek tendered an almost apology.

Lorcan nodded his acceptance of the warrior's regret. "When did the druid visit you?"

"Two nights ago." Hedrek replied, though the warrior was back to staring at the flames in front of him. "Eurwyn was in a hamlet near the fortress of Viroconium Cornoviorum when he was given the information. A tribesman of the village supplies pigs to the food stall that lies outside the fortress walls. He claims to have overheard talk of plans being made for the bulk of the Legio XX to move out soon."

Lorcan smoothed down the thick hair above his top lip with the thumb and forefinger of his right hand, a habit he had acquired when his beard first grew in, but found it sticky and matted. He took a quick glance at his fingers and realised they were the blood-encrusted culprits. "Did Eurwyn say when that might be?"

Hedrek shook his head.

Lorcan turned to Cynwrig. "This is really disturbing news. The Roman legions usually stay in winter quarters till their festival of trumpets has been celebrated."

"Festival of trumpets?" Cynwrig cawed. "What does that mean?"

Lorcan became aware of Alaw stopping just behind him, a large wooden bowl of gently-steaming water cradled in one arm and a bundle of cloths in the other. Another young girl carried a wooden beaker which she held out to him, a warm honey-brew from the tantalising aroma wafting up to him.

He smiled at the girl, and accepted the offering. "I doubt I will need too much of this to make me sleep soundly tonight."

After a nod from Cynwrig, Alaw knelt down, near his injured palm, and laid the items on the bracken-strewn floor.

Without a murmur, Lorcan felt her take hold of his wrist before she began to unwrap the filthy piece of cloth.

"Alaw is a good healer. She will tend to you without disturbing our talk," Cynwrig assured. "Now, tell us what you know of this festival, my friend."

Lorcan balanced his elbow on his leg, and let Alaw clean the wound, suppressing the pain-laced winces when the removal of the dried-blood pulled away lumps of ragged skin.

Focusing his attention on Cynwrig, he shared his knowledge of the Roman customs, information gained at the fireside of King Venutius. "If any of you have ever witnessed a Roman cohort marching out, then you will have heard their instruments sounding a call that is something like our own battle carnyx."

Cynwrig laughed again. "Our carnyx is much better than these Roman trumpets you speak of!"

"Aye." Lorcan was pleased to agree. "Ours are indeed, though we rarely have more than a few of our high-tubed horns at a battle site. The Romans, I am told, have a small trumpet for each cohort. And each cohort responds to the sounds of their own trumpet."

"How can that possibly be? I was told that a cohort could be hundreds of men." Hedrek stared again. However, this time, it was interest that prompted it, his brows raised in inquiry.

Lorcan knew his attempt to smile was more of a grimace, his back teeth clenched so hard they were likely to shatter into small pieces. Alaw was wielding a fine bone-needle and was drawing the ripped pieces of his flesh together.

"This time, Hedrek, I have to be honest," he gasped, his front teeth now clenching into his bottom lip like a startled hare on the moors when the stitching continued. "I have never yet gone to battle against our common Roman enemy. Though, I am assured that the soldiers respond to particular sounds made by their own cohort trumpeter. One sound might mean the men should all retreat, and…" He broke off to draw a deep breath. "Another might urge them to group themselves closer together. Roman soldiers obey every order issued to them, even when made by a metal instrument."

An older warrior further down the fireside was quick to scorn. "I doubt those Romans retreat very often. Our southern tribal neighbours have not been able to dispel them."

Cynwrig quickly suppressed the resentment that began to burble before Lorcan felt the chief's attention turn back to him. "Tell me more of this Roman trumpet festival."

Lorcan looked around to gain the interest again before speaking, inwardly willing Alaw to finish with her torture. He used the back of his free hand to wipe away the sweat that continued to form on his forehead and dripped down his temples. He was belatedly realising that his hand wound was a much worse gash than he had thought.

Willing himself to answer the question, he set his focus on Cynwrig, his words tumbling out.

"King Venutius knows a lot about Roman habits. He said that…before the beginning of winter…the legions usually stop their campaign battles against their enemies. They hunker down in their wooden fortresses during the poorer weather when it would be more difficult to live under leather tents. They use those moons to ensure all armour and equipment is in perfect condition for a new campaign season, though they still continue with their battle training. The *Tubilustrium*, their festival of trumpets, is a type of purification celebration, an acknowledgement that all is ready for renewed battle – men and equipment."

"Does this cleansing and renewal happen at the same time as our festival of *Beltane*?" someone shouted, from the second row of the gathering.

"Nay, I think it is more than one moon before *Beltane* when it is celebrated, though after the spring season is properly underway." Lorcan answered in the direction the question had come from, although he had no idea who had asked it, just relieved that Alaw had eventually finished her stitches and was wrapping a clean piece of cloth around his palm.

Cynwrig's hand gestures meant the gathering should listen first before slowing down the information sharing. "So, you think that the Legio XX will not move out till after their *Tubilustrium* festival?"

"I did not say that." Lorcan shook his head but immediately regretted the movements. He could not really confirm anything, since he was now feeling light-headed. "Their festival is old, as old as some of our own. Tradition keeps it aflame. Each legion may celebrate in their own way. Or perhaps the commander of the Legio XX does not keep to tradition?" Since nobody interrupted he found himself babbling on. "From what the druid Eurwyn said, it sounds as though the Roman commander has not waited for their *Tubilustrium* festival to be over, before organising the beginning of their new invasion campaign."

Hedrek raised his hand slightly to add some more information, ensuring Cynwrig could see it. "Eurwyn also mentioned that there may still be problems with discipline in the Legio XX. The druid says that the unrest still rumbles from some seasons ago, when that legion declared their allegiance to the previous emperor – the man who was named Vitellius."

One of the elders at the fireside chuckled heartily, "Since the emperor is now Vespasian, the Legio XX clearly made a mistake and did not choose the best man."

Different whispers rippled around the fireside. Lorcan could see that not all of those present in the roundhouse understood the complicated scheming it took to become emperor of the Roman Empire. It had taken him a long while to grasp many of the details, so he was not surprised they were confused.

Cynwrig held up his hand for silence. "Lorcan. Explain to them again, slowly, about all these men with such similar names. Especially about the two called Vitellius and Vespasian, so that we do not have more confusion and interruptions."

Lorcan nodded, and then tried to clear his head. "Like Hedrek says, the present emperor is named Vespasian."

He paused to make sure all were listening, fleetingly thinking of the many times he had already explained the complications of becoming leader of the Roman Empire. "I heard at King Venutius' stronghold that when the Roman Emperor Nero died nobody had been named as his successor. That caused great confusion and left the powerful men across their Roman Empire scrabbling around to nominate the next ruler. To stay in position as emperor means gaining the support of most of the legions, as well as having the backing of the men of the Senate in Rome."

Some eyes staring blankly at him made Lorcan pause to explain the Senate of Rome. Though, in truth, he was not actually sure if he was the only one who was unfocused.

"Are they similar to our tribal council of leaders who make final decisions for us?" asked one of the elders at the fireside.

"Aye, I think they are just like them," Lorcan agreed before continuing. "Someone...I cannot remember who...told me that there are more than five and twenty legions spread across the whole of the Roman Empire. That means a lot of commanders to decide who to give allegiance to. Vespasian was not everyone's favourite before he was put in place as emperor, but he has had enough legions maintaining their support for him."

Cynwrig interrupted, looking at Hedrek. "So, it seems, the Legio XX gave Vitellius their support but then they found it was not enough to keep him in the place of power. The problem now is that some of the Legio XX are arguing about having made that choice?"

Lorcan answered, "I believe what Druid Eurwyn means is that it will take more persuasion for the complete Legio XX to give Emperor Vespasian their sincere and full backing."

Lorcan noted Hedrek's enthusiastic agreement.

"Exactly that!" Hedrek declared. "Eurwyn also learned that a new commander is due to arrive at the Legio XX's fortress at Viroconium Cornoviorum."

Lorcan scratched the itching behind his right ear with his cleaned thumb tip, entangling his long, tuggy side-braid even further. "If a new commander has been sent, it might be to ensure better loyalty to Emperor Vespasian."

"Are you saying that some legions do not immediately give commitment to the new emperor? How can that be possible, Lorcan?" Cynwrig sounded confused.

"The Roman Empire is huge, and many of the legions – like the Legio XX – are stationed far away from Rome. It takes some time for news to travel and for things to be sorted out."

Though Lorcan shared the details, he was not entirely sure if he had made the conclusions himself, or if he actually had heard someone else voice them.

As he recounted more of what he knew of the complex situation, he tried to ignore Alaw. She was tending to his right ear and adding even more of her painful stitching. It felt as if she was re-attaching his whole ear to his skull, and it was smarting like fury, making his eyes water. The spear of his assailant that morning must have sliced off more of him than he had appreciated. Though, perhaps the wounds were the work of the wolf?

Her mild chuckles tempted at his ear, but he was not in the mood to appreciate any humour about his condition.

Turning his head slightly he whispered, "*Dè thu a dèanamh?*"

"You ask me what I am doing?" Alaw asked. "I am tidying your mess."

Her answer tickled, her lips being so close to him.

He felt her fingers undo the leather cord before she rifled through the braid at that side. Low giggles increased when a shimmering of his almost black hair fell onto his outer tunic, some of it snagging on the thin silver torque that encircled his neck.

He brushed the hairs away, and cleared his throat, having lost the continuity of his thoughts. "Err...indeed. The emperor named Galba was a brutal leader."

Cynwrig chortled. "Is that not a good thing for a commander to be?"

Lorcan returned the laughter. "Aye, though not if it gets you killed by someone you think is your friend. Otho had Galba assassinated after only six, or maybe seven, moons because Galba did not choose Otho as his successor."

Alongside Lorcan, Alaw was having difficulty rolling up the sleeves of his two tunics, her attempt to get at the scratches and teeth marks on his arm thwarted by the bunching material.

Her breath huffed at his newly-cleaned ear. "You need to take off the top tunic."

"But did Otho not become emperor after Galba?" someone asked.

"Aye," Lorcan replied, unable to stifle a small startle when Alaw slipped behind him and urged him to raise his arms, before she deftly pulled off his top tunic. She was well-practised. He did not even try to suppress a grin when those around him did not even blink. The loss of the heavy woollen tunic was not a problem: he was already overheated.

Summoning back his concentration he added more details, feeling almost like a bard telling the tribal stories.

"Otho was only emperor for about one season. Then came Vitellius, supported by legions like the Legio XX; however, he did not last long either. Vespasian proved to be even more powerful. He had the bulk of the legions across the empire in his firm grasp, and the knives of a number of Vespasian's soldiers ensured Vitellius was killed."

Cynwrig chuckled. "So, an emperor needs to have the obedience of most of the legions to stay in power?"

Lorcan nodded. "It appears so, yet it also seems to take the support of many powerful men in Rome to ensure an emperor keeps his throne. I think the current Emperor Vespasian must control many of those influential men."

"If the Legio XX's favourite was Vitellius, does that make them an untrustworthy legion?" Hedrek asked.

"I am not sure I am the one to answer that question," Lorcan said. "You all know how many Brigantes still favour Cartimandua, though in reality she is gone and Venutius is our king. Loyalties can linger and can be so difficult to relinquish."

Cynwrig nodded sagely. "Your words ring true, Lorcan."

The sigh that escaped from Lorcan was, in many ways, inevitable. "More than thirteen moons have waxed and waned since Vespasian became emperor. Any Roman legions who still do not give him their full allegiance must be very foolhardy."

Alaw was now dabbing at the wounds on his arms made by the wolf's fangs, clucking at the state he was in as she wielded her bone-needle a few times more. He broke off to stare at his arm.

"Do not fear," she chuckled, "Your inked star-brand of the Brigantes is still intact."

The stings of her needle were sapping his strength, and he suppressed the longing to just lay his head down to sleep.

"What of the other legions in Britannia?" Cynwrig asked.

"Vespasian is favoured by the Legio II Augusta. They are stationed in the territory of the weakling Bodvoc of the Dobunni tribe." Lorcan's words were broken off by someone interrupting.

"He was no more a weakling than your own Brigante Queen Cartimandua was, when Bodvoc accepted bribes from Rome."

Alaw wiped Lorcan's cheeks in between his answers, her skilful passes of the cloth from either side made in such a way that his sight was not impeded. He pointlessly wondered the extent of the wolf's clawing, though nobody had commented on the mess of his face.

"That happened some time ago. Keep focused on what is happening around us just now." Cynwrig snapped at his warrior.

Lorcan could tell that Cynwrig wanted no interruptions.

Hedrek drew back the attention of the gathering. "Does your King Venutius know who the new Legio XX commander is?"

Lorcan shook his head. "Nothing was mentioned while I was in his roundhouse. Do you know?"

Hedrek's expression was almost playful. "Eurwyn has ways of gaining important information. The new commander is named Agricola. Eurwyn said that Agricola served as a junior tribune in Britannia, with the Legio II Augusta, a good few seasons ago."

"How would that make this soldier important enough to become a legion commander, now?" Cynwrig sounded disbelieving.

Lorcan felt a shiver course down his back, though had no idea why. He had not heard of any Roman officer named Agricola. "That sounds like the strategy a clever Roman emperor would employ."

Cynwrig snorted. "A clever one? Were any of the previous three emperors clever?"

Lorcan grinned at his friend, albeit a weary grin. "Perhaps not. But consider what Hedrek has told us already. Would you not prefer to place someone in charge who would be known to the warriors, yet who would be loyal to you if you were their supreme ruler?"

The gathering was in agreement, their chuckles breaking some of the tension that had been rippling around the room.

Alaw's voice tickled his ear another time. "Do you have yet more wounds that need my needle?"

He pointed to the tear on the left leg of his braccae, below the knee.

Alaw rolled up the woollen material and after a quick look at the nasty wound, she whispered. "Oh, that is nasty. I need cleaner water for this one."

"I have heard enough talk of our Roman enemy!" Cynwrig's declaration was unexpected. "Marsali! Do we have any of the honey brew left? Or has Lorcan been given our last?"

Cynwrig's hearth-wife chuckled. "You always make sure we have plenty of that. And no, Lorcan has not nearly finished it."

"Then share it out! We have no bard here, but we will do our best. There are songs to sing and tales to tell." Cynwrig beamed at his gathering. "Who will entertain us first?"

A short while later, Lorcan felt the nudge at his elbow. He had not noticed Alaw's re-entry to the roundhouse. As before, she wiped the gashes on his leg and pulled the torn flesh together with deft strokes. Unfortunately, the bone needle felt much less sharp than it had been during her first stitching. That the present entertainer was recreating a bloody battle fought and won by the Carvetii tribe made the process almost unbearable.

He glugged down the last of his honey-brew, exhaustion and discomfort now so hard to banish.

"Do you wish this refill to be watered down?" Alaw smirked after half-filling his cup again, her gaze playful. "You fell asleep far too soon last time you visited here, though this night is yet young."

Lorcan stared at the bold grin on her face when she continued, "None of your wounds are serious, and not anywhere that is really important."

She was comely, and very spirited, but the day had been long and so very wearisome. A coupling for the sake of the opportunity held little appeal. He used his wounded hand to cover the beaker.

"I am not certain that I am in any better condition than I was before."

His response was met with more of Alaw's chuckles before she departed with the bowlful of bloodied water.

"Are you convinced of that?"

Lorcan managed a weak grin. "Nay. Not entirely."

Alaw's last words were enticing.

"I can heal more than the outside of a weary traveller."

Nara

A Slender Doe
Forest near the Lochan of the Priestesses

"When we get deeper into the forest glades there will be fewer opportunities for us to talk."

Nara's words were hushed.

She looked intently at the two young acolytes of the priestesshood who stood opposite her. Both were of a similar age of around thirteen summers, but there the comparisons ended. It was a tale of two opposites. One of them looked more than a bit apprehensive, but the other seemed quite unconcerned.

Whatever their dispositions, both were just as drenched as she was herself.

The day had dawned misty, with a fine penetrating drizzle, weather that she deemed very fortuitous for what she planned – if not the most pleasant to be out in. The double layer of mid-thigh-length tunics, and the checked woollen breeches that she wore beneath, afforded her some protection from the cold, but provided little resistance to the all-pervading dampness.

Dragging the girls from the beds in their roundhouse, in the pre-dawn gloom, had meant questions for her to answer as she directed them to wear similar garments to her own, the ones she donned for hunting. Though, in fairness, her novices had not made any grumbles in her presence, and had merely accepted that her reasons for stirring them a little earlier than usual were good enough.

The young women were already proficient with their spears during target sessions, aiming for non-moving objects like stacked oat stooks, or tree trunks. They could use their long knives reasonably well for many different purposes, and they were used to being in deep forest areas, but they had limited personal experience in tracking and hunting.

Branwen, the raven-haired anxious one, almost stuttered. "Nara. You will tell us what to do when we need to do something, will you not?"

Nara's low chuckles rippled around the slender alder trunks that populated the forest fringe at the far end of the Lochan of the Priestesses.

"Branwen! We have already discussed the many possible tactics that you can use. Why would I need to repeat myself when silence is necessary?"

"Is it because we must remain silent when in the realm of the god *Cernunnos*?" The response from the other girl, Rhawn, was confident.

"Well done," Nara praised. "That is definitely an excellent purpose to mention, Rhawn. We must respect the forest god at all times, nevertheless there are other equally good reasons for us making silent progress across the undergrowth."

Branwen's sudden smile made all the difference to the girl's dark-eyed expression. "We must not alarm the forest creatures in any way, so that we can track them properly – I know that, but I am fearful that I do not know enough about how to avoid causing upset to the forest god."

Nara's smile faded.

"None of us know very much about that. *Cernunnos* can be generous to all humans who enter his dwelling, nevertheless when he is offended, he can be fickle," she warned. "Just remember what I told you about the hunt today. We are here to fulfil the wish of one of our priestesses who has the desire to taste some deer meat during our forthcoming festival of *Imbolc,* before she passes to the Otherworld."

"Is the old one nearing her end in this realm, Nara?" Rhawn asked.

Nara could not prevent the instinctive smirk that widened her lips. "Our oldest priestess has changed very little since I arrived at the nemeton, many summers ago. Nevertheless, when *Coinchend* – the warrior from the Otherworld – will come for her is yet to be revealed. In the meantime, as the old one very well knows, late winter and early spring are good seasons for hunting."

Though keen to begin, and to dispel the early-morning chill that nipped at her bones, Nara decided a few more moments of clarification might be a good idea. "Before we move up to higher ground, remind me of what we should be doing?"

To her surprise it was Branwen who answered first.

"We should avoid hurried actions, since the roe is good at noticing movement."

Acknowledging the answer with a nod, Nara looked to Rhawn to continue.

"A roe is likely to be more nervous in this weather." Rhawn seemed pleased with her response, though Nara wondered if the reply was too confident.

"And why would this be, Rhawn?" she persisted, since the acolyte still needed to learn the value of sharing with her companions.

Rhawn wiped some of the moisture from her forehead and smoothed down wayward spirals of her thick and wiry blonde hair behind her ears before she answered. "Like me, they cannot see far in this mist and it dulls their sense of hearing."

"Are you nervous about being out in this damp mist?" Nara asked Rhawn.

"I do not like it overmuch, though I have no need to be as worried about predators as the roe has to be."

Nara was disturbed by the girl's assumptions. "That is a naïve answer, and could be so misguided, Rhawn. I can see that my teaching has been lacking, if you can possibly think that. There are many hazards for us in this forest, and the god *Cernunnos'* whims is only one of them!"

She turned to Branwen, whose expression betrayed her shock that Rhawn could be so sure of herself.

"What threats must we be aware of, just as much as any hunted animal?" Nara asked.

Branwen listed a few she could think of, like unstable branches after a violent storm. Her ideas were interspersed with acknowledging nods from Nara.

"Or a lone wolf?" Branwen's eye expression carried some doubt; however, it was as likely as her other responses.

Unable to wipe the amusement from her face, Rhawn's addition was dramatic. "Prowling warriors from another tribe intent on attack?"

"I pray that does not happen to us today, though it is definitely something for us to be aware of, and no laughing matter." Nara made sure the tone of her reply held a note of censure. "Now, move on, both of you. Keep going till we reach the burn."

Rhawn adopted a mock-threatening expression and deepened her tones. "Never fear, Branwen. My spear is at the ready."

Continued whispers and bold gestures were designed to make Branwen giggle as Nara watched the two girls step forward through the spindly birch saplings, past the plentiful willow and alder growth that lay near the Lochan shore, the trees still seeming vulnerable and winter-bare.

Rhawn's irrepressible good humour was mostly optimistic, and often improved the mood around the nemeton. However, it would not be a positive approach if it meant that the girl was careless of her own safety. Furthermore, it would be especially bad if she was reckless and not mindful of preventing harm from befalling on the other nemeton inhabitants. Selfishness was not an acceptable trait for a priestess to have. The novice was very likeable, yet Nara had, so far, been unable to dispel the occasional misgivings she felt about the girl's dedication and suitability.

It was a rare occurrence for an acolyte to be informed that she was not acceptable for continuing in the priestesshood, even if the novice had spent many moons in training. Nara knew rejection was possible, though it was so rare she had never known anyone to be expelled from the nemeton by the High Priestess Swatrega. She prayed to the goddess *Dôn* that Rhawn would never need to confront such a horror, yet she could not be sure that it would not happen to the girl.

As they padded on towards the burn, Nara chose not to add that a similar threat may also come from a marauding Roman patrol, though they had not recently discussed the possibility of Roman army invasions at the nemeton. Nevertheless, many seasons ago, news had reached Swatrega that Roman legions had sailed across the god *Manaan's* watery realm from Gaul, and had settled in southern Britannia. That invasion had happened before Nara's birth, but the Roman aggressors had gradually moved northwards and had occupied even more tribal territory. Nara's Selgovae lands had never been marched into, but she knew that was only because the Brigante tribes – who lived beyond the high hills – had made treaties with the Roman leaders.

Swatrega had bemoaned that some of the occupied tribes had adopted Roman customs and almost lived like Romans. Nara, being younger when she had heard this, had no idea what that could mean since she could conceive of no life that was different to her own. In truth, she still could not imagine what being Roman was about, and never wanted to learn. To reject her own way of life at the nemeton, and be forced to adopt a Roman one was something, she vowed, would never happen. She would rather die than endure such a disruption.

Roman fort building had also been mentioned. Yet, she could not quite grasp what a Roman fort might look like since they were said to be different from the typical settlements of the Selgovae. Apart from her father's hillfort at Tarras, she had visited only one other large settlement on Selgovae territory, since most of the tribe lived in small villages or clusters of roundhouses. The notion that the Roman army had built lots of wooden forts, housing thousands of soldiers, was seriously disturbing. It seemed like a salutary fireside tale because it was happening so far away. Nevertheless, she regularly made pleas to the goddess *Rhianna* that the Romans would never ever build on her precious Selgovae lands.

"Bear in mind all that we have talked about," Nara cautioned, when they all stood on the far side of the rippling burn. "You will take the lead first, Rhawn, though be ready to swap with Branwen when I give the signal."

Treading forward with assured steps, Rhawn made swift progress deeper into the forest. Underfoot in many of the hollows, the newly-sprouted green leaf-growth – of the little flowers that would bathe the area in a swathe of purple-blues come early summer – dulled any missteps on brittle twigs that had come down during the ferocious storm of the previous moon. The snaking trail that Rhawn created around the undergrowth demonstrated to Nara that the girl's attempt to avoid disturbing the creatures of the forest floor was successful.

Branwen trod a handful of paces in Rhawn's wake, taking prompts from her leader, momentarily pausing when Rhawn silently made them all aware of something worth noting. Sightings of small animals were rare, the creatures seemingly happy to be snuggled up tight in nests and holes, protected from the penetrating mist. Not so the forest birds.

Some were not silent, the birdsong of the tiniest ones a cheery companion on their trek.

Regularly glancing back, Branwen ensured that Nara was close behind. Nara was content to see that the girl was not doing it out of fear of the hunt, but was practising the tactics she had been taught. Being aware of the whereabouts of all members of a scouting group, or a hunt, was one of the important skills that she wanted both girls to demonstrate that day. Teaching the younger acolytes normal life skills was one of the joys of her position at the nemeton.

Helping with their spiritual development was important too; however, the bulk of that was imparted by the fully-fledged priestesses.

The morning was well advanced by the time they were into the predominantly oak forest, where the 'chiff-chaff' song of the tiny grey-green backed birds, the ones that liked to sing higher up in the taller trees, was drowning out most other sounds.

Branwen, currently leading, paused to watch the flitting ascent of a couple of those particular little birds. Nara watched the girl point to a clump of bramble bushes. About half way up one of them, the tell-tale signs of dead leaves poked out, indicating the nest the birds had been departing from.

Branwen grinned, opened her arms wide and mouthed some silent words before turning to move on. "This wet mist never bothers them."

Nara indicated when it was time for a change of lead, mainly using low whispers to the girl ahead of her, a particular whistle, or hand signals, but there had not been a single sighting of a deer.

She found it encouraging to see that both girls were getting much better at reading the signs underfoot. She had halted their progress many times to check that they could tell her which animal had left a soggy footprint, or what was likely to have made a disturbance to the leaf mould that lay under a beech tree.

A questioning glance from Rhawn gave Nara a moment of doubt about her teaching because she was not sure what the girl's expression meant. For the last little while the mist had been dissipating, ebbing and flowing, giving momentary clear sight then snatching it away again. They were very close to the tree line, approaching the area where the trees found it much harder to thrive, the soil being thinner and much more difficult to maintain a good root system at that elevation. The space between the trunks was extensive and the bush cover scrawny.

Without warning, Branwen, who was in the lead, dropped into a crouch then darted her way from one spindly tree to another.

The mist floated in again masking the novice from Nara's view.

Indicating that Rhawn should follow, also keeping low down, Nara headed in a wide curve. Branwen must be seeing something she could not. Perhaps Rhawn had noticed something, too? And had been intending her expression to be cautionary, rather than questioning?

Branwen's raised hand, the agreed warning signal, halted their progress. Nara watched the girl lift her spear and ready herself for a throw, then the weapon thundered a pathway towards the target.

The first sounds of the distressed animal reached Nara just as the mist cleared. The startled doe hesitated for a moment before it began to bound off in the opposite direction, the spear embedded in its rump.

Nara sent her own spear flying at the same time as another weapon whirled through the air from a different location.

Then a howl of agony from Rhawn almost drowned out the dying struggles of the wounded animal. Dragging her gaze from the writhing creature, Nara located Rhawn and dashed off towards her, wondering what had made the girl call out.

Splayed out on the forest floor, almost as prone as the doe, Rhawn was attempting to rise up onto one knee when Nara reached her.

"What happened?" Nara reached forward to assist the girl to her feet.

Rhawn's smile was one of disbelief, yet it was also of wry amusement. She pointed to the twisted knot of gnarled roots that still snagged her left leg.

"I was too bent on making a really good throw, to make sure the doe was dead, that I did not even notice what was beneath me," Rhawn gasped.

Branwen was out of breath when she reached Nara, an exultant smile wreathing the younger girl's face.

"The doe is a weak one, but we have been successful," Branwen gushed.

Nara watched the smile fade on Branwen's face. It was as if the girl had just realised that she had not inquired about Rhawn's squeal.

"What made you cry out?" Branwen asked.

Nara pared Rhawn's leg free of the trapping roots and bade the girl sit back down again. Releasing the cross-straps that held Rhawn's braccae material in place, she pulled up the cloth. There was already considerable swelling at Rhawn's knee. Using her fingertips, Nara tenderly checked the injury. The kneecap was still in place, but there was clearly damage to the flesh around it.

Nara bit back a sigh. Having recently wrenched her own foot, she could see that her injury had been insignificant and had quickly healed, compared to what Rhawn was now suffering. It was going to be a very long and slow progress back to the nemeton.

"I am sorry, Nara." Rhawn was in tears, the initial frustrated mirth having given way to the more practical reality of her situation.

"Accidents happen, Rhawn." Nara consoled the girl before she delved into the small sack that she had been carrying, slung across on her back.

Inside was the last of the flatbread that she had brought for them to eat, and a water-skin that now only held little more than a few drops. Offering the last of it to Rhawn, she rummaged around to find the strips of cloth that had multiple uses. They were not the best for strapping Rhawn's knee, not quite wide enough, but were better support than nothing at all.

She made quick work of binding the injury. "If the goddess favours you, you will walk on it soon enough. Though with a knee swelling like this one, your patience will be tested. This is a painful way for you to learn that elation at the success of a hunt should never be diminished by careless tracking."

"My spear thrust was not enough to kill the animal, it needed yours as well, Rhawn," Branwen said.

Nara was pleased to see that Branwen's comment and smile of reassurance was intended to lighten Rhawn's disappointment.

Rhawn's gasp of pain when she tentatively put her foot down, and immediately raised it up again, was only barely masked by her next words. "*Tapadh leat*, Branwen. I think, though, that you will find my spear went wide and it was Nara's that dealt the final blow."

"Come, let us all limp over to the kill and then we will make plans for returning to the nemeton," Nara joked. "Do either of you have any thoughts on how we will manage that?"

As Branwen had remarked, the doe was a small one, yet heavy enough. In addition to finding sufficiently strong tree-falls to make a frame for pulling the doe, Nara instructed Branwen to find a stout branch for Rhawn to use as a support to help her get down the hill to the lochan, where their coracle was tied up.

Nara collected Rhawn's spear from where it had fallen, though made no mention of it not being the one to kill the doe.

Even though wracked with pain, Rhawn still managed to make light of her limping gait, "At least we are not fleeing from wormy Roman soldiers slinking their way around our forests after disembarking from their ships. If that were the case, I would be urging you to run off and get reinforcements to help get me home."

Nara was astounded. When had the girl heard about Romans arriving in ships? And if it was true, that the Romans had made landfall, why did the High Priestess not inform the rest of the priestesses?

Keeping her tone casual she asked, "Who told you about Romans being anywhere near here?"

Rhawn shrugged one shoulder, all she could manage since her other was draped around the supporting branch.

"It was when I was last helping at the nemeton horse pens. A warrior who was bringing a message to the High Priestess mentioned it to the priestess who was on duty," Rhawn said.

Nara pretended not to hear Branwen's suppressed squeal of horror.

"What, exactly, did this warrior say?"

Rhawn shrugged again. "I cannot remember his exact words but the message was that Roman ships had been seen near the Selgovae sea coast. He did not say that any soldiers had stepped onto the shore, just that they had been spotted."

Nara continued to be stunned. The girl did not even seem to be distressed in any way by the news, her face now quite devoid of expression. "When did he say this sighting happened?"

"I am not sure. I think it may have been sometime before our last festival of Samhain."

"Why have you not talked of this matter before, Rhawn?" Nara questioned.

Rhawn's head dipped, her voice unaccustomedly sad. "I kept it to myself because I thought the news might be too alarming for the younger novices."

Nara gave the girl a swift hug, realising that she had perhaps been far too critical of Rhawn. Maybe the girl had hidden depths and sensitivities that maturity would enhance?

However, since Swatrega had mentioned nothing of the incident then there must be no reason for immediate alarm. The unsettling thing was that Nara had never heard of any Roman soldiers ever being so close to Selgovae territory.

Lorcan

The Newest Roman Commanders
Stanwick, The Settlement of King Venutius

Lorcan had found Cynwrig's extended hospitality most welcome. For more than a se'nnight, he had rested at his friend's Carvetii village giving his wounds some time to heal. Alaw's continued attention had been flattering, though he found it had ultimately meant as little to him as it had done on his previous visit. He had no qualms about taking his leave of her, and had made no plans to return to her enfolding embrace.

More positively, the respite was long enough to receive further updates about the Roman fort building, and the latest news meant his responsibilities could not be shouldered aside for ever.

Relieved that his present journey across the highlands and moorlands of Central Brigantia had been incident-free, apart from some delay caused by more heavy snowfall, Lorcan was now approaching the settlement of Stanwick. The huge hillfort was currently occupied by King Venutius of the Brigantes, yet in the past it had also been the official dwelling place of Queen Cartimandua. There were multiple pairs of guards to pass before he would be allowed through all of the defence ditches and ramparts, but he had visited a few times before and knew what to expect.

He had perhaps given the impression at Cynwrig's gathering that he was personally familiar with Venutius. That was stretching the truth more than a little bit. It was more accurate to say he had been in Venutius' company, though only when attending large gatherings with many other men. However, he was well-enough known by some of the chiefs who tended to spend time at Venutius' headquarters, and it was those men who vouched for his loyalty and helped gain him entrance to Venutius' advice-givers.

After a considerable wait at the innermost-gate, Lorcan was given permission to enter.

"Go straight to Thoft. He will give you accommodation," the guard said, before he whistled forward a young lad who had been playing with another stripling close by. "Your horse will be taken to the animal enclosures by this idle one..." The man broke off speaking for a moment to playfully cuff the lug of the older boy before Lorcan felt his full attention again. "And my little brother, Efan, will guide you inside."

While he removed the pouches that had been strapped onto his horse, Lorcan found the man was pleasant enough, though not exactly talkative, when asked what had been happening of late.

"How would I know about that?" The warrior, who Lorcan reckoned to be a few summers younger than he was, just laughed dismissively. "I spend my days standing at this post and my nights getting enough sleep to do it all over again."

Lorcan halted the older lad before his horse was led away to the communal horse pens.

"Dubh Srànnal has been cantankerous, snorting more than usual, and I warn you he does that a lot. Ask the horse-handler if he will check him over and see if he can find something wrong that I cannot."

The expression of disbelief on the lad's face made him smile.

"Does the snorting not mean your horse is happy to have you ride him?" the boy asked.

"Aye, sometimes it does mean he is comfortable with me," Lorcan explained. "But Dubh Srànnal seems more anxious than usual."

Lorcan moved off in the direction the younger boy pointed, glad that he was not the one standing at the gate for lengthy periods. He had certainly done guard duty at his home hillfort of Garrigill, but being the son of the chief – and a prince of the tribe – meant those times had been merely lessons of strategy to be learned. He was glad that Arian, his older brother, was now the designated overseer of the defences of his father's hillfort, and if any brother was likely to do regular guard duty, it would be Arian.

Since the last days of the previous summer the health of his father, Tully, had been in decline, though his stubborn parent was doing a grand job of pretending all was still well. Lorcan worried for his father who had been the formative presence that made him the warrior he now was. Tully had always been so strong, yet now it seemed to be more than just old age that was creeping up on him, too fast, far too fast. His pleas to the goddess *Brighid of the Hearth* were going unheard, because during his last visits to Garrigill, his father was less and less able, and increasingly suppressed abject pain.

As he strode forward in the wake of the almost tripping little lad – who did a power of chattering and pointing out of things the boy thought impressive and important about the huge hillfort – Lorcan vowed he would not fail Tully in the duty allotted to him.

His father had instructed him in how to be a good listener. Tully had trained him to speak well in company, and it was Tully who had given him the confidence to be the warrior son who carried information from dwelling to dwelling.

Since the fall of the druid base on Mona, half his life ago, messages were more frequently carried by people like him, and negotiations conducted between rivals and allies. He had learned a lot about negotiation, yet he knew there was still much more knowledge to be gained before he would be the best.

Efan halted at the entrance tunnel to one of the roundhouses near the centre of the hillfort. It was not a large house, however the spiralling smoke rising through the reed-lined roof meant a good fire was warming the interior, which probably meant it housed a good few warriors. Lorcan had heard of the chief named Thoft, though had not yet conversed with him.

Patting the tangled mass that lay above the boy's side-braids, he gave his thanks. "Efan. I will remember your skill should I need a guide another time."

Spaces where the boy's adult teeth had yet to fully form made the grin that came Lorcan's way lopsided, and added a sparkle to the little lad's cheeky inquiry.

"Do you know Chief Thoft?" Efan asked.

"Nay. Do you?"

"Aye, I do! I have felt the back of his hand more than once, so I will just be leaving you right here. You should be nice to him, or else maybe you will find he is not too much your friend, either."

Efan grinned at him a further time before he sped off, clearly having enjoyed his escorting role.

Before Lorcan dipped his head down to pass through the wattled entrance tunnel that was no more than two strides-long, he took a look around. The king's hillfort had many roundhouses of different sizes, widely spaced around the area. Some of the smaller ones he imagined would be communal storehouses, though others would house smaller family groups. The larger ones, he knew from before, tended to be ones which gave temporary shelter to visitors. The largest one of all – formerly named the Queen's House – was where he would find King Venutius.

But first, it sounded as though he had to ensure that Chief Thoft would help gain him entry to the dwelling of the king.

91

Later that day, King Venutius stopped abruptly and turned around to face Lorcan. "Did you witness this building of the fort near the western shores?"

"Nay, but I received the news on good authority, during my recent visit to Cynwrig of the Carvetii," Lorcan answered.

He had been invited to accompany the king on what Lorcan knew to be a daily inspection of the outer defences of the settlement, but which was probably also an excuse for Venutius to be out of the confines of the King's Roundhouse for a little while.

He added, "The information came from the Druid Eurwyn who covers the western coastline."

Venutius harrumphed, his hand gesturing back and forth imperiously to waft away the senior chief who had been plodding alongside him. "Make space for Lorcan of Garrigill to walk next to me."

The man nearest the king moved away allowing Lorcan to slip forward.

"When did you get this news?" Venutius barked out.

"Close to a half-moon ago." Lorcan had already learned that the king required answers without delay. He was well-used to cranky old men, since his own father was just as irascible, even before Tully's decline had set in. "My journey to Stanwick was hampered by snowfall on the western moors."

He declined to mention the days spent resting and recuperating at Cynwrig's dwelling.

"Ha!" Venutius' countenance brightened. "We have had no snow at Stanwick. The weather god favours us more than your Carvetii…friends."

Lorcan knew what had caused the king's hesitation. The Carvetii tribe of the north-west were reliable enough associates, though they had preferred not to join the main Brigante alliances. He watched the king's expression drift back to an appraising one.

"Nevertheless, Tully of Garrigill never sends me false information. On the strength of that, I will listen to what else you – Tully's negotiating son – have to tell me." King Venutius rattled on, briefly acknowledging the sentries who guarded the outermost gate as they moved through it and veered around the perimeter of the high turf embankment.

In between the many questions King Venutius fired his way, as they strode along the perimeter of the settlement, Lorcan shared his information.

"Agricola?" Venutius stroked the grizzled grey hair that sloped from upper lip to beneath his wrinkled chin a few times with a thumb and a forefinger before the king came to an unexpected halt.

Lorcan felt the king's full gaze turn towards him before the king spoke again. "I do not recall that name, yet you say he was a tribune of a Britannic legion some time ago?"

Before Lorcan could reply, he watched Venutius' upper body swivel. The king stared behind at the elders who walked in his wake, his expression inquiring. When no response came from any of his advisers, Venutius carried on walking.

"I had thought that we may only need to pay great heed to this newest Governor of Britannia, a soldier they name Cerialis, but perhaps there are many more senior Romans we must also monitor," Venutius said.

Lorcan dared to ask, "Cerialis? That name is new to me."

The king snorted. "Emperor Vespasian's doing. He has recently installed a new governor for Britannia, one who will do his bidding without question."

One of the king's retinue, clearly a battle-survivor from the scars that adorned him, grunted behind Lorcan. "My hillfort lies on our Brigante border with the Cornovii tribe. I have infiltrators rooting out orders that come from Emperor Vespasian. Though, finding out commands in the names of Cerialis – and this Agricola – will need to have equal importance, now."

Lorcan walked alongside the king, engrossed in the conversation that rumbled around him. He learned more about the brand-new Governor Cerialis, King Venutius' aides being well-informed. He wondered how they could come by such information, and be so sure of it being genuine. Mostly, he was highly impressed by their ability to gather the information.

Venutius hawked up thick phlegm and spat it out, his aim well-rehearsed as it landed perfectly onto the grassy bank of the rampart they encircled, the resultant slide of the slippy mess down the turf-blades as sneering as the king's expression. "Like all the Roman scum I have had dealings with, this man Cerialis has many more names, but two will suffice to mark him."

Lorcan had only heard of the man referred to as Governor Cerialis and reasoned it had to be the two the king meant, but curiosity made him wonder if he had missed something more interesting.

He was surprised when Venutius asked him why Agricola had become the new Legion Commander of the Legio XX.

"My Carvetii informer mentioned that rumours still circulate about members of the legion continuing to be rebellious," he explained. "The Legio XX may still be having problems with giving allegiance to Emperor Vespasian."

Venutius' lips pursed, his head making a series of small abrupt nods. "I would promote someone I trust to rally up the men. That must be the reasoning behind Vespasian giving the command to this Agricola."

After a few more questions, Lorcan had no further information to give his king. But before his formal dismissal, Venutius' grey-eyed stare was piercing. "Emperor Vespasian is not like the last three weaklings. Many seasons ago, I recall that Vespasian was in command of a Britannic legion, just like this soldier Agricola. And I also remember that Vespasian was a thoroughly ruthless commander."

Lorcan did not doubt the king's judgement. Venutius continued on with further updates on what Vespasian had been doing.

"Vespasian has begun something new in Roman leadership." A contemptuous heckle spat forth before the king continued. "Lorcan of Garrigill, did you know that Vespasian is not properly high-born?"

Lorcan had not heard this information and was unable to prevent an automatic lift of his eyebrows.

The king rattled on. "This man Vespasian comes from dubious second-class status. And, not being of their Roman Senatorial class, he will have his work cut out to continue to mould and keep the empire under his control."

Lorcan felt Venutius' gaze land directly on him.

"If I were Vespasian," King Venutius suggested, "I would post men in positions of power all over the empire who would give allegiance only to me."

Venutius suddenly stopped his determined strides. Lorcan felt the king's concentration on him become even more intense, a glint within it of challenge, yet also of a warped amusement.

"Lorcan of Garrigill, you will find out if this man Agricola's background is similar to that of Vespasian! You can expect brutality born of ambition, if you discover that he does come from less-elevated stock, since proving loyalty and demonstrating his ability to his emperor will be paramount."

Lorcan held his breath when Venutius' attention swivelled around to encompass all of the men who were gathered around the king.

"Whatever Lorcan discovers, we can all be sure that Brigantia is now threatened like never before."

Much later that night, Lorcan wended his way back to Thoft's roundhouse, many things rumbling through his head. Venutius was definitely preparing the Brigantes for renewed pitched-battle conflict – but now it was against the forces of the Roman Empire.

The following day Lorcan was called to the King's Roundhouse. A young woman, with a babe in arms and a toddling infant of no more than two summers at her feet, stood near Venutius.

The king wasted no time on greetings.

"This foolish woman of Brigante beginnings – found wandering by one of my patrols in the west – was trying to return to her kin, but the guards brought her to me."

Lorcan nodded acknowledgement though he held his tongue. It was clear that Venutius was not in a hospitable mood.

Turning to the woman the king's expression was disdainful, his words scathing. "Tell Lorcan of Garrigill what you have just told me."

Lorcan watched tears hover on the young woman's eyelids before they dripped down onto hollow cheekbones. Deep grief was evident in her expression and in the tense clutch of the baby, who was becoming fretful. The gauntness around the other infant's eyes told a tale of its own, silent tears also tracking down the little one's dirty cheeks.

"Their father is a Roman centurion, of the Legio XX." The woman was unable to hold back her sniffles. "I mean he used to be, but I am no longer sure…"

Lorcan's interest was immediately piqued on hearing the legion named. "Is this centurion that you mention attached to a unit stationed at the Roman Fortress named Viroconium Cornoviorum?"

The young woman nodded, her sobs increasing. "I begged him many times to think more carefully about who he talked to, and who he claimed to still support, but Marcus never heeded what I said."

The child clutching her leg whimpered on hearing the father's name being mentioned before burrowing deeper into her calf.

Lorcan looked down at the little mite, unsure if it was male or female, a downy thatch of curls still wispy around the crown.

After a nod from Venutius he asked, "Is your centurion dead?"

"He cannot be!" The woman's head shook vehemently, her whole face crumpling. "Marcus would not take me with him. The new commander sent other centurions to new postings as well."

Lorcan turned to the king, raising his eyebrows in inquiry.

"Aye. It would seem that this new man Agricola is already unearthing those of the Legio XX who blindly followed Vitellius, and is punishing them." The king was matter of fact about it.

The woman was now shushing the mewling baby who was reacting to its mother's suffering.

Lorcan questioned again. "Has Agricola given orders for the whole of the Legio XX to move out soon, to march north and invade Brigantia?"

The woman's head shook. "I have not heard of that. Marcus told me he was preparing to go south-westwards with his century to quell new unrest in the lands of the Ordovices. That was just the day before they came for him."

"Who came? Was it other centurions?" Lorcan prompted.

Venutius snorted. "Nay, they were much more important than that!"

Lorcan was intrigued. The king's mood was so changeable. He turned back to the woman who was almost collapsing, her words barely heard through her anguish.

"It was the new Legate Agricola and the Primus Pilus – the senior centurion of the whole legion – who came for him." The woman buried her head in her baby's neck, her gulps almost choking her.

Lorcan hated to distress the woman further, but some things remained unanswered. "Are you sure your Marcus was sent away from the fortress of Viroconium Cornoviorum? Did you see him leave? Or being escorted alive out of the gates?"

The woman could contain herself no longer, her howls deafening all around her as the implications of his words sank in.

King Venutius intervened, ushering forward a woman from one corner of the roundhouse. "Take this traitor to Brigantia away from me. Feed her brood and find a place for her to do menial work. She will have no status here, but she can slave for anyone who will house her. And if none come forward to offer this, cast her and her Roman offspring out of my hillfort!

Lorcan expected to be dismissed, too. It came as a surprise when the king ordered him to sit down alongside.

Nara

A Precious Legacy
Islet of the Priestesses of Dôn

"Nara? Are you in there?"

Nara knew from the volume of Branwen's voice outside that something must be urgent.

The younger acolyte entered the tool store at the home of the priestesses.

"Ah, there you are. Cearnach has sent word that the warriors are practising today. You are to meet him at the training field."

Nara looked up from the sword that she was sharpening. It was old, and had been used by many hands before it reached hers, yet that made it all the more precious to her. She had not been at the bedside just before her mother had died, but had been told her mother had insisted that the sword be given to her elder daughter. At that time, it was not likely that Nara's only brother would live to maturity. Nara cherished the weapon that had once been wielded by her grandfather, who had been a small wiry warrior. The sword was a perfect fit for one of her size and strength, yet she used it with a degree of guilt because her younger brother continued to live, and the old sword remained in her possession.

"*Tapadh leat*, Branwen. I will make my way there soon." Nara's thanks were met with a puzzled look across Branwen's features.

Nara watched the girl point to the sword.

99

"Someone else must have managed to give you the message already."

"Nay. Not at all." Nara was quick to answer, her chuckles and ready smile intended to put the girl at ease. "I just made time to clean it. Though I did not know it, the war goddess *Andraste* must have prompted me to make sure I am ready to best Cearnach today. He is such a good teacher, but he is also an extremely fit warrior and very hard to triumph over."

"All that, and handsome too?" The look on Branwen's face was unexpected.

"Branwen!" she chided. "Such opinions are not worthy of an acolyte. You know that already."

The girl looked abashed. "I do not mean I have any unworthy thoughts about him. I just mean that the gods have given some of us more gifts than others."

"Ah." Nara softened her tone. "Coveting the qualities of other people is not productive, Branwen, and is not the way of the goddess. But I do understand your yearning to widen your training and skills."

Learning to wield a sword, even a first wooden one, was not attainable by all young people at Tarras. Warrior training was a privilege given to those of high birth. Branwen came from good stock, but her forebears had never been in the upper tiers of the tribe.

"I understood that you had put aside all thoughts of sword wielding. Was I wrong?" Nara asked, more to ease the disappointment Branwen must feel than to encourage any false hope.

"I have tried. I really have, but I still hanker to be one of the priestess guards…"

Nara patted the girl's arm. "None of us ever know where our true path in life will eventually take us. Not what we will be required to learn, nor whether we are fit for a task."

Branwen managed a small chuckle in spite of her disappointment. "The only way I will have sword training would be if we were to go to war, and I needed to defend the Islet of the Priestesses from more than small neighbouring war bands."

Nara agreed, though said nothing. Such a threat would need preparation, for sure, but till such a misfortune happened only the privileged by birth would have the opportunity to bear a sword. Swords were valuable weapons and there were never any spares.

Nevertheless, she sought to soothe the hurt the girl felt.

"There are many things in life that are not fair, so we must make the best of what we are given. I cannot ever promise to train you to use a sword, but I am permitted to ensure that your spear-throwing and sling skills are the best they can be. When you acquire that degree of expertise, I truly do believe learning to wield a sword would not be so difficult for you, if you ever have to."

Branwen's smile was heartening. "Then I shall practise and practise and I will be ready. I am strong and healthy."

Nara thought of one person in the tribe who was being instructed in sword skills whose health did not merit the opportunity. She deeply regretted that a persistent weakness caused her young brother, Niall, to be less robust than most of his fellow young warriors. Her brother was rarely fit enough to even lift his own sword – a reluctant gift from their father after much prompting from the tribal elders – yet her father forced him to attend the training sessions.

The only positive thing about Niall's condition that she could think of was that as a result of her brother's poor stamina, her father had eventually bowed to persuasion and had allowed her to have full warrior-training. It was not uncommon for the daughter of a tribal chief to learn sword skills, though what was surprising was that Callan of Tarras had permitted it. He seldom did anything for her, and not much for Niall either.

"My poor brother," Nara whispered.

"Your poor brother? What do you mean?"

Branwen's voice intruded and jolted Nara out of her contemplation. The girl's expression was wary of what Nara was talking about when she lifted her head, because Niall's condition was no secret.

"Ignore me. I was wool-gathering."

"Do you need help with anything?" Branwen was babbling. "I mean, perhaps I could do something for you while you are at the training ground?"

"Ah, you make me a very good priestess sister." Nara's compliment earned a beaming smile from Branwen. "You could start by finding my two spears that are buried in that pile over there."

Nara's thoughts were still on her own birth family. It was a strange notion that she had a young sister, born a few winters after her brother: a little girl that she had never got the chance to know. The induction process at the nemeton had taken many summers, and during that early period Nara had hardly ever been allowed off the crannog of the priestesses.

Only occasionally had she had glimpses of the babe, who grew into a comely young child. Those instances were when she had visited the Hillfort of Tarras with the priestesses, for one of their important seasonal ceremonies.

It had been heartrending to watch Callan doting on Gaenna, well-named because the girl truly was his little fair one. Nara bore her sister no ill will, nevertheless, Callan's attitude to Gaenna was so peculiar, given his antipathy towards her and Niall.

Nara abandoned her sword sharpening, set down the file and stood up.

"Do you know that I have a blood sister, as well as a brother?" Nara asked Branwen who stood waiting patiently near the door for further instructions.

"Aye," the novice answered, though the girl was quick to ensure that she was not known as a gossip. "I only heard that you had one because I asked old Wynne, though she could not tell me anything more about Callan's other daughter."

"She is close to your age. When my mother died, my father sent Gaenna to be fostered at the hillfort of my mother's kin. I have not set eyes on her since then."

Branwen absorbed the information. "What age was she when she went away?"

Nara had to think. "She would have been about five summers old."

"Perhaps you will hear word of her progress if she is ages with me?" Branwen hinted at the changes that could be coming Gaenna's way. The blossoming of womanhood was often marked with a betrothal, especially if it was a high-ranking female.

"Indeed," Nara agreed. "I have not yet heard of any alliances for Gaenna. Though perhaps it has happened already? Callan has never been keen on following any of my mother's deathbed wishes, and he never shares news of Gaenna with me."

Only pressure from the elders had made her belligerent father change his direction over things that were related to her own progress.

"Are you not keen to train today?" Branwen's question was tentative.

Nara laughed. "You are right to chide me. I should make haste."

She glanced down at what she held. The carving on the sword hilt was beautifully done. She traced her finger along one of the worn swirls before she reached for its leather scabbard. She always checked to ensure there was nothing that marred the blade's smoothness, but in reality she just loved owning the sword. The home of the priestesses was bereft of personal belongings, its ethos being a sharing of all goods and sustenance. The sword was a guilty luxury.

The weapon normally resided in the weapon rack that sat just inside the door of the roundhouse where she slept at night. It only saw the light of day when she cleaned and sharpened it, or on days like the present one, when Cearnach – or another warrior from Tarras – was ordered to practise with her.

Untying her leather waistbelt, she slipped one end through the loop on the scabbard, settled the sword in place and retied the belt. As always at this stage of donning the weapon, she raised her chin and held her arms aloft.

"*Andraste*? Make me a worthy bearer of this fine weapon."

Branwen's own plea was fervent, if almost silent, so Nara had no idea who was the recipient of the appeal. Perhaps the girl was telling *Andraste* that she still desired to bear her own sword?

Nara took the spears held out to her, and then the shield that Branwen had also collected.

"There, I am ready now. *Tapadh leat*! I will not keep Cearnach waiting any longer."

"Are you not changing your clothes?" Branwen asked.

Outside the tool store, Nara gave Branwen another task to see to before she set off towards the roundhouse where she slept at night.

Dropping her weapons just inside the door, she untied her leather belt before grasping the neck of her dress to pull it off over her head. The watery-yellow woollen garment that was commonly worn by the acolytes of the priestesshood was dropped onto her sleeping platform, before she lifted her checked woollen braccae and tunics off the iron hook alongside her bedspace. Tying the breeches on tightly at the waist with a thin cord, she pulled on her double layer of tunics that hung to mid-thigh level.

Though they were the typical acolyte hunting clothes, Nara also wore them when practising combat. Wielding a sword and shield with her long dress on was not an impossible task, but the heavy material made it harder to dart around an opponent.

The weather god *Ambisagrus* had sent them a fine enough day, though still a chilly one. She wrapped her brown cloak around her shoulders, clasping it in place with her iron pin. She would not be wearing the bratt when practising her sword skills; however, it would keep her warm till she got to the combat field.

Picking up her weapons she stepped out, allowing herself a huge smile as she scanned above. "My thanks to you, *Ambisagrus*. Yesterday was a rainy day, though today will suit the warriors very well."

Once across the walkway between the crannog and the shoreline, she greeted the priestess who was in charge of the shoreline nemeton animal pens.

"Eachna is ready for you," the woman declared, pointing to the tethered horse at the far end of the mid-height wattled partition.

"You did not need to spoil me," Nara chuckled, and gave her thanks. "I will return the favour when I am finished and will do something to help you."

"Ha!" The woman's laugh rumbled around. "Let us wait and see how you fare. The last time you came back from training with Cearnach you could barely lift a bundle of straw."

It was Nara's turn to giggle as she swung herself up onto Eachna's back. "I see that you forget nothing. I will double my usual prayers to the goddesses *Epona* and *Andraste*."

The priestess patted Eachna's rump. "Off with you, while I see to our hungry and snuffling pigs." Twinkling hazel eyes looked up at Nara. "I think I will take you up on your kind offer. On your return you can clean out the pig pen, if *Andraste* has been looking after you well enough."

Not the worst job Nara had ever undertaken, she grinned her agreement. More encouragement followed at her back as she moved onto the pathway that led across the flat ground to the training fields.

The priestess' voice carried a long way.

105

"We also have some stray sheep to find, if you are fit to walk," the woman shouted. "I know you really love that job."

Twisting herself around, Nara's answering smile was a huge beam. Wandering sheep were sometimes a challenge to collect, since they tended to head up the hillside around dusk, a time when the priestesses who worked with the animals went across to the crannog for the night.

Lorcan

Lorcan was aware of Kesar sidling his horse up closer to Dubh Srànnal.

"Have you ever yearned to ride as far south as this before today?" Kesar asked.

"My answer to that is both yay and nay." Lorcan's chuckles were cynical as he studied the wiry young warrior alongside, who was a good few summers younger than he was.

Lorcan had guessed the third warrior in their small band to be around his own age, though he had met neither of his companions before King Venutius had made his recent request.

Kesar lived up to his name of "small black one". When Lorcan looked closely, the man's hair was almost as dark as his own, though Kesar's locks were fine and straight and hung flat against the skull.

Lorcan didn't need anyone to tell him that the bulk of his thick side-braids were more out than in the weaving that was intended to keep the wavy hair off his cheeks. The tuggy mess that was the rest of his long mane was grasped back with a leather thong.

Just thinking about his hair made him scratch at his nape, jostling his thin silver torque in the process. Few Brigantes wore a decorative neck ring but, sometimes, it had its uses in proclaiming his status as a prince of Garrigill. As the son of a Brigante chief, it was an entitlement to be named a prince, though he preferred to have people judge him for his deeds and not his family origins.

He did not think of himself as vain, but he occasionally liked to free his tresses and comb out the debris that had got trapped in them, though that had not happened since he left Stanwick. He scratched again, the itching now too hard to resist.

Lorcan had learned that Kesar liked to talk.

"I am guessing that the yay in your answer is because you are a man who is not content in one place for too long?" Kesar declared.

Lorcan studied his companion carefully wondering how the warrior could make such assumptions.

Kesar grinned. "I asked Thoft what he knew about you."

Lorcan watched Kesar's gap-toothed grin spread even further.

"King Venutius issued me a task, though told me nothing about you." Kesar shrugged his shoulders before he continued. "It is true I need to gain experience, however, I want any I receive to be positive and not…deadly. To be sure of that, I have needed to know more about the men I am accompanying."

Lorcan looked ahead at the warrior who was leading them across a flat scrubby area that had once been tilled farmland though was now spent earth unable to produce good crops. Part-tumbled walls still separated fields that had reverted to a wilder state, and a burnt-out roundhouse had its own story to tell. Farming folk were often forced to move on to more productive ground, and it was especially necessary to live where plentiful wood supplies grew nearby.

"And what of Cuinn up ahead? Does he merit the same scrutiny?" Lorcan asked.

Kesar's grin never slipped. "Aye, but I had already met him before this errand."

It was a half-smile that Lorcan allowed to slip free, one that curved up only one side of his mouth. "In truth, Kesar, I have become accustomed to travelling the length and breadth of the Brigante territories over many seasons now, though I am gradually coming to realise that being permanently settled in one roundhouse might bring its own advantages."

Lorcan sighed before scratching yet again. This time it was at his ear, the wound there now well scabbed-over but very irritating.

He looked at the tempting river that they had been following downstream and berated himself for not making better use of the cascade of frothy water that they had passed the previous day, at the waterfalls of the goddess *Suala*. Though more than inviting, there had unfortunately been no time for dawdling. Scooped up onto his face, the water had been invigorating. It had stayed cool in his water skin for a good part of the day but, realistically, it had been probably been far too frigid for a full submersion of more than a couple of moments. That was a great pity, because all of his almost-healed wounds would have benefitted from a long spraying of *Suala's* healing waters.

"When we reach that fork up ahead, we will take the smaller track to the right," Cuinn called back to him, before urging his mount to walk a little faster. "There is a hamlet not far off where we can rest overnight."

Cuinn, the nominated leader of their small group, was a southern Brigante who knew where to deviate from the river's edge, taking paths across the flat valley floor which shortened their journey.

"Are you certain of that?" Kesar asked.

Lorcan thought Kesar was definitely a wary one, though remembered what it initially felt like to be in territory that was unknown. He had been particularly vigilant during those earliest times when his father had delegated him to make visits on his own.

Cuinn looked back over shoulder, his expression reassuring. "One of the women who lives there is kin to my father. I have stayed there before. My last visit was a good few seasons ago, but I was made very welcome."

Cuinn had the approval of King Venutius and that would have been good enough, but Lorcan had formed his own opinion of the man over the last two days of journeying. Decisions that the warrior had made had been good ones. Cuinn was not much of a talker, and more of an observer, but that made Lorcan esteem the warrior even more.

Sure enough, the sight of the spiralling smoke seeping through the pointed tops of the small cluster of roundhouses, in the closing dusk, was a welcome view.

Before darkness properly descended, Lorcan was settled around a spitting and sparking fire and his belly was already full of a fine barley broth. Herbs he could not identify had been added to the flat bannock that he was still chewing on, which made it more tasty than usual, and the wooden beaker of watery-beer at his feet was almost empty.

It was only a small gathering that sat around the fireside. Ailin – the chief – and Orlagh his hearth-wife, had summoned a couple of other local warriors to join them.

Lorcan realised it had been a long while since he had been in such limited company around a fireside, and found it very relaxing. Cuinn was more talkative amongst familiar people, so there was no need for Lorcan to lead the conversation. Being able to just concentrate on the expressions of those around him was a welcome luxury. He had learned a long time ago that it was often the unsaid that required more attention.

Cuinn repeated the question he had just put to Ailin. "Have you definitely seen these Roman soldiers on the move, during the last few days?"

"Aye, we have." The chief nodded a few times, signs of antipathy creeping across his well-worn features. "Small groups of Roman scouts traipsed around here last summer, but those groups showed no signs of staying longer than a night or two. Oh, they made plenty of observations, but they did not bother us here at our hamlet."

Noting a startle shatter Orlagh's expression, Lorcan asked, "That is surprising. They did not approach anyone?"

Orlagh fiddled with the beaker in her hand and looked at Ailin. "You know that is not quite how it happened, husband."

Ailìn grunted, his disgust even more evident than before. "I do not think a conversation was in the mind of those particular Roman cavalrymen."

Orlagh sighed. " Nay, it was not."

Lorcan felt her gaze turn to him, her explanation clearly full of solemn memories.

"Delyth, from the roundhouse at the far end of our cluster, was out collecting the little blue berries we use mostly for dyeing our cloth. The nearest bushes are a good distance from here, in the woods that you travelled through after the fork near the River Swale. A small mounted patrol came upon her."

Lorcan saw the glisten in Orlagh's eyes as she stared into the fire, her words sorrow-laden. "We have no idea if they had any kind of conversation. The poor woman did not fare well."

"Delyth is dead?" Cuinn demanded.

When the woman's nod confirmed, Cuinn slapped down his beaker so hard Lorcan watched the contents spraying up and then they dripped onto his feet. He ignored the splashes on seeing the anger in Cuinn's expression mingled with a much deeper emotion.

"Delyth took a liking to me during my last visit." Cuinn's words indicated his feelings. "She was a comely woman, full of life and with a great heart."

The chief solemnly agreed, "She was that, and knowing Delyth as we did, she would have been courageous and would have resisted them right to the end."

Lorcan realised his question might appear insensitive, but he needed the circumstances to be clear. "Are you sure she was attacked by a Roman patrol?"

"Aye, she definitely was." Orlagh was vehement. "When she did not return as expected later that day, a few of us went looking for her. It was most unlike Delyth, for she was one of the most capable women of our village, who knew every blade of grass hereabouts." Her voice hushed, the anger replaced by a more profound anguish. "She was still alive when we located her, though barely. She had been ill-used by more than one man before they battered her with their weapons, and she was left a broken shell. All she could whisper was that there were eight of them."

Orlagh was now openly weeping and clutching Ailin for comfort.

"It was her pride, Delyth said, that made her their plaything." Ailìn's words were bitter. "Her pride! She was outnumbered by those *Diùbhadh*! Marauding scum cowards!"

Orlagh sniffled. "Delyth detested the Romans, and her reaction to them must have been confrontational."

The conversation continued around the fireside, but the mood in the roundhouse was graver than when it had started.

"Aye, we can show you how to reach that particular hill come the dawn," Ailin said.

The chief referred to the best place to see the Roman encampment that had recently sprung up where two rivers merged in a flat valley floor, a morning's ride away.

Back to being practical, Orlagh added, "Stealth is what you will need come the morn, not confrontation of any kind. There are hundreds of those *Ceigean Ròmanach* pigs. The turds mill around all over that valley."

Before sleep claimed him, Lorcan's words were meant to be only heard by Cuinn and Kesar who were bedded down close to the fireside, like he was. Though chief of his clan, Ailin's roundhouse had no extra stalls for visitors set around the room as in the huge settlement of King Venutius at Stanwick, or as at his father's hillfort of Garrigill.

"When we get closer to this encampment, we must keep our presence unseen. King Venutius wants only information just now." The last words were almost wiped out by Lorcan's huge yawn while he got as comfortable as he could manage on his pile of skins.

Nara

Sparring Partners
The training grounds at Tarras

The training grounds at Tarras were on the reasonably-level land below the hillfort, which was built on a low plateau further down the valley from the Lochan of the Priestesses. She counted the sparring figures as her horse trotted closer to them, idly wondering why there were more people than usual out training. Callan had allowed her to train since she was a young woman, but there were men out there that she had never practised with. It looked as if her father had drawn in men from further afield, though from where she could not imagine.

It would be most unusual to demand that the lower orders, below warrior level, train with more than a spear, yet that must be what Callan was doing. Men from the wider Tarras Territory would be very skilled in fighting with a long knife, and some might have had experience of training with a longer wooden sword, but she thought that few would have had the opportunity to use a deadly-sharp metal sword.

Spying Cearnach talking to a cluster of the younger warriors, she drew Eachna to a halt, jumped off and tethered the filly to a nearby berry bush that grew well back from the combat. It came as second nature to her to inspect the bush, to check if there was any spring growth. In the summer time, the shrub had tiny, easily-squashed, nearly-black fruits. The tart purple-blue pulp inside was sometimes eaten, but the women of Tarras mainly picked the fruits during the

Lughnasadh festival and used them for dyeing cloth. She, on the other hand, more often picked the fresh leaves. They made an effective remedy when overindulgent drinking led to messy and soft discharges. However there was presently no need to lick any juice from her fingers, since the little pink buds had not even appeared yet, and the leaves were not yet unfurled enough to pick.

The far end of the combat area was where the men tended to show off their prowess with their spears, but curiously that was not happening.

Deciding to leave her spears at the base of the bush, she undid her cloak and tossed it across Eachna's back. She settled her arm into the arm-guard of her shield, balanced the weight, and set off. A quick lope took her along the edge of the fighting area towards Cearnach.

"Did they have trouble locating you today?" Cearnach's words held suppressed amusement when she reached him. "Or did you forget where the practice grounds were?"

"No more than usual." Nara's reply was equally jocular, knowing that her father had set Cearnach many tasks during the last moon. "And you are as much to blame, as I am, for me not being here."

"Ha! Will your skills be as rusty as that old bit of iron?" Cearnach joked.

Nara enjoyed sparring words with Cearnach as much as with their swords. "Time will tell, faithless one."

A degree of affinity had grown between herself and Cearnach, who was only a few seasons older than she was. He had grown up at her father's hillfort, though it was only recently that he had been given leave to train regularly with her.

"Iola asks that you do not injure me too badly today." Unsurprisingly, Cearnach did not look in any way contrite when he said it.

Set on a different path in life from most of the women at Tarras, Nara's role meant no opportunity to indulge in a normal close friendship with another female. She believed she was held in high esteem by some of the women who recognised her skills, though she had no doubt that she was spiritually feared by plenty of others who were in awe of her priestess powers.

Cearnach's hearth-wife, Iola, was the one exception in the whole hillfort. Iola was naturally friendly, without any loss of deference or respect for Nara's status. She was comfortable in Iola's company, and in turn became just as relaxed with Cearnach's presence, as well.

The warrior's continued mirth made her suspicious about his request.

"And what have you been doing to merit her asking this of me?" she asked.

"It is more about what your father has been asking me to do: tasks that have been stealing me from her side. So perhaps we had better get out there on the field, or you may find you have no training session at all if Callan requests me again."

"Ah." Nara paused till Cearnach moved past some other warriors to access a good space for them.

"And like the elders who keep their mouths locked when I ask what prompts my father's recent flurry of activity regarding the safety of Tarras, will you be the same?" she asked.

"What I can say is that your father has had me out of the hillfort gaining information more times than my hearth-wife is happy about."

Nara ensured she had his full concentration. "But this is surely good news. Callan must regard you now as a reliable messenger."

Sarcasm dripped from Cearnach's laugh. "That would be definite progress for me. The truth is that there are plenty of warriors ready to grovel at his feet, but they will do anything to steer clear of dangerous situations. They find ready excuses for them being unable to undertake Callan's missions. Whereas I can never find credible reasons to avoid his errands."

Cearnach held his sword ready as she whipped hers free of its scabbard. Talking during a practice session was not easy; however, they continued the conversation in snatches as they circled each other, intent on finding a weak spot to take advantage of.

"Why did he send you to Novantae shores?"

The clang of Cearnach's blade striking on hers, parry after parry, sent strong ripples up her arm, even though she knew he was still holding back the bulk of his strength. He had the weight behind him, but she knew her feet were more agile than his.

She changed her foot stance, adjusted her shield angle and stabilised her knees before the next sword strike came her way. She doubled her grip and held firm when their blades clashed, blocking the chance for him to flick aside her weapon.

Cearnach withdrew his blade and readied it again. "Word came that Roman ships had been patrolling around the far tip of the firth."

"I heard about that some days ago," she gasped.

"Did you also hear that they may have made footfall on southern Selgovae shores?" Cearnach did not even seem winded when he talked. It was so annoying.

Nara took time to digest the words before she could speak again as the attack grew more intense. More moments of sword on sword ensued, and sometimes she managed to block his thrusts with her shield, till her arms ached. They covered some distance within their practising space. Cearnach's power behind his blade increased as he tested more of her stamina and expertise. When she was almost at the point of making a mistake Cearnach jumped back from her, retracting his sword.

"Concentrate on the challenge, Nara. Put that fiery dark-red hair of yours to good use and claim the tempestuous nature that usually goes with it. I could have had your arm off with that last swipe. You definitely need more exercise."

She breathed deeply with the exertion, not yet acknowledging his last comment, her head bent, arms braced on her knees and her sword hanging limp at her side. Instead she asked, "Did you find anyone who had actually seen these ships?"

The clanging of iron blades around the field was formidably noisy as the opponents did all they could to win their bout.

Cearnach looked barely winded when she lifted her head.

"Not personally," he said.

She circled slowly, while she watched him get ready to tackle her again.

"What I heard was from someone who had been told of ship movements by another person." Cearnach's voice rose as he raised his sword to swing. "Not the most reliable method of getting information."

"And that would not be good enough for Callan," she cried before she whacked Cearnach's weapon out of reach. "He rarely gives time for reports to get back to Tarras. You will be back out of this hillfort in a blink."

For a while she prowled around Cearnach, awaiting a best time to lunge, and took opportunities when Cearnach's shield cover looked fragile. Her head was soon ringing, and she was sweating as though she had just walked out of the Lochan of the Priestesses. For some time she was unable to make any replies while she wielded her sword and used her shield to gain the upper hand, parrying skilfully enough to keep Cearnach at bay, the swords meeting high, low and in between.

"Keep up the foray, Nara!"

The voice from nearby distracted Cearnach just enough for Nara to flip his sword away in one desperate flick, after which her own sword point was close to his chin.

"Not fair play!" Cearnach mumbled to Iola as he held up his hands in defeat. "That was cheating."

Iola stood waiting for them at the side of the field, her grins as wide as the open cave that lay high on the hillside above the Lochan of the Priestesses. "Nara never cheats. You know that, Cearnach the weak!" Iola's giggles were irrepressible as she ran off before retribution could come for her remark.

Cearnach jumped over his sword that lay at Nara's feet and sprinted after his woman. Grabbing Iola up, Nara watched him swing Iola around and around till it seemed that the spinning made the woman dizzy.

"Put me down! This is not good for me or the…"

Nara grinned to see Cearnach almost drop Iola. Since he happened to be facing her as he let go of Iola, she could see his puzzled expression.

"I know nothing of this. Do not ask me." Nara excused herself with a laugh.

Iola was beaming. "Aye, Cearnach, I will soon bear you another child, if the goddess wills it."

"So you say that I am not so weak after all?" Cearnach grabbed Iola again, though this time to give her a resounding kiss.

Nara waited a few moments before intruding, her comment laced with all the delight she felt for Iola who had not become with child as readily as many of the women at Tarras. Only one young bairn of three summers shared their hearth, whereas many women of Iola's age had already birthed three or four. "Since you have plenty to celebrate, Cearnach, I will find someone else to practise with."

Cearnach ended the kiss and looked down at Iola who was much shorter than he was. "Nara is in need of more training today, but I will not tarry."

Iola's little quip was quiet as she turned to go. "Nara has my blessings. But steer well clear of Callan, if he comes anywhere near you."

119

Nara was subjected to a furious sparring, Cearnach clearly energised by Iola's news. Their earlier drawn-out discussion was not repeated as they concentrated on honing Nara's techniques.

It was a howl of agony, from somewhere among the combatants on the field, that pierced Nara's preoccupation and ceased her sword in mid-swing. Cearnach's reaction was just as acute, since he also pulled his weapon back before spinning around to see what was amiss.

"Cearnach," she urged, dropping her sword and shield. "Fetch my sack from Eachna…"

She loped off leaving her words trailing. Cearnach had already sprinted off to do her bidding.

The ringing around the area eased off as other pairs stopped to see what had occurred, by the time Nara reached the injured man. Accidental injuries were not uncommon on the exercise area, though they were rarely really serious. Part of the art of practising sword skills was to avoid unintentional harm.

Nara looked at the blood flow that ran down the side of the man's tunic, and at the fingers which were clamped to the gash.

"He slipped just before our blades made contact. I thought I had missed him," his opponent explained. "He is new to wielding a sword."

The initial surprise of the blow now over, the injured tribesman shook his head. A grimace shielded the obvious pain he was feeling. "Nay! You did not miss me. But the blame…was mine."

The man's breathing became so worrisome that Nara thought he might pass out. She could tell that pride alone kept the man standing. "The mud… slick beneath my feet."

"Give him some support," Nara instructed the man's opponent then spoke directly to the injured warrior. "You need to remain upright for me to check your wound. Or, if you prefer it, lie down."

The shaking of the man's head showed his dislike of seeming pitiful.

"I thought I had retracted my blade swiftly enough," The sparring partner's apologies continued to trip out.

"You…did."

"No more talk. Think only about your breathing," Nara ordered, before turning her head to reassure the other warrior. "The injury would be much worse if your reactions had not been so quick." "

Looking directly at the injured man's eyes, Nara issued further orders. "I need to examine the cut. You need to let me see it."

Gingerly removing his hand from his side, the tribesman looked down. "No blood spurting out. That is a good sign, is it not?"

"Aye, though I need to look more closely," Nara ordered, realising that he was not of the warrior class and was one of the new recruits Callan had sent to the training field. She beckoned Cearnach who had just reached her side, and another person who stood nearby, and bid them hold the injured man's arms out. Pulling her small knife from its pouch at her belt, she sliced open the sewn-side of the man's tunic before replacing her blade.

On inspection, the wound was not too deep.
She looked up at the young man who now seemed deeply embarrassed at causing the disruption.

"Your practising is over for today, or you will lose too much blood."

Opening her sack she pulled free some long strips of cloth.

"Hold up his tunic," she asked Cearnach.

When the upper body was bared, she wound the lengths around it. "This will staunch the blood flow till you get back to your roundhouse."

A few more questions and Nara knew which farm the man came from, glad to learn that it was one that lay not too far from where they were. She would give his wound better attention when she got there.

"Nay," the tribesman insisted when his practising partner offered help to get him back to his home. "I can walk by myself."

Nara watched the young man's awkward retreat, his pride keeping him from staggering too much. She hoped the injury would not dispel the honour he must have felt to be asked to take up a proper sword.

Cearnach's wordless inquiry made Nara smile. "We could spar for a little longer, but I think Iola will be far more pleased with your early return than that young farmer's hearth woman."

The grin that slid her way was catching.

Laughter lingered while Nara lifted up her sack and went back to collect her sword and shield that lay where she had abandoned them. Her day was not nearly over, since she still had to replenish some of her salves. The collection of the herbs and the preparation of the unguents was often a long process, but she wished for nothing different.

Lorcan

Eboracum Rises
South East Brigantia

The following day, the golden orb of the god *Bel* had long since passed directly above Lorcan when he entered a thicket on the foothills of one of the many low rises that edged the valley floor.

He had found the morning's journey an easy one. *Ambisagrus*, the weather god, had favoured him – an auspicious and welcome sign. The early morning mist and chill had dissipated quickly, and it was now an almost clear day with light winds, making it easier for him to see ahead for a good distance. He had not yet needed to purposely evade any Roman patrols, because he had not spied any.

"I will remain here with the horses while you take a look." Berwyn, the warrior that Ailin had sent to guide them, added, "There is no cover once you have passed above this belt of trees, but it will not take you long to clamber up to the top. Follow the course of that stream over there."

Berwyn paused to point it out before he continued with his instructions. "Track it to the edge of the woodland and follow the trickle up to its source. Beyond that, you will find faint animal tracks that lead up through the heath cover to the scree at the top. This side of the hill is steep, but there is a much more gradual, gentler slope on the other."

The previous evening, Ailin had confirmed that this present position was the best one around to view the encampment. Even though the chief had warned that they needed to take a long curving route to reach it, in order to avoid confronting any patrols in the valley.

A short way above the treeline, Lorcan stopped to pay homage to the goddess of the spring, at the spot where her water source gushed forth from under a large flat rock. He needed of all of his weapons, could offer her none of them, but rummaging around in a pouch at his waist he pulled free one of his favourite sling-stones. He had no idea what the now well-rounded stone was made of, though its white surface glistened with shiny tracks. For many moons he had handled it, and smoothed it in his palm when decisions needed time to form.

"Accept my offering, goddess, and know that it holds meaning for me," he whispered. "Now, I gladly give it in to your keeping and will appreciate your life-giving waters."

Bending down, he tucked his familiar stone under the overhang of the spring. Then he cupped some of the cool clear water up to his mouth, and took time to fill his water skin.

Before climbing any further, he looked all around him. Large birds soared and cawed above the treetops, swooping here and there, but none showed the panicked movements that would have indicated a disturbance below. The base of the hill he had just scaled showed no signs of small animals rooting around, but that was to be expected at the time of day. Most importantly, he could detect no signs of humans tramping nearby. He was acutely aware that he needed to be listening for any rattling made by metal chainmail – Chief Thoft at Stanwick had impressed that caution upon him since his own personal experience was, as yet, limited.

Leaving his companions to pay honour as they chose, he followed a faint animal track up through the barely-flattened heath cover. A short way up he stopped to look around him again. No cover for him meant extra vigilance and many such examinations of the land below.

Keeping low to the ground was necessary, as the slope was indeed a steep one. He stopped just short of the summit and then crawled on hands and knees up the last part of the rise and over to the far side of the peak, where he lay splayed out to take a look.

The wide valley floor beneath him stretched out endlessly, any slightly higher ground being mere fringes at the sides. Two substantial rivers meandered over the low-lying area, one from the north and the other from the west, eventually converging to encase a shallow plateau. The elevation snuggled within the last convoluted bend before the two water-flows became one.

Lorcan was still at a good distance from the encampment, but the hill he was on was high enough for him to make a good estimate of how many tents were pitched below.

"Look!" Kesar whispered after he sidled in bedside him at his right, Cuinn doing likewise at his left. "More soldiers are arriving from the south."

Lorcan praised Kesar's keen eyesight. The column just pointed out to him was so far away it showed up as the tiniest dark trail. But it was a very long trail.

"Do you think that is more than one cohort?" asked Kesar.

Lorcan cleared his throat. He felt he had already learned a lot about the Roman invaders, but he had never actually seen them up really close. King Venutius had mentioned that a cohort numbered about five hundred men but the line approaching could well be a lot more.

"I have no idea. I think they will need to be much closer before we can make a judgement like that. I cannot see how many men form the width of the line. Can either of you work that out?"

Cuinn shook his head. "Nay, but what I am sure of is that we can judge how many soldiers are sheltering in that camp down there."

That seemed a much easier task since the Roman tents were pitched in regular rows.

Only after many tries, they eventually came to a conclusion that there might be around two hundred tents.

"You are sure that King Venutius said that one of those tents is for about ten men?" Cuinn sounded disbelieving.

"Nay," Lorcan said. "It was Thoft who mentioned that a tent was for the eight men of a patrol but might also be used by more, if they had one or two slaves."

Lorcan was not surprised that his words soured their anti-Roman mood even more. The idea of being forced to slave for a Roman patrol was not a notion any of them wanted to gain first-hand knowledge of.

"Move!" Cuinn warned. "There are figures tramping around in those woods right below us. It looks as though they are heading up this hill. We need to go now."

Bel's dwelling above was mostly a blue wrap, spattered here and there with thin fluffy stains around the strong golden orb – perfect conditions to pick out the faintest glints of metal down below. As the soldiers snaked a pathway through the trees, their armour flashed in the undergrowth.

Lorcan found that slithering back down the hill was much faster than the climb up. Not far from where the beasts were tethered, Cuinn's second warning came almost too late.

"By all the gods!" Cuinn barked. "There is another of those rummaging turds over there. I detest those *An cù*. Run!"

The large group of Roman infantrymen that Lorcan could now see must have been around the side of the hill, shielded by the tree line cover.

He judged the distance between him and Berwyn to be not much shorter than that of the Roman patrol, but by the grace of the horse goddess, *Epona*, Berwyn was already on the move. The warrior was mounted and was hauling all of their horses behind him. It was no easy feat, since Berwyn had to dodge around the saplings and more mature trunks, snatching backwards glimpses to make sure the leather reins were not entangling, or snagging on the undergrowth.

Taking to his heels, Lorcan sped through the trees, the other two forging their own routes towards Berwyn. As soon as Dubh Srànnal drew close enough he vaulted on, grabbed the leather strap that was tossed his way, and followed Berwyn who forced a pathway through the shrub cover. Lorcan heard more than one Roman javelin whizzing his way, but his prayers to *Andraste* kept him safe from the sharp tips. A squeal blasting from behind, followed by some very noisy curses, indicated they were not all similarly protected.

"*Ceigan Ròmanach*!" Kesar bellowed. "Those Roman shite will pay!"

Whipping his head around, Lorcan winced at the furious expression on Kesar's face though the clenched fist urged him onwards.

"Keep going!" Kesar shouted.

A Roman javelin shaft bobbed near Kesar's shoulder, the arm on that side hanging limply, but Lorcan could see that the wiry warrior was still holding himself upright. The immediate reaction to reach down and pull his spear free of its sheath to retaliate was halted by Cuinn's shouts from behind.

"Nay, Lorcan! The Roman scum will not outrun us once we are beyond the woods. They will be out of spear reach. I have Kesar's rein now and will keep him close. Make haste!"

Lorcan agreed, though a reprisal would have made him feel much better. It was more important that they get their information back to King Venutius – but they had to get out of the wood first.

Urging his horse faster towards the forest fringe, he bawled encouragement to the two behind him to keep up. Following Berwyn, he blasted out of the trees.

127

With the yelling of the furious Roman infantry fading at his rear, he rode hard till Berwyn halted at a place where there was long sight in all directions. It was a location where they would not be taken unawares by any other Roman patrols while they tended to Kesar. The warrior was now slumped over his horse's head but, thankfully, had not fallen off.

Lorcan found he was gratified that Cuinn continued to take charge after they slid Kesar down to a sitting position on the ground. King Venutius had definitely made a good choice when he had given Cuinn the leadership.

The javelin had gone through both Kesar's woollen cloak, and the tunic worn underneath, close to the rise of his shoulder.

While Lorcan undid the iron pin that held Kesar's cloak together, Cuinn's knife made short work of cutting the blood-sodden material free from the spear shaft. Once the cloak was fully removed, it was an easier task to rip open the tunic to reveal the wound. Though it bled freely, it was not a gushing injury.

To Lorcan's surprise, Cuinn actually seemed relieved when he pulled down the tunic material at Kesar's back.

"Look here. The tip has already penetrated the skin at the other side. It has gone through the fleshy part of his shoulder, but has not embedded itself in any bone," Cuinn said. "You two, keep him still."

Lorcan took up a kneeling position. He braced his forearm under Kesar's uninjured armpit, and drew the almost senseless warrior's weight against him, while Berwyn secured Kesar's legs.

Cuinn broke off the javelin shaft as close as possible to the shoulder wound without fuss, and then used his knife to trim off the rough splinters. A few swift cuts at Kesar's already shredded cloak produced some wads of material that Cuinn deftly folded before he popped them onto Kesar's splayed knees.

Lorcan had seen something similar done before and knew what might come next. At Cuinn's silent nod, he drew Kesar's attention to him, the words meant to provoke. "Just think what you will do, Kesar, when you get close enough to the Roman scum the next time you are near them."

As hoped for, he felt Kesar's pain-filled gaze turn towards him and away from Cuinn who was wrapping his own cloak around his palm, to strengthen it.

Kesar's teeth clenched, his words menacing. "I will run those *Ceigan Ròmanach,* turds through with my own..."

A huge gasp interrupted Kesar when Cuinn used the heel of his hand to thump at what remained of the spear shaft sticking out of Kesar's shoulder, the blow forcing the wood almost all the way through at the back.

"...spear." Kesar only just managed the last word before he passed out.

A swift tug on the now protruding spear tip was all it took for Cuinn to clear the broken shaft from the gaping wound. Lorcan swept up one of the wads of material and pressed it against the entrance wound while Cuinn did the same at the back with the other pad.

After a few moments, Cuinn peeked underneath the soaked material. "There is no spurting blood. I think it a good sign."

Berwyn helped Lorcan to keep Kesar upright while Cuinn set about cutting the cloak into wider strips, which were then wrapped around Kesar's chest to hold the pads in place.

Lorcan looked around him. "He needs to rest but this is not the place."

Kesar's eyes were closed though his voice was thready "I can hear you."

Nara

A few days later, on hearing her name being called, Nara looked up over Eachna's rump towards the wooden walkway.

"Nara!" Owaina repeated her shout as she covered the distance between them. "The High Priestess summons you."

Nara handed the woollen rag that she had been using to rub down her filly to the novice who stood alongside her, at the horse-pens that were situated just along the shoreline. "Take care of the rest for me, please."

Picking up the hide sack that always went with her, she stepped along to meet Owaina.

"You are sure it is Swatrega who sent you to fetch me?" Nara asked the girl, who was now moving around the nemeton area at a more reasonable speed.

"Of course I am sure it is her. How could I not know the High Priestess?" Owaina confirmed.

Nara acknowledged the information with a short nod, though was not convinced that Owaina had learned much else.

The girl explained further, "I was told to keep watch for you returning. You have been a long while away."

Nara laughed. "You are not going to tell me that you have been waiting at the nemeton gates all day doing nothing?"

The girl looked shocked. "How could that ever happen?"

"Then, I trust you were given some tasks to keep you occupied?"

As soon as the question was asked, Nara almost regretted it. Owaina's tale of the work she had done while watching for her arrival was a long one, given that the girl had mostly needed to remain near the nemeton gates.

Nara was already across the walkway by the time the inquiries came about what she had been doing that morning at Tarras. She could not fault the girl's general interest. Owaina was still in the newest learning phase, and had only been to Tarras Hillfort a few times in Nara's company.

"The elders at Tarras asked for my help," Nara explained.

The amazed look on Owaina's face made her smile.

"You mean the herb-wife at Tarras could not help, so they called on you to give aid? Why did the sick person not send for you first?" Owaina seemed genuinely puzzled.

"Tarras shelters many tribespeople, Owaina. Sometimes they do come to me immediately, though they also know that I have other duties as well as being a healer. If it seems something simple that the herb-wife can deal with, then they ask her. That is, in fact, what happened yesterday."

Owaina trailed through the nemeton gates after her. "But the herb-wife could not fix the problem, so the elders sent for you today?"

Nara was tired. Extra patience had to be summoned.

"An unknown sickness caused some of the tribesfolk to be in the firm grip of a deep bellyache after dawn yesterday morning."

Nara stopped to absorb the girl's expressions, Owaina's palm having immediately rested on her own stomach.

"They were sweating, and some had high fevers." Nara paused. Owaina was listening so intently she almost tripped over a wandering hen that pecked around the pathway.

"Did they vomit?" Owaina asked after she righted herself, mimicking the motions.

It made Nara smile again. "Aye, some did, yet others just felt really sick. The herb-wife at Tarras gave them potions to help them, but only some of the people were recovering today. That is why the elders at Tarras sent for me."

"Did you have something better for them?"

Nara thought Owaina seemed intrigued, even excited. That really did make Nara laugh, yet she knew it was a little unworthy of her. "Well, I did, though I am not sure they liked it overmuch."

"Why?" Owaina asked.

Nara looked the girl straight in the eye to ensure her attention. "Would you like to be fed something that made you immediately vomit, and heave really badly?"

"Nay!" Owaina's expression was a different sort of horrified. "Why did you do that?"

"All of those affected lived in roundhouses in one area of the hillfort. Whatever was causing the upset, it was not affecting the whole of Tarras."

Nara was pleased to see that Owaina was thinking hard about that. "You think it was something that they had eaten?"

"Or perhaps something that they had been drinking," Nara confirmed. "I will be checking their progress in the coming days, and will make sure that other people in the hillfort do not get sick."

"Will the tribespeople still ask the herb-wife for her help, even though she had to ask for yours today?"

Nara could see that a bit of reassurance was necessary. "Sometimes it takes the effort of more than one person to achieve a good result. Between us we have made a difference, but had the herb-wife not called on me today, tomorrow she might have tried what I used. The goddess *Rhianna* of the Hearth has guided us and we have given her our thanks."

Nara paused at Swatrega's roundhouse entryway, trying to recall if there had been anything she had done that could merit a summons. It was most unusual to be called in this way; in fact so unusual she could not remember any recent time.

Having thanked Owaina for fetching her, Nara pulled back the heavy leather cover that kept draughts from entering the roundhouse and ducked under it.

The first thing she noticed was the pall of aromatic smoke that lingered and danced high up in the roofbeams, and the heavy burning smell that permeated the dwelling. Swatrega and the priestess diviner had been casting prophecies.

At the far end of the large room, Swatrega sat alone in silence. The eyes of the High Priestess were closed, though Nara guessed the woman was not asleep. She stood awaiting the invitation to go further into the room. It came eventually, by which time Nara was feeling extremely unsettled, wondering what she could have done to merit the censure she now feared was coming to her.

"Come and sit by me, Princess Nara of Tarras."

Swatrega's tone was not angry. For some reason, this disturbed Nara even more. The use of the term 'princess' was yet another reminder of her tribal status, and not a good sign at all.

Nara made her way to the end of the fireside, to a low-burning fire that gave out just enough heat to warm the priestess, who sat on the stool that had specially carved sides and was created for the one who led the order. Swatrega was enwrapped in a thick blanket of close-woven wool of a mud-brown colour. The material was similar in colour to the wool of the acolyte cloaks.

Only after Nara was settled on the short wooden bench beside her did Swatrega begin to speak again.

"You have been here for many seasons and, for my part, you have always given the impression that you would eventually rise to become one of our best priestesses." Swatrega broke off, a gruff laugh coming unexpectedly.

Nara was dazed by the words, a sudden thrill overtaking her natural caution. Was she now to be given her final priestess rites? The elation she was feeling she quickly suppressed from sight – it was not a worthy trait under the eyes of the goddess.

She also knew it was not her place to answer…though it was her place to listen,

Swatrega broke eye contact, her focus drifting towards the doorway at the far end of the room.

"In time, believe that I had even envisaged that you might take my place as High Priestess, here at this sacred home."

Once more Nara had to wait, confusion now reigning. The word 'had' that Swatrega used did not seem to indicate that she would remain at the nemeton. Did that mean she would leave and go to another priestess settlement? Nara's head whirled. For some reason, conversations about other priestess villages had been rare, although a visiting priestess was not a completely unheard-of occurrence.

Talk with the High Priestess about her future had never transpired before. Many times Nara had wanted to ask why her final vows of the priestesshood had been delayed, and further delayed, yet it was never a conversation that she could start. When the goddess willed it, it would happen. She felt her eyes glisten as she focused on the hearth stones.

Was it about to happen now?

Nara listened to the huge sigh that came before Swatrega's attention returned to her.

"Know now, Princess Nara of Tarras, that time will never ever come. You will never be a High Priestess at any sacred place. The goddess has spoken. She has prophesied a new pathway for you."

"A new pathway that is not as a priestess?" Nara could not control the wobble in her voice that bordered on a squeal, and could only repeat Swatrega's words. "What does that mean? I do not understand."

"The goddess has newly spoken today. There is no longer a place for you here. You must leave the Islet of the Priestesses. You have only a few things to claim as your own. You will collect them and leave now."

"Leave? What have I done?" Nara was horrified. Dread cold replaced the heated excitement that she had been trying to suppress. "Why does the goddess not favour me? Why does she send me away?"

"Your future is freshly foretold, Nara of Tarras. You are no longer an acolyte of the priesturehood. You must take your place once again at your father's side in his stronghold...as a woman of the people."

Nara fell to her knees beside the High Priestess and grasped Swatrega's thin and bony fingers, tears stinging and dripping from her chin.

"I still do not understand your words. My father has never had any need of me at Tarras. He hates the very sight of me. Why must I return there?" Relentless tears continued to stream down Nara's cheeks. "I have been a priestess in all except name for many seasons now, bar the final rites. Why cannot I continue? Even as I am now, still uninitiated?"

Soft pats at her cheeks only barely registered.

Swatrega's tones softened, though the High Priestess did not properly claim her gaze. "The goddess *Dôn* has spoken – and as her servants – we must obey, Princess Nara. Your path is no longer as a priestess."

Nara was distraught.

"But how can I now be a princess of the tribe at my father's side? What shall I do?"

"The goddess *Dôn* has foretold that you will be the mother of a son who will become one of the greatest leaders the northern territories has ever known. In this time of great threat from the legions of the Roman Empire, the tribes of the north will desperately need strong men and women to defend our way of life."

Nara could only gape, open mouthed. What the High Priestess Swatrega was saying to her was totally incomprehensible.

"Our forthcoming Beltane Festival will be a crucial time for you along your prophesied journey. Before then you must find a worthy warrior to sire your son. It cannot be just any man, but will be the one whose destiny is linked to yours. Pray to the goddess *Dôn* because she will always guide you."

"A mother?" Nara was dumbfounded.

Swatrega's expression lost its momentary softness. "You must leave immediately and prepare for your new future."

"How can I be a mother?"

Nara had never ever cried so hard. Beside her, Swatrega just sat and stared at the doorway, uttering not a word, her expression more and more resolved.

The gulping tears eventually subsided enough for her to ask, "Is this why I have never gone through the final initiation ceremony? Can you at least tell me that? Did the goddess *Dôn* warn you earlier that this was likely to happen?"

"Nay, Nara." Swatrega's tone was almost belligerent. "The goddess works in mysterious ways. However, my doubts about conducting your final initiation rites were always my own. Your father..."

"Is this his doing?" Nara's hard-won control snapped again, her hands fisting at her hips.

"Not at all. Nevertheless, he knows now. I have already sent the Priestess Diviner to inform him of your immediate return to Tarras."

All Nara could do was stare at the woman she had thought to be her guiding mentor – never a mother figure, but a high influence during her progress to adulthood. Her voice cracked, though she was past caring. "I really have to go? Leave my nemeton home?"

Swatrega's expression became even more forbidding. "The goddess wills it. Be strong, Nara. You have never shown cowardice in all of the seasons you have lived here."

"But what will I do at Tarras? How am I to become a mother? And find the sire?" She sought hard to control the shaking that beset her. "I am so confused."

"You will continue to be a healer. That training is part of you now, and those skills will always be needed. The goddess will guide you in the rest of your quest." Swatrega's tone indicated she was done with the conversation.

Nara was not sure her legs would support her as even more of the implications hit her.

The High Priestess' voice intruded, the tone imperious. "The goddess *Dôn* has not abandoned you, Nara. She has another, much higher, purpose for you. Now go and change your clothes!"

The best that Nara could do was stare down at her pale-yellow acolyte priestess gown. Swatrega's last words before gesturing her to leave the room were no comfort either.

"Your life is far from over."

Lorcan

Beneath Lorcan, Dubh Srànnal plodded forwards despite the extra weight the horse was presently carrying. At his back, Lorcan could feel that Kesar's slump against him was deepening, the warrior's blood loss having taken its toll. It was as well that Cuinn had strapped them together when travelling over rougher high ground, or Kesar would have slipped free.

His own fatigue was barely much better, since they had maintained a punishing pace during the journey, Cuinn leading them straight back to King Venutius' stronghold. By day, they had only stopped to water the horses, taking some welcome sips themselves when they forded streams. By night, they found a safe refuge, places their small fire would not be detected. Their fare was limited to the hazelnuts they could gather and the small birds they managed to kill when they walked the horses. Two out of three beasts needed to rest, with one horse bearing Kesar whose condition was worsening.

They had chosen not to stop at Ailin's village for fear of a Roman patrol following their trail – endangering Ailin's people was unthinkable.

Lorcan's sigh of relief on reaching the first rampart gate at Stanwick was hampered by Kesar's iron-tight grip at the front of his waistbelt. The security around the area was still as thorough and vigilant as during his previous visit, yet he passed through the defence entrances more swiftly. He wondered if the outer guards had, somehow, been looking out for them.

"Take Kesar to Thoft's roundhouse. There are women there who are ready to tend to him." The guard at the innermost defence gate confirmed Lorcan's thoughts, the man's gestures urging him to dismount.

He chuckled as though carefree of burdens, though in truth his back protested at bearing Kesar's weight for so long. "It might be a good idea to get Kesar off first," he said. "But wait till I free his fingers from my belt, or they may snap off."

Alongside, Cuinn slipped off his mount, and threw both his own rein and that of Kesar's horse to a waiting horse-handler who led away both of the beasts. Approaching Dubh Srànnal, Cuinn's tone was sharp. "Kesar! Wake up."

Lorcan waited till Cuinn untied the leather strap that bound him to Kesar, before he prised Kesar's grip free of his leather belt. With the help of the guard, Cuinn then slid the dazed and awakening man to his feet.

"I can walk," Kesar protested, though he was unable to remain steady without support.

"I am sure you can," Lorcan agreed, his chuckle affable as he made an awkward dismount.

After Dubh Srànnal was led away, he carefully propped Kesar up on the damaged side, while Cuinn supported the other.

"If you are feeling so well," Lorcan grunted, as they set off into an unsteady lurch. "You will be able to help me straighten out the kinks in my back. But that will be long after we make it to Thoft's roundhouse."

"I am told that your experiences have been painfully formative?" King Venutius declared.

Lorcan admired Kesar's strength of character when King Venutius slapped at the young warrior's healthy arm before

139

urging him to be seated at his fireside the following evening. Though not nearly recovered, Kesar now looked more like himself.

"Tell me everything, Lorcan of Garrigill!" King Venutius ordered as they took their places.

Lorcan was honoured to be asked to speak first. With no embellishments, he told the king of their observations from the spot that Chief Ailin had recommended.

King Venutius nodded more than a few times as Lorcan continued, the king absorbing the details of their estimated troop numbers and the general situation of the encampment.

"Did you see any intentions to make the encampment permanent?" Venutius asked.

"There were carts going in the camp entrance gates, some of them piled high. We were too far off to see clearly, but, aye, it was probably wood. Though whether for cooking fires or for construction was impossible to tell."

Venutius gestured Cuinn to speak, the warrior almost impatient with his information.

"When I first spied the units of soldiers below us in the belt of trees, some of them carried wooden pails," Cuinn added. "I saw one soldier make markings on the trees at the commands of another. They were too close for us to remain safely above, so we hastened back down to the horses."

Venutius' snort was derisive. "And that was when you foolishly realised that the sneaky *Ceigan Ròmanach* pigs were all around you!"

Lorcan swallowed. It was true that they had made mistakes. His king did not need to remind him in such fashion, yet it stung deeply when Venutius did exactly that. He vowed silently to the goddess *Andraste* that he would never be so unprepared ever again.

"You! Lorcan of Garrigill." The king's tone grated. "How would you avoid a similar situation in future? Because as sure as the goddess *Cerridwen* relinquishes the dark of the night to the brightness of the god *Bel*, those

Roman legions will invade all of Brigantia, unless we halt their progress."

Lorcan faced his king. He answered as objectively as he could, but knew that it was nigh impossible to clear regret from his expression. "You sent three of us. We should have arranged ourselves in a way that we monitored that hill from all directions. We should have each observed what we could see, and then discussed and agreed on our findings afterwards. During a safe return journey."

To Lorcan's surprise the king laughed. Not a snide one but almost appraising. "You are as harsh on yourself as your father Tully declared you would be, when he set you to your tasks."

Lorcan stared, unable to mouth anything. To his knowledge Tully had not left his own Garrigill hillfort in many moons. He had no idea what prompted the king's opinion.

"You are as silent and wondering as you should be, Lorcan of Garrigill." The king stopped talking on hearing the arrival of a newcomer.

Lorcan looked to the entrance tunnel that was longer and higher than all others at the settlement. The figure standing at the entrance was distinguished by the cromach he carried at his side – a tall staff adorned with a canine skull that marked him out as a druid.

"Come and sit here, Maran!" The king's traditional welcome continued in an affable manner, more genial than Lorcan had heard used for any other guest.

At Venutius' request, Lorcan shuffled along the wooden bench, those seated alongside him also managing to move along a space.

Lorcan had met a few druids during his journeying, but Maran was new to him. The man was probably slightly shorter than he was if they stood shoulder to shoulder, but Lorcan sensed a strength to the druid that went far beyond his wiry outer layers. The druid's age was hard to guess:

perhaps more than thirty summers, the hair of his side braids being a lighter grey than the rest that fell in waves down his back. However, Lorcan knew that a change of hair colour as a man got older was no reliable indicator of real age. He felt it keenly when piercing light-coloured eyes alighted on him as the druid padded up the roundhouse to King Venutius.

After the tiniest nod of greetings to encompass the whole gathering, Maran sat down next to Lorcan. Though unable to decide why, it made Lorcan feel uneasy.

"Your timing is impeccable, as always, Maran. A druid truly does sense all!" Venutius' guffaw rattled around the roundhouse, though Lorcan had no idea what humoured the king.

Venutius continued his welcome, addressing Maran, "Do you know Lorcan, a prince from the Hillfort of Garrigill?"

Lorcan again sensed the keen eyes assess him, though the man's facial expression was unchanged. Up close, he could see now that the penetrating eye colour was more grey than blue.

"I do not – yet – know him." The druid's odd answer came with a hint of a smile.

King Venutius chortled, "Your neighbour, Lorcan, was just sitting there wondering how I could have had a recent exchange of information with his father."

Maran's answer was softly spoken, but Lorcan could tell that it was a voice that would be easily heard when raised inside, or outside at a large mustering of people. "I have come straight here from Garrigill, my mission being to fetch you back, Lorcan."

Lorcan felt a cool sweat begin to trickle down the back of his neck when he turned to fully face Maran, questioning what he could have done that merited being summoned back home in the company of a druid. But before he could utter a word Maran continued, the druid's expressive eyes conveying a degree of merriment, though a reservation was also discernible.

"Your father, Tully, boasted of your awareness that druids have few brothers to cover the northern territories," Maran said. "And that you do a fine job already to help us."

Lorcan felt numb. To agree would be unthinkable, given his recent failures.

Maran continued, "Knowledge is gained from experience. And that, in itself, brings trials and errors."

King Venutius interrupted, his tone mildly indulgent. "Nothing happened that cannot be fixed in time. Is that not so, Kesar? Do you wish that some other warrior, instead of Lorcan, had been sent with you to do my bidding?"

From the opposite side of the low-burning fire Kesar's words tripped over each other. "Nay, it was not Lorcan's fault that a Roman pilum became embedded in my shoulder."

Lorcan stared at the willow twig that Venutius had been moulding in his fists when it pointed towards him. However, the words that the king voiced were still directed at Kesar.

"Did you learn anything useful from Lorcan?"

Kesar nodded so heartily that Lorcan felt the painful twinges that were fleeting across the younger warrior's expression. "I did. He has been to many Brigante villages and I have not. I may not remember all of those he spoke of, but I am sure I will remember which still show a hankering for Rome and Cartimandua." Kesar stopped, then seemed to recall some more. "And Lorcan freely shared all of his information with me, without appearing prejudiced in any way."

Venutius nodded in agreement. "And is there anything else you learned that was useful to you?"

"During our journey, Lorcan taught me to look at the landscape around us and decide what might make the local Brigante chief prefer the seemingly protective cloak of

Rome, as opposed to being his own master in all things." Kesar was becoming more and more animated. "Lorcan encouraged me to consider what might drive that chief to make his decisions, should his land be under direct threat from the legions of Rome. He made me think about whether what was chosen was because of the self-pride, or the greed, of the chief. Or even because it was thought to be best way forward for the people under the chief's care."

Lorcan felt Maran's nudge at his shoulder, though the druid's words were directed to Kesar. "So, you blindly believed everything this man of Garrigill told you?"

"It was not like that at all!" Kesar looked uncomfortable, the druid's question making him defensive. "I used to look at things but only acknowledged what was easily visible in front of me. Lorcan has taught me to ask myself questions as to why something should be. And through the answers to my own questions, I believe my judgements are much better than before."

Lorcan felt heat rise at his cheeks. He had not realised that Kesar had been influenced by him in this way.

Relief was profound for Lorcan when King Venutius' head bobbed once to Maran, and once to him.

Then…the king changed the subject completely.

Nara

Banished from the Nemeton
Hillfort of Tarras

Nara pondered Swatrega's final words as she approached the innermost gates of Tarras, her legs quivering around her filly so much that Eachna's irritated sidestepping was difficult to control.

Callan stood there, his legs spread apart, his arms folded – an aggressive stance if ever she saw one. She knew her father's mannerisms fairly well, even though she had not lived at Tarras since she was seven summers. She was now almost three times older and she had changed over the time, but Callan remained much as he had been when he had sent her away.

Always angry and confrontational.

As an acolyte healer, Nara never needed to give reasons for her entry through the two outer rampart gates of Tarras. The guards had always greeted her in a sociable enough fashion, though never familiarly. Respect for the priestesshood was inherent, and a certain feared distancing was generally universal.

It was the changed attitude of the outer guards that had just shaken her to her core. Their first affront was their demanding her purpose at Tarras, as if she was a complete stranger. The next was forcing her to wait till they verified her entry. Witnessing their contemptuous expressions had almost broken down the false confidence she had summoned on the ride to her father's hillfort.

"Swatrega demands that you return to me, here at Tarras. Though I fail to see why I should harbour a failure." Callan's declaration, delivered at high volume and intended to be heard by everyone nearby, reached her before she had even brought Eachna to a halt.

Being named a failure stung, deeply, yet Nara forced the tears from her eyes and lifted her chin. She was determined not to let his cruelty make the already dreadful situation even worse.

Callan continued with his bitter harangue. "If the goddess *Dôn* no longer wishes you in her service, what am I supposed to do with a creature that she has spurned as useless? One that she has cast out from the sacred home of the priestesses? Tell me that?"

Nara swallowed down the abject lump that lodged in her throat. What answer did she have for him? She had, in truth, been thrust from the sacred nemeton home. She was definitely not useless, yet how could she defend her new situation? Her prophesied future was not to be divulged to anyone – not even to her despicable father. The goddess *Dôn* and Swatrega had her promise on secrecy, and she could never break her oath.

On the point of forcing out some words in her defence, two of the most venerable tribal elders stepped forward and fell into place to flank Callan. The men exchanged a low conversation, too quiet for Nara to hear, but it clearly enraged her father.

"I do not ever wish to set eyes on you again. You are no daughter of mine!" Callan's angry expression was even more pronounced before he turned on his heel and strode into the hillfort.

One of the elders, a man she had known all of her life, beckoned forward a young lad of some eight summers to stand alongside him.

"Fergal will take you to an unused roundhouse, Princess Nara. It is not in your father's nature to offer you a place in his own, but we will not leave you completely without shelter."

The other elder added, "There may be little we can do to help you. Nevertheless, there will be no harm in asking the two of us. I cannot say that for anyone else here at Tarras: they fear your father's wrath too much to challenge his order that you be ignored."

Nara could only nod. The man spoke the truth. The tribespeople would be terrified to go against any of Callan's dictates. His punishments were usually severe, and at best harsh. Before the elder walked away, she quelled the trembling at her lower lip and asked him, "What of the horse? Is Eachna also to be spurned, as I am?"

"Nay. The filly will be cared for at the horse pens, as normal, till someone from the nemeton fetches her. It is only you who is to be rejected, Nara. Your father would prefer you were an outcast, banished forever from Tarras. Nevertheless, he cannot go against the will of the High Priestess who decrees you must live here. It will take some time, but be assured that we will try to make Callan accept your presence."

Nara had no need to be escorted to the horse pens though since young Fergal had a task to fulfil, she trailed after him. The horse handler took the reins from her without the evident hostility the outer guards had shown. At least she thought so, though the young man would not make any form of eye contact. The respect that she was usually shown was absent, as if the horse handler had no idea how to treat her. Not talking at all seemed to be his way of dealing with the situation.

"You will take good care of her for me, will you not?" Nara forced him to make some kind of answer.

With down-bent head the man agreed. "Aye. While the filly is here, I will."

The realisation that she may not be allowed to ride Eachna again swamped Nara.

The filly had been given to the nemeton horse pen stock, and as such belonged to no one. Swatrega had given her permission to use the horse to return to Tarras, but the High Priestess had not said the filly could remain at Tarras for her use.

Clutching her arms around the horse's neck and trapping the mane, Nara dipped her head and momentarily breathed in deep of the scent that she could not be sure of smelling again. But she kept it brief. To spend a lengthy time saying a final goodbye was too gut-wrenching.

Pulling back from Eachna, she looked up above her. Willing her emotions to calm themselves, she inhaled some deep breaths and forced the tears away. Nothing about her situation made sense.

Turning back to the lad Fergal, she hoped her shaky reactions were not evident. "Where you lead, I shall follow."

It was not Fergal's fault that he had been given the undertaking of being the escort of someone who was almost an outcast.

On the way they passed few people, since avoidance was the more common reaction. On seeing her coming, the tribespeople had mostly scurried away, or diverted themselves round the back of nearby dwellings. Those who did walk past were silent in their staring. They either appeared embarrassed and kept their heads down, or they made it seem that they could not see her at all.

The first thing she recognised about the small roundhouse that she was escorted to was not its poor condition, it was that it was about as far away from Callan's central roundhouse as was possible, and was near the inside perimeter of the hillfort.

Having arrived, it seemed that her young guide had no notion of what to do next.

"My orders were only to escort you here…" Like the horse handler, Fergal kept his gaze lowered.

Nara felt sorry for the lad. "*Tapadh leat*, Fergal. You have fulfilled your task well."

Fergal ran off, his kicking heels indicating how glad he was to be free of the woman that nobody seemed to know how to treat. Or want.

Nara took a deep breath and stepped through the open space that led into the ramshackle dwelling. The roundhouse was not large enough to have a wicker-sided entryway, and the opening was merely a gaping space. There was no wattled door, and no drape of thick woollen or hide material hanging from the support beam to repel the biting winds.

The small room held only some flat firestones set around a central fireplace that looked, from the amount of dust and ash that almost obscured the worn surfaces, as if it had not been used in a long time. There was no iron weapon rack, no fire tools set near the end of the fireplace, and not a single cooking pot to be seen.

The sleeping platform that had originally been formed along the base of the interior wall, built up of stacked and packed wattle and daub, had not seen repairs for many seasons. The dried mud and straw mix was now crumbling and unstable.

The tears that formed and engulfed Nara were now too much to bear.

"*Rhianna of the Hearth*, my most revered goddess, what have I done to deserve this? I understand nothing of what is happening to me."

Slipping down to the floor, which looked as though it had not had clean rushes added to it for many a season, Nara folded her arms around her knees. She tucked her short cloak around herself and rocked and rocked till her sobs eventually subsided, and her tears ceased to make a soggy drip-pool on her braccae.

Wiping the dampness from her cheeks and chin with the back of her hand, she unfurled herself and got to her feet.

Pacing about the empty room, her head was in a whirl as she thought through her impossible plight.

"I could walk out of that doorway and never return."

No answer came, since only the goddesses were her companions.

"*Rhianna*, where can I go that is beyond my father's influence?"

Though she stared at the hearth stones as she bypassed them, her uneven breathing was the only sound that broke the silence in the room.

Every single outer farm was bound to the territory of Tarras.

She halted her agitated striding and stared out through the empty gap. Not much outside was moving in her sight line, bar a young child who lugged a heavy wooden pail that bumped at her legs as the little girl made slow progress in the opposite direction. A hound barked nearby, yet Nara could not see it, nor the clucking hens that must be alongside the next roundhouse. The space around the dwelling she presently occupied was barren.

Closing her eyes, she imagined herself striding away through the outer gates of Tarras. On foot, with nothing but the clothes covering her, and a short cloak billowing behind her.

Her eyes popped open again. Her gaze trailed down to the two woollen tunics she was wearing that came almost to her knees, and at the checked woollen braccae that she wore below them. She looked nothing like a woman of the tribe. No mother at Tarras wore what she had on.

The long dress of the acolyte still lay in the house that she had occupied at the home of the priestesses. As did the mid-brown cloak of the attendants. Swatrega had forbidden her to take anything beyond the clothes she used for battle training, the knives that were strapped onto her belt, and her bag of herbs and tools for potion-making that hardly ever left her side.

Her fingers drifted to her neck, to the thin silver torque which declared her princess status and which she almost never wore. Swatrega had produced it from her own dwelling where it was always stored, and had insisted the neck band be worn. A threadbare short woven cloak had been thrust into her hands before the High Priestess had ordered her to lift up her sword, shield and two spears before being escorted to the gates of the nemeton.

Now, patting the sword at her side made Nara feel only a little better. She could use it to protect herself, though the question was why that should be necessary at the place she would now be calling home?

To ask for refuge on the lands of another tribe was unthinkable. Her banishment from the Islet of the Priestesses would likely now be transported far and wide, since Swatrega's influence as High Priestess was over a huge swathe of land, in similar form to a druid who covered a wide area.

Nay, taking herself from Callan's territory was impossible.

Most important of all, Swatrega's final words to her had bound her to an oath that she had to fulfil by the Beltane Rites – only a couple of moons hence – and she could not defy the will of her goddess. To birth her prophesied son needed a man's seed. But not just any man.

She had no idea how to proceed!

How could she do something she had foresworn from for so much of her adulthood?

How could she now accept a tribesmen of Tarras as her own lover?

Lorcan

Travelling with the Druid
Brigantia

"Do you have a special woman?" Lorcan asked Maran.

The druid looked over at him from atop his ageing grey mare, a cynical grin on his lined face that displayed sharp eye teeth. "Do you?"

Lorcan knew his inquiry was audacious, and was not daunted by the question being immediately thrown back at him. The druid was better known now that they had been journeying together for six days, but it was the first time he had asked anything quite so personal.

His anticipation of travelling, from King Venutius' Stanwick stronghold, directly to his Garrigill home had been quashed when they had initially headed due west across to the borderlands that were common to the Carvetii and Brigante tribes. Though they had remained on Brigante territory, they had then turned northwards and were currently still following the tribal border. The trek would have been much shorter if they had traversed the spine-like hill country that straddled central Brigante territory. When he had asked why they had taken their present longer route Maran's explanation had been simple. They both had things to learn before going to Garrigill.

Lorcan had quickly realised that the details Maran had wanted to learn were largely regarding him, and he found it impossible to chafe about the delay in returning home to his father at Garrigill.

Their nights spent at hamlets along the way had mostly been constructive. A few had been very enlightening, especially when he had acquired useful mediation approaches from the druid. Some of those visits had made him realise that persuading tribesmen to change course from being hankering supporters of Cartimandua, to responding to the rallying call of King Venutius, needed the greater threat of impending Roman invasion to be emphasised much more than he had been doing.

While assessing Maran's strategies, he had sensed the turning points when those villagers accepted that joining with Venutius to repel the invading Roman legions had double purposes. It was a way of them saving face, their dignity preserved. It also became less of an abandonment of Cartimandua and more of an excuse to act for the good of all Brigantes.

It was unfortunate that other visits had been of a menacing nature, yet Maran had shrugged off those dangers better, Lorcan felt, than he had managed to do. They had been experiences which had tested his resilience and tempered his impatience. Maran was learning about those less-well-honed traits, but Lorcan found that he was also seeing a different side to himself than before. Used for some time to only looking out for himself, Lorcan found that accompanying someone of such elevated importance meant different responsibilities. And, for him, that had meant many compromises.

The situation right now was a perfect example of him having to adjust to compromises.

Lorcan did not even try to suppress a grin as he stared back at the druid, daring him to answer the question about whether, or not, he had a special woman.

Maran's eyebrows rose in inquiry, amusement still evident.

Lorcan had learned that Maran often delayed answering a question, though in fairness the druid did tend to reply after some parrying. He had found that the less serious he himself was, the more he learned from Maran.

"Nay. Not for a long time." Lorcan eventually answered his own question as he steered Dubh Srànnal around rubble that had fallen to the track from higher up the hillside they had been skirting around. It had been extremely windy with driving rain the previous day. "My father bound me to a hearth-wife when I was barely sixteen summers, but she died soon after during her first childbirth."

Maran's teasing smile slipped away, leaving a more sombre expression. "Do you still mourn the loss of both woman and child?"

Lorcan shook his head. "Nay. I mourn their passing, since Gweirmyl was as gentle as could be, and the girl-child never had the chance to grow."

Maran nodded, just once in acknowledgement. "And you have never loved again?"

Lorcan grunted, a sound that was somewhere between derisive and disbelief that the druid could think that of him. "She was the daughter of a southern Brigante chief. Our union was the usual kind of pairing, organised by our fathers to bring different blood to our clan. I had never met her before the hearth-blessing. Afterwards, she lay by my side at night for many moons, yet I shared no bond of love with her."

"But you would have liked to know your daughter?" Maran's finger-flick indicated they would be following the riverside track.

This time Lorcan's snort was sufficient to outdo those of Dubh Srànnal. "Show me a tribesman who can tell if the child born to his hearth-wife is truly his own? By the time a boy-child is a man, he may see the youth as he believes himself to look like, but which warrior can tell when a babe is newly born?" He shrugged his shoulders in Maran's direction. "Gweirmyl may have been faithful to me. She was overly timid and took time to settle at Garrigill. She appeared to miss everything about her former home. I never saw her favour any other warrior, but we did not spend all our waking moments together."

When his answer faded to nothing Maran drew back his attention. "Lorcan, some men never make a true bond with a woman. They may have someone to tend their hearth and bring up any children they acknowledge, yet true joy eludes them. We cannot know whom the gods will favour with a pairing that speaks deep inside a man as well as any urges to spill seed."

Lorcan knew it to be so. Women often chose him to couple with. Sometimes it was more pleasurable than others, yet no woman had ever drawn him strongly enough for him to want them to share a new roundhouse. He had resisted all efforts by his father to choose a new hearth-wife for him, and Tully had eventually given up.

He was surprised when Maran shared some personal information with him as they wended their way along the track that followed the curve of the low-flowing river.

"Druids rarely have one special woman. Some women show me favour, yet it is only those brave enough, or those females who are highly curious to find out if I function as a normal man who send out the lure. Unlike you, the reputation of a druid still tends to instil fear in many tribeswomen."

Lorcan contemplated what Maran did not say. Stories of sacred ceremonies with sacrificial female victims were sometimes shared by a bard around a fireside, but he knew them to be tales of long ago.

"I do not feel the lack of a permanent hearth, tended by one woman." Maran sounded pragmatic. "My training has always meant a different purpose for me."

Lorcan snared Maran's gaze. "Perhaps I should join the brotherhood? I feel destined to have a solitary life."

"Lorcan of Garrigill!" Maran's raucous laughter rang free, startling some riverside birds that were flitting among the still-winter tired reeds. "The priesthood is not for men who are disgruntled because a fruitful hearth eludes them. You know very well that a druid is chosen."

Lorcan's grin oozed abashment. It was not news to him.

"How many summers had you reached when you were selected?" he asked.

"Less than ten. The training was long and hard on the course set for me by the gods, though not so long as others since I am presently not much more than a druid guide." Maran's smile remained in full force. "Soon you will appreciate that some of my fellow druids have a much more rigorous training than I have endured."

Though Lorcan asked for more information Maran would not be drawn, the subject firmly closed. He had learned some things about the druid, one of those being that although there was a certain companionship developing, Maran was still also very much the stranger.

They were approaching the outskirts of their next destination, the largest one they had stopped at, so far, on their journeying. Maran had told him that the village of Chief Nudd housed a sizeable number of tribespeople, and the guard with the angled spear at the entrance to the outer ditch defences confirmed it. Small hamlets around the area needed every man to break the soil during this early spring season, and could spare no one to do permanent guard duty, though larger ones could afford the luxury of at least one guard.

"We did not expect you back so soon, Maran, though it is always good to see you." The watch pulled back his spear to allow the druid to pass.

Lorcan felt the warrior assess both him and Dubh Srànnal.

"Lorcan of Garrigill has accompanied me from King Venutius' stronghold." Maran's tone was matter-of-fact as he urged his mare onwards, as though that information was sufficient for a companion of his to gain entry.

After a nod of acknowledgement from the guard, Lorcan followed Maran.

"Urien's roundhouse will accommodate you," the guard chortled at their backs. "She can summon enough friendliness to give personal attention to two of you at the same time."

"We will lodge somewhere else." Maran's remark was loud enough for Lorcan to hear, though not the guard.

From the glint in Maran's expression when he glimpsed over his shoulder, the druid had a story to tell about the woman named Urien. It seemed that he was in no hurry to revisit her.

A short time later, Lorcan was seated at the fireside on the opposite side of the flames from Maran, who sat in pride of place next to Chief Nudd. The gathering was a small one with only some of the elders in attendance, their allegiance to King Venutius having been confirmed during Maran's previous visit.

The formal discussion had not yet begun, since hospitality was being tendered by a few female servants who scurried along behind the seated people with various bowls full of food. Though not a feast there was plenty for sharing around. Lorcan's hunger was swiftly sated. The thin broth and large chunk of flatbread that was handed to him was quickly consumed. The small portion of roasted boar strips was fare he had not tasted for some time and was well appreciated. He was soon supping from a third refill to his wooden beaker.

Chief Nudd's boasts about the skills of his brew-woman were justified, because Lorcan was resisting the creeping drowsiness that comes from a full belly. He accepted a handful of dried fruits and nuts from the bowl a young serving girl held out before him, and popped a few into his mouth. Crunching them was more to keep him alert than to stuff himself with even more food.

"I have never travelled as far north as your Garrigill hillfort." The elder seated next to him mumbled as he picked at fragments of hazelnuts that had got stuck in his worn back teeth. "Is it a large place?"

"Aye, it is. The largest in northern Brigantia. You would trek for at least a day in any direction to reach anything as big as Tully's hillfort." Lorcan replied to more of his neighbour's questions, about his brothers and sisters, giving the slightly-deaf elder the respect due to him, yet he also watched what was happening around the room.

A warrior of a similar age to himself had just arrived.

"Sit there, Bradwr," Chief Nudd declared, waving the newcomer into place on the far side of the man who was positioned next to the druid. "Eat first and then we must talk."

Lorcan watched Bradwr acknowledge the presence of the druid with a brief nod before he slid down onto the wooden bench, food appearing at his elbow almost immediately. The village women were clearly skilled at feeding many mouths.

Lorcan's gaze shifted to Maran. He now knew the druid well enough to see that the latest arrival caused some disquiet. There was a subtle tension to Maran's lips that had not been there before, and a glint in the druid's expressive eyes that held more than a trace of repressed anger when he looked sidewards upon Bradwr.

After wiping drips of broth from his above-lip hairs with the back of his hand, Bradwr's words were loud enough for Lorcan to hear. "It is not that long since you visited us, Maran. I thought the surviving druids were too busy to make return visits so soon."

Lorcan's concentration became distracted when the elder next to him sighed and continued the conversation about Garrigill.

"My time for making long treks is over," the old man said. "But I can tell you are proud of what your father has achieved at his Garrigill hillfort. A man with many competent sons is a man well-favoured by the gods, indeed."

Lorcan found that the elder might be hard of hearing but the old man's stare commanded his full consideration. However, something prompted him to heed the talk across the fireside, as well. The questions Bradwr put to Maran might appear harmless to some around the fireside, but to him they seemed increasingly probing. And the druid's responses seemed more terse.

The elder drew back his attention. "You may tell your father of my compliments when you return. The gods granted me only one son who lived to maturity, but he is long gone to the otherworld after a thoughtless argument with someone much more powerful than he was with a spear."

The momentary flash of regret Lorcan detected in the old man's expression was replaced with the slightest turning up of the man's wrinkled lips, a warmth of approval now in the stare.

"I believe your father has nurtured patience in you, Lorcan, and I trust it will have been the same for all of your other brothers."

While Lorcan was working out the most diplomatic reply, the elder's gaze shifted to peer across the fireside. A darkness descended across the eyebrows before the old man hawked up some thick spittle which he spat onto the logs in front of him. The following words were bitter, almost stripping the bark from the logs that awaited being added to the fire.

"There are some young Brigante warriors in this room who have no patience at all, and no proper concept of trust." Disgust dripped from every word the elder grated out.

Lorcan could see that it was not the druid who was the focus of the elder's attention but that it was the newcomer named Bradwr.

Those around the fireside were drawn to pay more attention when Chief Nudd's voice level increased almost to a shout.

"Bradwr. Now you have eaten, I want to know what delayed your return for so long." Nudd demanded of his warrior, his taut jawline indicating extreme displeasure. "You must have been at King Venutius' hearth at the same time as the druid and Lorcan of Garrigill."

Lorcan felt the chief's gaze seek him out over the fireside, an imperious finger pointing in his direction.

"You do not have the excuse of visiting villages along the route as they did, Bradwr. So what detained you?" Chief Nudd was persistent, his intent focus demanding complete attention from his warrior.

Lorcan studied Bradwr. He did not remember having seen the man at Stanwick, but in all fairness Nudd maybe did not realise just how many men congregated around the king's dwelling. And few were allowed to be at Venutius' hearth at the same time.

"King Venutius gave me a task to do before I came home." Bradwr's tone was truculent.

Lorcan noted the man could not meet the chief's gaze properly, Bradwr's head turning aside as he found a place to put down his empty bowl at the fireside. A gesture that was both fidgety and discourteous.

"Did he now?" Nudd's unimpressed and sarcastic tones drew even more of Lorcan's attention. Something was definitely amiss.

"Did you perhaps visit a southern Brigante village?" Maran asked Bradwr. "Before returning here?"

Across the fire-glow, Lorcan noted the tiniest flare of anger across Bradwr's eyes.

The chief's impatience was rising further. "Tell me where you have been!"

Lorcan watched Bradwr's chin firm, the pursing of the warrior's lips indicating his own growing annoyance, yet

160

there was a careless arrogance that Lorcan felt was misplaced given the circumstances.

"I headed southwards." Bradwr's answer was brief and unrepentant.

It did nothing to dissipate his chief's anger.

Nudd's chin jerked upwards to stare at the junction of the beams of his roundhouse, exasperation and other emotions causing him to smash his beaker down onto the floor rushes without a care of who might be hurt by it.

Maran probed further, his tone insistent, though Lorcan could see it was supremely controlled. "Did the king order you to inform one particularly important man about the next Beltane feast that is being organised at Stanwick?"

"What?" Bradwr's instinctive question spilled out, the first signs of real panic flashing across his face. He sought out his chief rather than facing more of the druid's questions. "What gives the druid the right to ask me such a question?"

Lorcan could see the tension that held Bradwr's shoulders rigid, curled fists pressing against the spread of the warrior's thighs.

Maran continued as though the outburst had not happened. "Or perhaps King Venutius instructed you to take news …" There was a definite hesitation before the druid continued, his focus entirely on Bradwr. "…to others in the south that there would be a larger than usual Beltane gathering at the king's dwelling?"

Lorcan observed the druid closely. There was something about Maran's expression that was the angriest he had yet experienced. There was a determined edge to Maran's tone he had not heard before, and something well-repressed about Maran's posture.

Chief Nudd's anger was palpable when his piercing gaze dropped to focus entirely on Bradwr, his clenched teeth a terror in themselves. "What have you not yet told me, Bradwr? I want to hear about all of your doings, of late."

161

Bradwr flinched away from the stripping glare, the cornered look of a snared animal replacing his earlier arrogance, though he summoned enough courage to spit back.

"Venutius' Beltane gathering might well be a large one, but Maran is unlikely to be there!"

Maran jumped to his feet. Pointing across his neighbour's head to Bradwr, his words were for the chief. "Your warrior, sitting right there, is a traitor. He has been to no Brigante village. His information was taken to the Roman Legate of the Legio IX."

Bradwr leapt up to his feet, screaming, "Death to all of the druids!" Launching his fist beyond the seated figure at his knees, Bradwr's well-honed eating blade was embedded in Maran's upper arm before anyone could stop him. Bradwr's screams continued as he drew his knife free for another assault. "The Romans will be better friends to us than that traitor Venutius!"

Lorcan was around the fireside in a blink, but others nearer the chief hauled Bradwr free of the knife hilt before more damage could be done to the druid. Bradwr wriggled and squirmed but the grip around him was impossible to break.

The furious chief confronted Bradwr, chin to chin. "Traitorous scum. By your actions we can see you do not dispute the allegations of Maran, our druid messenger who has faithfully brought us news for many, many seasons."

Even though trapped, Bradwr continued to deride, "Roman rule is welcomed by many tribes to the south of us, and they now have a much finer life than we have. You have been foolish to resist Roman rule for so long."

Nudd could no longer tolerate the conspirator in his midst.

"Haul that scheming filth out of my dwelling, and summon all of my people right now so that they can witness his punishment outside!"

Nara

Nara alternated between an agitated pacing around the room, and forlorn slumps to her knees while she stared out of the gap. A door cover should have shielded her anguish from anyone passing, though the lack of one made no difference.

The golden orb of the god *Bel* steadily moved westwards, the day dwindling, but no aid of any kind arrived at her dwelling. It sluggishly came to Nara that she had to help herself. The nights were still cold, and a fire in the abandoned hearth would be necessary later to banish the chills and to nurture her spirits.

After the largest sniff she ever remembered making, she looked up towards the bound-beams that formed the conical roof. She vowed that whatever treatment her father meted out to her, she would never again be cowed by his antipathy.

"Callan of Tarras cannot ever hurt me more than he has done already."

Resolving to leave aside the question of whether she should leave Tarras for ever, her practical nature won out on her fragile feelings. She had learned to be resourceful, and she would continue to be so.

Tumbling out the contents of her hide sack, she took stock of the contents. The wooden bowls for mixing her potions were tiny, too small for preparing food in – food which she did not have. The wooden spurtles would just about do for swirling some broth around in a small iron cooking cauldron – but there was not a single one of those around the room.

"And a fire will not build itself."

Her words echoed forlornly in the empty space while she popped her sling and a pile of sling-stones back into the pouch. Her leather water-bag followed, since there was no wooden bucket of any sort in the room to gather water. Her small iron fire-steel and piece of flint she set aside for later, but then changed her mind. They were not particularly heavy, but they were essential for fire-making, and she could not countenance either of them going missing. She added them to the bag before she slung it over her neck and set it to lie slantways across her chest.

Patting the long knife attached to her plaited-leather belt, to make sure of having a cutting tool with her, she debated leaving her sword. It was cumbersome to wear when doing some tasks, yet to leave it in the uninhabited roundhouse did not seem wise.

Her palm squeezing the hilt, she again spoke to the empty silence.

"I fear you must be my constant companion. If ever I need reassurance of your sword's worth, grandfather, then this may be a good time."

The shield she used was almost as old as her sword, however, it was so distinctive that it was unlikely it would be removed in her absence. She stared down at her two spears. Taking both of them might hamper her carrying of a wood pile, but one spear in hand was more easily seen from a distance than her sword would be. She bent down and fisted only one of them.

Not at all sure if she would be challenged by anyone, her steps took her out of the dwelling. She spent time doing one full circuit of the roundhouse. It was as she expected. The door entrance was dilapidated, and the rest of the dwelling was just as tired.

Having made the inspection, she trod onto the nearest path that led directly to the gates of Tarras.

"Off you go! Play elsewhere." The strident cry came the moment she was near the little ones.

Some of the young children, shooed away by the shouts of the adult, were confused. Yet others were more inquisitive as they reluctantly ran off.

A number of the adults working outside their dwellings chose to stand and silently stare rather than confront her, though most could not meet her gaze. Many were tribespeople she had helped in the past, in some way or another. A few who did look at her seemed trapped, their regret suppressed, since they too were under the scrutiny of the others around them.

Callan's influence was overpowering.

Collecting wood for the fires at the home of the priestesses was a duty usually assigned to the younger novices; therefore it was a very long time since she had done it. At Tarras it was little different. There was normally a steady stream of young children trailing off to the nearby woods to collect brushwood. Larger log piles were stacked under the roundhouse overhangs, in the space where the circular roof timbers overlapped the low wattled walls. Servants, or male members of the household, generally took on the task of providing those larger split logs.

When she reached the horse pens, her breath hitched. It was a different man from earlier, however it was one of the young men that she knew reasonably well.

"I need Eachna to go for a short ride, though I will be back well before dusk falls."

The horse-handler stood in silence, shaking a denial. Nevertheless his expression was pained. "I am not permitted to allow you access to any of the horses." The poor man's gaze dropped, unable to maintain eye contact with her. "I have my orders..." His words trailed off. "I am sorry Princess Nara."

Fury bubbled up, but the horse-handler was not the person to blame. "And I know very well who issued those orders!"

Turning on her heel, she strode on to the inner gates, determined not to take her ire out on the blameless. The man had not relished his task. Belatedly she realised that he had named her as Princess Nara. Perhaps that was the doing of the two elders she had spoken to earlier? She could not, at that moment, envisage her father being happy with the reuse of her tribal status.

Firming her chin, she walked on towards to the inner-gate guard who stood propped against the stout post.

Finding it difficult to summon an amiable tone, she nonetheless tried. "I need to collect firewood."

Her eyes flickered when she saw the minute flash of astonishment in the guard's eyes, yet he maintained a sober mien and said nothing as she walked past him. The young guard was probably as confused as she was about what was happening at Tarras.

The reaction at the outer gate was different. The guard there sat cross-legged whittling a piece of wood. A new dread filled her. It was Afagddu. Her immediate thought was that he made no attempt to rise to his feet. That would not have happened the previous day, and not even early that morning. A deferential nod would have been normal once up to standing, though in this man's case the nod might have been missing given their last conversation. The warrior stared insolently, even aggressively as she approached, his sharp knife still paring away thin slivers of wood that pinged around him.

Now, from the man's visibly hostile attitude, it was evident his fear of the wrath of the goddess had faded away.

"Are you leaving Tarras so soon?" he asked, but he did nothing to prevent her from moving on.

Nara could have said nothing, yet his impertinent tone bristled so much the words tripped out.

"I need the warmth of a fire tonight." Though she had not meant her words to be misconstrued, they were.

Afagddu crowed. "Have you not realised yet that there is no warmth for you here at Tarras? We admire champions. Never failures. If the goddess, and the priestesses of the nemeton, have all spurned you, then we shall do likewise."

Doing her utmost to ignore his spiteful comments, she headed off in the direction of the nearby forest. Raising her head to check above, she realised that the day had all but gone, so steeped had she been in her misery. Dusk was not far off. Though she did not feel at all hungry, she knew that food would become a necessity, if not for that night then for the next day to come. The treatment she had just been given at Tarras assured her that an invitation to feast at her father's hearth, or at the fireside of anyone else, would not be forthcoming.

Fending for herself meant collecting fresh water, a brief forage for food, and a swift gathering of firewood. There was a spring-fed well in the hillfort, but she had no intention of being turned away from it. She would not give her father that satisfaction.

She knew where the nearest spring-fed burn was situated, only a few copses away, so she made water-gathering her first task. As she passed through a hazel grove to get to the burn, she collected the few nuts that she could find still littered under the decayed leaf fall and popped them into her sack. From the dearth of nuts lying around, she could tell that others had been successful in seeking them moons ago, and not just the squirrels in preparation for the long sleep of winter that they were now awakening from.

On reaching the burn, she paused to pay homage.

"I come in great need, *Coventina* of the spring. Accept my humble thanks for your life-giving waters."

Unable to donate any of her personal items, she added a pledge to do better on her next visit then bent to fill her water skin. She tied it tightly at the neck and attached it to her belt, knowing from the growing dimness around her that time for her tasks was scarce.

One good thing she knew about dusk was that the small creatures of the forest tended to rise from their rest to look for their own food. Pulling her sling free from her leather pouch, she looped it over her left wrist and fisted some sling-stones, thankful that she always maintained a good supply. Though having a few at the ready did not mean she could throw caution to the winds. The animals of the forest did not make the hunt easy, and nor should they. She would have fed off some oats if she had them, rather than unnecessarily kill any of the small creatures, though it was unlikely she would be having a share of the Tarras cereal crops.

The scurrying of a squirrel descending from one of the oaks ahead set in motion the perfect hunting conditions. Her spear flew from her fist, but shockingly it fell far short of the target. How that had transpired was mystifying because her aim was never normally so poor. She looked down at her hand. It was trembling. And must have been trembling before she fired the spear, though she had been unaware of it.

"*Andraste*? Have you also deserted me?"

Flurries of the littlest brown birds rose into the upper branches on hearing her wail, but it was one of the slightly bigger ones that she kept in her sight as it tapped away at gnarled old oak trunk. The startlingly coloured feathers striped black and white, with a red underside, meant only a small feast would be had from that type of tree-pecking bird, though it would suffice till the new dawn. Sidestepping very slowly, she concealed herself behind a gnarly-trunked holly tree.

The whirling of her first sling stone only served to warn the bird enough for it to fly off to a nearby rowan, not its preferred place as far as Nara had observed when hunting.

Affixing a second stone as silently as she could to her sling, she sent a silent plea to *Cernunnos* to afford her one small kill. Without unnecessary movement, she sidled around the trunk and let it fly. This time it made its mark and the bird plummeted to the ground from the rowan that was still leaf-free.

Bowing her head over the dead bird when she reached it, she gave thanks to the forest god. "My thanks to you *Cernunnos*, lord of all the creatures within your domain. I appreciate your bounty. Know that I only kill to survive another day."

The bird carcass was added to the collection that hung from her belt before she began the task of retrieving her spear.

On the way back to the forest fringes, one by one she plucked up an armful of longer branches and dragged a few even heavier ones behind her. The routine task kept only some of Nara's swamping thoughts at bay. What mostly filled her mind was what she needed to do to continue to survive her dreadful situation.

Near the edge of the forest she dumped her pile on the ground, removed her short cloak and opened it out. Yanking out her long knife, she hacked at the branches to make them a tidier pile for carrying, and set them onto the opened material. Her last gathering up was of smaller twigs; mosses to dry for tinder; and long dried brackens to make a torch.

When the pile was as much as she could reasonably manage, she bound it up tightly with grass twine from her pouch and swung it up onto her shoulder, bracing her arm around it to balance the weight. She plucked up her spear from where it was propped against a bush, dipped her chin and closed her eyes.

"My thanks to you *Cernunnos*, lord of the forest. I promise I will use your gifts wisely."

By the time she was out of the trees, darkness had fallen and the clear dark blue above was being replaced by a deeper bluish-black. Her trek back to Tarras was lit by the goddess *Arianrhod*, her full silver globe having replaced the yellow disc of *Bel*.

Nara sighed and awkwardly shifted her burden to her other shoulder, her spear transferring from hand to hand, when the looming presence of the outer ramparts of Tarras came into sight. Few visitors, or tribespeople, entered through the outer defence ramparts at night. She guessed that her arrival would not be a welcome one, but prayed to her favourite goddess *Rhianna* that she would be given some clemency – especially if it was the hostile Afagddu who was still at the gate.

Lorcan

"When did you realise Bradwr had been spying for the Roman Legate of the Legio IX?" Maran asked.

The question was almost drowned out by the fidgets of Dubh Srànnal as Lorcan followed the druid on foot along the narrow and muddied riverside track the following morning, the horse protesting at the slippery uneven surface below its hooves created by heavy rains through the night. Gentle neck pats to soothe the beast gave Lorcan a valuable few moments. He was almost ashamed to answer.

"Far too late to stop him from harming you."

"No matter," Maran said. "The traitor is no longer a threat to our Brigante friends. And that was just one wound among many."

Maran's chuckle sounded drole, with an inevitability to it that Lorcan found depressing. However, the druid's eye contact that came his way was reassuring.

"You were at the other side of the fire. You have nothing to be guilty about."

"I was suspicious about the questions he put to you, though I could only half-hear them." Lorcan's answer held none of Maran's mirth, the wounds he himself had suffered still too recent for comfort. "Bradwr was too keen to know the whereabouts of your brethren, and how many of you would gather at King Venutius' dwellings for the Beltane feasts. I knew he was hiding something, but never for one

171

moment thought he was spying for an important Roman officer. Though you knew he was a traitor long before last night."

Maran's head dipped a little.

"I did. He had been in my sights for a few seasons. I was warned that he had been seen a number of times near the Roman encampment of the Legio IX, at the place they name Eboracum. As you learned after he was removed outside, I could only unmask him when I had enough evidence to convince his chief."

"Knowing that he had been passing information to the Roman Governor of Britannia was an overwhelming accusation for Chief Nudd to hear," Lorcan said. "I would never have thought that possible."

He had also been stunned to realise that Bradwr had been colluding with General Cerialis.

"Even I was surprised to learn that the traitor had gained access to highest levels of command." Maran's head nodded, his eyebrows raised and his eyes alight with incredulity. "We know that it is only recently that General Cerialis made his decision to travel north from Londinium. But, since Bradwr has been an informant of the former Legate of the Legio IX for many moons, he was able to find that out."

Lorcan was impressed with Maran's knowledge of Roman ongoings. "You said last night that Cerialis has taken command of the Legio IX himself. Why has he done that?"

Maran shrugged his shoulders before climbing up onto his mare. They were on firmer ground now that the riverside mire was left behind them.

"Who can tell what is in the mind of the usurper beyond taking control of us? What I do know is that Cerialis is familiar with the Legio IX. He was the senior officer of that legion some ten summers ago, when he suffered defeat at the hands of the forces of Queen Boudicca of the Iceni."

"And…he now commands all of the Roman forces in eastern Brigantia?" Lorcan asked as he deftly mounted Dubh Srànnal.

"That he does, and what is equally as worrying is that this new Legate of the Legio XX, Agricola, commands just as many men in the west. Both Agricola and Cerialis, I am told, answer with alacrity to the orders of Emperor Vespasian."

"You are well informed, Maran."

The druid's amused chortle startled a couple of small yellow-breasted, blue-beaked birds into flight that had been chirping merrily in nearby low-growing bushes that bordered the pathway. The new leaves rustled as the birds flurried off, but no harm came since the tiny dark blue berries that would be collected come the festival of *Lughnasadh* had not yet formed. The women who were most skilled at colouring woven garments would not pick the berries for three or four moons, the staining properties of the berries well-known to all around the area.

"We druids who still cover northern Britannia have many sources who help us monitor those *Ceigan Ròmanach!*" Maran's tone was deceptively light.

The path widened even more as it turned away from the river course sufficient for Lorcan to draw his mount forward at Maran's beckoning.

"Bradwr's activities were not the only ones I have been monitoring. I have also been following others."

Lorcan felt the druid's candid eyes seek his own, and did not even try to suppress the smile that widened his cheeks.

"Aye, I realise that now. You are the one who has been following me, at times, during the last few seasons." Lorcan's head dipped slightly in Maran's direction.

"That I have. I am impressed that you noticed." Maran's smile was complimentary.

Lorcan laughed. "Nay! I never ever saw you. I just had a sense of being watched. I reasoned it was not one of the gods but someone I believed to be a mortal man." Sufficiently comfortable with his companion he dared to continue, "Though if truth be told, I am not sure what you are. The wound inflicted upon you last night would have laid many a man low with the amount of blood that was lost, yet you show no discomfort at all."

Maran's eyes glittered with amusement but also with another hidden emotion. "Oh, I feel the wound, Lorcan. And I most definitely am mortal, but druids have ways of curing their inner-selves which are not known to everyone."

A small pause followed before Maran continued. "When I was sure that you were heading where you were supposed to be going, I slipped away and saw to more of my own business." The comments were all matter-of-fact. "All I needed was the certainty that you had no hesitation over carrying out visits to the known challenging circumstances, to those hamlets and villages that still clung to their support of Cartimandua."

Maran slowed his old mare to a standstill.

Lorcan did likewise, wondering what was coming.

"Are you familiar with that fork just ahead?" Maran's question rang with serious undertones.

Lorcan assessed the surroundings again before he nodded. He had been aware of the route they followed but confirmed it, in case their conversation had distracted him. "In as much as I have always taken the route that leads towards Garrigill. I am less familiar with the left-hand pathway."

"Would that be because it leads northwards across the valley floor, and then uphill to the Sacred Groves of my brotherhood?" Maran's hushed tones were as solemn as his probing observation.

Lorcan swallowed down an immediate anxiety that could not be expressed in words but that he felt instinctively. He knew of no mortal man who had entered those Sacred Groves who could properly relate his

174

experience afterwards. All the tribes around knew of the existence of the place of the gods, but none would ever dare to enter the hallowed area on their own.

Many terrible stories abounded of strangers who had blundered into those groves unwittingly, but who had not come out in the same manner as they had gone in. Their lives had been irrevocably changed by their terrifying experiences.

He managed a nod.

"Then prepare yourself Lorcan of Garrigill, because this very day is one that you will be taking the route that leads into the Sacred Groves of the Druids." The druid spurred on his mare and took the left-hand track, expecting to be followed.

A moment of sheer panic made Lorcan feel unsteady on Dubh Srànnal. He was no coward, yet every known dread swamped him simultaneously. His head was brim-full of panicked questions.

Should he flee along the right-hand track to Garrigill? Nay, he could not do that!

Follow Maran and trust the druid to keep him safe? Did he know the man well enough for that? Nay, he still did not, but his king had ordered him to accompany Maran back to Garrigill.

Lorcan felt wrenched apart, yet he knew where his duty lay.

His throat felt scratchy but he raised his voice loud enough to be heard. "Will I still be the same man who reaches my father Tully's roundhouse after a visit to the Sacred Groves?"

Maran smirked over his shoulder, faintly amused by the question. "That will be entirely up to your destiny. In this instance I am merely a messenger like you are, Lorcan. I may be the one who is a changed man and not you, but we will never know this if we fear the future the gods have in store for us."

Lorcan watched Maran turn away from him, though the druid was not finished speaking.

"Follow. We are expected."

Expected where?

Lorcan knew they were expected back at Garrigill, his father Tully awaiting his arrival, but nothing had been said at the roundhouse of King Venutius about making a visit first to the Sacred Groves.

Fleeting thoughts of what Tully would do in his present situation had Lorcan recall some of his father's words. Embrace the unknown, Tully had advised. Work with the unexpected. Make sound judgements about choices that required to be made. Think well about the situations and consider possible outcomes. Tully's advice had always, so far, been useful. But Tully had never ever made him imagine a setting where he was in the Sacred Groves of the gods!

Deep down inside, he also knew that his father would have been unblinking in the belief that a druid might sometimes have dread things to impart to the chiefs of Brigantia, but that a druid's purpose should never be casually dismissed out of hand. Sometimes it might be tentatively questioned and not necessarily blindly followed, till understood. Though, blatantly disobeying a druid was not something Lorcan had ever been taught, or even heard of.

As he urged Dubh Srànnal into motion he forced down the turmoil inside and concentrated on thinking through the present state of affairs. Every new day had brought him challenging circumstances since he had undertaken his task for King Venutius, yet the goddess *Andraste* had favoured him many times of late, and kept him from moving over to the otherworld. Surely she was still giving him her blessings?

Maran's pace increased when Dubh Srànnal came right up behind him.

"Move forward, Lorcan. This part of the track is wide enough for both of our horses while we cross the valley floor."

Lorcan attempted a smile but was unable to form more than a lukewarm one. The druid's manner was as before and posed no threat. He had to believe that would continue.

The golden orb of *Bel* had passed well-overhead by the time Dubh Srànnal took the first paces away from the stream that was sparsely wooded on both banks and padded into the deeper forest that sloped up the hillside, though Lorcan thought it no different to any other forest he had ridden through.

The conversation continued to be useful and informative, *Bel's* light filtering down through the unfurling beech leaves, casting a twinkling lightness atop the green-brown mat of ferns that Dubh Srànnal stepped a careful way over. Lorcan's initial misgivings receded as he answered Maran's questions about his brothers and sister, since the druid knew little about the younger ones.

"Tully has maintained a full roundhouse!" Maran declared.

"Aye, my mother birthed lots of bairns, and was favoured that almost all lived beyond their earliest years." Lorcan chuckled, "She had many sons but only one daughter."

"Did your father foster-out his sons?" Maran asked.

"Aye, all of us. And since my mother's passing some seasons ago, my little sister – Mearna – lives with mother's kin in a southern Brigante clanhold."

"I know nothing of your sister Mearna, but a few moons ago I visited a village near the eastern coast of Brigantia which shelters a young warrior named Rhyss of Garrigill. Would he be your brother?"

Lorcan's smile beamed. "Aye, it could well be. Rhyss was sent to the east, but I have not set eyes on him for many seasons. How does he fare?"

Maran returned a chuckle. "The Rhyss I speak of is as blond as a field of spelt shimmering in a breeze, but he looks nothing like you Lorcan."

"Rhyss and Brennus have the lighter-haired locks of my mother's family, but the rest of us are dark." Lorcan negotiated Dubh Srànnal around a larger boulder that blocked his side of the pathway. "Tell me more of Rhyss."

"He has an admirable determination to succeed. He should make a fine warrior..." The druid's voice dipped, just a little but enough to make Lorcan uneasy.

"Should?" he asked. "What would prevent him?"

Maran's sigh was deep. "Roman supply ships have been regularly sighted not far from his coastal village. They offload goods which are afterwards transported up river in small flat-bottomed boats to the Roman encampment at Eboracum. My sources tell me that Rhyss' foster-father has not confronted them so far, but, should that situation change for any reason, all in that coastal area are under greater threat."

"How is such information passed on to you?" Lorcan worried about his brother's safety, but was impressed by the druid's familiarity with what the Romans were doing.

Maran's smile was enigmatic. "Druids have many reliable wanderers like yourself."

Though the fine details remained secret, Lorcan gleaned enough to realise that direct contact between the druids and trusted chiefs was paramount for the exchange of information.

Lorcan's disappointment was acute when the wider track narrowed down, and he was forced to drop in behind Maran's old mare. The lively chat that he had found so engrossing faltered after eye-contact with Maran was no longer possible.

As they moved deeper into the forest, he tried, unsuccessfully, to fill in the gaps that Maran had chosen not to divulge. The spoken word of the druid was clearly highly important, but there had to be other signs or signals that he was unaware of. Perhaps it was not just the fact that the druids brought word of developments, but it was the actual words used that had more than a surface meaning? Particular words he might be able to learn? And learn from?

Lorcan felt a smile grow and lifted his head to glance around him. He was staggered to realise that Dubh Srànnal no longer followed a visible pathway. He had no idea when the horses had left the beaten track to pad directly across the undergrowth, yet Maran's mount moved forward with confidence.

Dubh Srànnal plodded along after the elderly mare, but it did not take long before Lorcan sensed a growing unease beneath his thighs. Dubh Srànnal's tendency to snort and fidget was often annoying, but the horse had an unerringly keen sense of danger – even though Lorcan could see none around him. The tree cover was definitely more dense than before, and a lot less light penetrated down to the forest floor. The saplings and lighter green spaces of the forest fringes had given way to gloomy, sturdy trunks of ancient trees, whose trailing, twisting branches created gnarled brown arches which were all so intertwined that it became almost impossible for Lorcan to pinpoint the mother trunks. Heavy colonisations of shrubs, that were in early leaf, encircled the old trees and made their route a tortuous winding one, Dubh Srànnal having to step cautiously to avoid the snagging roots that lay disguised under the tuggy ferns and recently-greening brackens.

When Maran's horse stopped moving up ahead, Lorcan found himself jolted out of his absorbed and wary monitoring of the sinister surroundings. The druid dismounted, a soft command stilling his mare.

Maran padded the few steps necessary to move back to him, yet Lorcan found he was not the focus of the druid's attention. Maran took a soft clasp of Dubh Srànnal's mane before he sidled his head in to caress the horse with his forehead. Low murmurs then escaped which soothed the beast almost immediately. Under his spread thighs, Lorcan could feel the edginess leave Dubh Srànnal as though the horse was discarding an unseen burden.

Lorcan looked down towards the druid's crown, amazed at the immediate understanding between his fretful horse and the man who was clearly entrancing his mount into a settled state. It took only a few moments, but during that short time it emphasised to Lorcan just how still and quiet the forest was around him. It was as though dusk had swiftly descended, yet he did not think natural nightfall was imminent.

Dubh Srànnal might be now be less fretful but his own deep misgivings returned. He did not at all like the prospect of being in the Sacred Groves when darkness fell properly.

"From this point on, what we do is in the hands of the gods." Maran's declaration did little to jolt Lorcan out of his growing foreboding. "Dismount. From now, we walk in the presence of all of those who dwell in the inner sanctuary."

Nara

Unfortunately for Nara, Afagddu was still on guard duty.

Two blazing reed torches, one on either side of the gate, brought him into prominent view as she trudged up the pathway, her burden now an almost unbearable weight.

The man had the audacity to step into the gap between the posts. He stood with feet apart and with his spear held across his body, barring her way. The derision of earlier was evident in the black eyes that glistened in the flickering torchlight.

"Who comes late to the gates of Tarras?" he challenged.

Nara acknowledged that they would have been the usual words if an unknown person was arriving at the outermost entrance.

She desperately wanted to take to task his disdainful disrespect, yet she was weary of everything. The long trek. Her physical burden. And the draining weight that lodged inside her body.

"You know very well who I am." She hoped her tones conveyed a calmness she definitely did not feel.

The impudent warrior leaned forward and peered at her.

"Oh, I do. The acolyte whom the priestesses have rejected as an abject failure. The healer who would have had me punished by the goddess many a time, though for some strange reason, that did not happen." The warrior sneered, baring his crooked teeth, his breath indicating that a recent

181

supping of an early brew had been drunk. "Why should I allow a useless outcast to enter Tarras? I have no instructions to do that."

Nara stood her ground. Her attempt to not be fazed by this repulsive warrior was waning, though it was her best. When she eventually made Afagddu realise that she would not be drawn into any more conversation, the warrior still had the nerve to add further jibes.

"Of course, a communal servant entering Tarras – to be used by anyone for any reason at all – is another matter entirely." His raucous laughter continued in the same cruel vein. "I believe I just might bring myself to make use of your services, after my turn at guard duty is ended."

When his spear was set upright and he moved aside, Nara wasted no time in moving on through the gate. Refusing to turn around, she felt his eyes raking her back as she slogged on up the slight slope towards the inner gates.

"I have never seen a wood collector bearing a sword like that one at your hip," Afagddu called, not yet done with her. "I wonder if your father knows you still have it? Perhaps I will let him know."

His shouts increased in volume as she doggedly put one foot in front of the other.

"Princess Nara?" The scorn was now dripping from every word. "Will the goddess *Andraste* still give you the power to wield it?" Cutting guffaws rang around the empty ramparts.

Nara tramped on, out of patience with Afagddu in particular, though really with everything. She refused to be baited by him, though actually she had no answer to his question. She had no idea if she had lost the favour of all of the goddesses, even the all-powerful *Brighid* whom she rarely invoked. She certainly hoped not.

Prepared for antagonism at the inner gate, she drew in a long breath and forced herself to keep going. It was not the same guard as earlier, and to her great relief the warrior made no objection to her walking through. He either recognised who she was, in the light provided by the two torch brands that flanked him, or more likely it was because her passage had been allowed at the outer gate. Whatever, the warrior saying nothing was a blessing, and she routinely gave him her thanks as she staggered on. The weight at her shoulder was agonising, but she did not halt till she was on the pathway that lay around the inner wall of the settlement and out of his sight.

Bracing herself against the upright posts, she snatched a brief rest. Her legs trembled with the exertion and her thoughts raced on. Perhaps asking for the help of the goddess *Brighid* truly was a good idea?

"My thanks to you, all-seeing *Brighid*. Soon my hearth will be warmed by these offerings, and with your benevolence I will, too."

Her pleas given, she prepared herself for the last part of her return journey. Along with the light of *Arianrhod* up above her, the occasional torch brand held by someone walking from one place to another gave off enough just enough light for Nara to find her way.

Not far from the dwelling she had been given access to, she watched a tiny child run headlong out of its roundhouse. Intent on playing an amusing game in the dark, it was the only thing in a very long while that had come close to making Nara smile.

But the game was not to last. The little one tripped and fell over, its howls of surprise and fury quite deafening.

Sliding her burden to the ground, Nara moved forward and bent down to help the child.

"Leave him alone!" The child's mother rushed from her roundhouse doorway and whisked the boy out of her hands.

"I was only..." Nara could not continue.

Before turning away, the mother looked terrified that she had dared to touch her infant.

How could a day make so much difference?

What untruths had her father been spreading around his hillfort?

Stooping down to pick up her cloak-wrapped firewood, Nara forced the despair to remain hidden. The woman was now her near neighbour.

Fighting against her feelings, she dumped the burden just outside the door of the dilapidated roundhouse. In the weak light given to her from above, she unwrapped her cloak and separated out the long dried brackens that would make a firebrand, if she had any fats to dip the ends in. Since she did not, she added some twiggy material to the bundle even though she knew they would not make the torch last much longer.

The brackens and heathers that been laid on the interior floor seasons ago were useless for keeping the chill off the beaten earth, and for keeping the doorway draughts at bay, though they were still dry enough to help with fire-lighting. Stepping just inside the dark room, she scooped up some handfuls and took them outside.

Rummaging around the items that were in the sack at her belt, she located her fire-steel and piece of flint. Both had seen much use, but it took little effort to create the sparks needed to light the dried material. In moments her torch brand was lit. She used it to light the inside of the room, setting it into an iron bracket that was, thankfully, still attached near the top of one of the doorway beams.

Looking up towards the conical roof beams, trickles of faint light seeped through where parts of the thatching was worn, some even completely missing. More sighs escaped her lips. Another job for another day. The completion of such mundane tasks, she determined, would surely ease some of her pain.

The contents of her spread cloak were soon dragged inside and a small fire lit in the central hearth. Conserving her wood stock was essential till she could build up more fuel. When the fire took hold, she appreciated the better light to see by. Kneeling down beside it she decided that the fire's edge would definitely be where she would lie wrapped in her meagre cloak for sleep that night. There would be no heather-filled pad on a sleeping platform for her comfort, as she had had at the home of the priestesses.

Glancing around the shadowy room, she was startled by a dark shape that was just along from the doorway. The spring to her feet and the hand at the sword hanging from her belt were instinctive, though she immediately realised she had over-reacted. The shape was not large enough to be a human threat, nor a predatory animal either.

But whatever it was, it had not been there earlier. Wondering what it could be, she padded over to it.

Blankets. Three threadbare, though still usable, covers had been left in a neat pile. The tidiness of the arrangement told Nara that the delivery had been deliberate. A huge sigh escaped, though this was one of relief.

At least one person at Tarras was prepared to go against her father's wishes.

She just wished she knew who it was.

Had the person sneaked in to make the offering an anonymous one while she was out gathering wood? Or was it simply that she had missed talking to the bearer of the gift? It would be encouraging if it were the latter, though she was less certain of that option.

She used two of the three poorly-made pieces of cloth to block the doorway gap, tucking the edges into the wooden frame as best she could. The makeshift door seal would prevent some of the night chill from entering, and would insulate her from an immediate entry by anyone untoward; however, it also blocked out *Arianrhod's* welcome full orb of light.

"Please let the firewood keep me warm...and safe from predators, whether they be animal or human."

Instinctively, she bowed her head in further obeisance but kept it brief, knowing that more tasks awaited her.

While the bird roasted on a stick frame set over the flames, she sipped from her water bag, her head nodding. She forced herself not to slip into exhaustion – physical and spiritual – before she ate her scant meal.

Short sleeps were beset by vivid images, dreams that woke her up. Those moments were used to feed the tiny fire which was hopelessly inadequate in bringing warmth to the bone-chilling room.

Lorcan

The Sacred Groves
Northern Brigantia

Slipping down from Dubh Srànnal, Lorcan swallowed down a feeling of impending doom.

Now, every step he took behind Maran brought an acute awareness of his surroundings that he did not just see, but felt deep in his core. Smells of well-rotted vegetation were usually something he was so used to that he ignored – till now. Each ancient knotted trunk he passed was possessed of a face, some merely inquiring but others malevolent. He barely needed to hold Dubh Srànnal's lead-rein since the horse padded over the twisted roots on the forest floor much more successfully than he did, his tripping feet almost upending him many a time.

"Ssh!" Maran cautioned, raising his arm aloft and halting his mare.

Lorcan stood transfixed, hardly drawing breath. Almost too afraid to listen.

In the stillness around him, there was one sound that penetrated. The tiniest scuffling of claws on bark heralded a downward-scampering animal on a nearby tree. It was the lightest streaks of cream on its bushy tail that drew Lorcan's attention to its outline in the dimness. The reddish-brown animal hesitated, stretching up on its hind legs at the bottom of a long-lived oak. It seemed to stare around before its gaze settled on the druid. Just in front, Lorcan watched Maran whose head dipped silently, just once towards the squirrel.

Turning away from the oak, the animal leapt into action. It hurried ahead, sometimes scurrying up a tree trunk before leaping across to another close by, before it halted, still within sight.

Maran followed.

Lorcan, in turn, trailed after them as the sprightly animal led them even deeper into the ever-darkening, oppressive sheath of foliage. It seemed an age before he detected the faintest glimmering of light up ahead. The flickering of reed torches was a welcome sight, yet they somehow served to make the shadowy faces in the tree trunks even more frightening.

Cernunnos, god of the forest, had many watchful followers.

Maran stopped at the edge of the clearing that was partly illuminated, the torches set into deep hollows in the bark of a few of the trees which lay directly ahead of them. The squirrel paused one more time and stared at Maran. After yet another silent acknowledgement from the druid, the squirrel's tail flicked up once before the creature ascended the oak at a rate that left Lorcan robbed of breath.

"Leave your horse here, Lorcan. It will go nowhere on its own. Come up alongside me, now."

While Lorcan did the druid's bidding a different voice boomed a greeting from the far side, though no one was visible in the shadowy low-lights the brands provided. What they did emphasise were the twisting branches of an impressive time-aged elm. A weighty branch had dipped to the ground and had sprouted a new trunk, in the process forming a natural waist-high platform between the mother-tree and its offspring.

"All is ready for you, Lorcan of Garrigill. Step forward."

The disembodied greeting was personal, but was definitely not one that gave Lorcan any reassurance. Breathing normally became incredibly difficult as he stumbled towards the table alongside Maran.

Without warning, the pathetic bleating of a goat broke the near silence around the area. At almost the same time, Lorcan became aware of one figure emerging from the side of the mature tree trunk while another appeared from somewhere behind it, dragging the protesting animal towards the table.

The figure who trapped Lorcan's full attention was the one who had stepped from the tree-hollow, holding a slighter torch brand. He was well-used to seeing a masked druid officiating at important ceremonies, but the headdress that confronted him was the most awe-inspiring one he had ever laid eyes on. He felt he was facing the god *Cernunnos* himself.

A pair of glittering eyes were the only human like characteristic, since the carved headdress – dripping with ivy and similar greenery – flowed down over the shoulders of the figure and seemed rooted to the very ground beneath him.

A living tree stood before him!

"I am Irala! Chief Druid of these Sacred Groves. Lorcan of Garrigill, your fate will now be revealed."

Lorcan's knees almost failed to hold up his weight. If he had not heard Maran's voice alongside him, he feared he would have succumbed to the overwhelming dread that trapped him.

"Do you have the sacrificial knife ready?" Maran asked the acolyte who had lifted the squirming young goat up onto the natural table, and had begun to pin it down beneath the strong cords that were already criss-crossed over and around the twisted ridges of the levelled-off tree platform.

"It is already there." Irala pointed to the far end of the platform from where he was standing.

Lorcan could not prevent himself from noting the glistening and highly decorative knife hilt that protruded from the wood. The blade-tip set into a crack held the weapon in an upright position.

Once the still screeching and squealing goat was deftly trapped, the cords were tightened fast. Its head reared desperately to free itself till the acolyte took another short cord and fastened the mouth shut, leaving the head lolling slightly over the table-edge next to Irala. The Chief Druid's nod indicated that the acolyte's role was over and that the novice should step to the side.

"Join me here, Maran," Irala instructed before he began to intone.

Feeling even more vulnerable without Maran's presence at his side, Lorcan watched his druid guide step along to the mother-tree trunk. Maran disappeared inside the base, immediately emerging again from the side opening, as Irala had done earlier.

"Step closer to the altar, Lorcan of Garrigill!" Irala ordered. "Observe. It is important that you see what the gods predict for you."

Irala's command left no confusion as to what Lorcan's role now was. He could not say at which point he truly believed that the knife was about to be used to sacrifice the goat and not himself, since he felt close enough to still be the victim.

Maran's chants began as a whisper, but steadily rose in intensity as he stretched past the goat to fist the weapon before withdrawing it from its wooden cradle.

Animal sacrifices were common during purification ceremonies, but the chants Lorcan was hearing were not ones that he was familiar with. When Irala joined in with an even gloomier-pitched-fervour, Lorcan's fragile security dipped again. He was unprepared when the loud intonation abruptly ceased.

With eyes that remained rigidly open, he stared as the knife slashed down to slice open the animal's neck. The acolyte darted alongside Maran and whipped a metal bowl under the goat's neck to collect some of the blood flow, before the low incantation began again.

Once the bowl held sufficient liquid, the novice moved away.

Maran slowly raised the knife again, the incantation volume rising once more. Three swift slits were all it took for Maran to slice away the pelt and reveal the innards.

Lorcan was confused. During previous sacrifices the animal had been laid down to face the diviner. Was he now supposed to extract the entrails himself? His gaze sought Maran's, but the familiar druid solemnly set the blade down near the almost-decapitated head. Then Maran and the acolyte both moved aside for Irala to stand directly in front of the sacrifice.

Lorcan watched in fascination as Irala's hands appeared through the drapes of greenery. Each palm cradled a leaf-shaped flat blade, the flickering lights around the area illuminating the different colours of the metals that were used in the construction of the decorative touches.

Scooping both blades into the peeled-open carcass, Irala extracted a bundle of innards and held them out in front of Lorcan. Another entreaty was made to the gods, before Irala stepped along past the sacrifice and allowed the animal guts to slip free onto the polished surface of the natural table. More intoning of chants that Lorcan had never heard before accompanied the Chief Druid's blade edges as he used them to open up the entrails, to lay bare the interiors.

Lorcan could hardly breathe. Irala seemed to be staring at the signs for too long before Maran was invited to come closer to make his own judgements.

Both heads dipped and soft mutters were emitted, words he was not intended to hear. When both druids eventually raised their heads, they stared at him in sombre silence and Lorcan knew that the time had come.

Was he to fall under the lethal knife?

It seemed far too late to pray to his goddess *Andraste* but his wittering was instinctive.

Irala's voice boomed around the clearing.

"You do well to ask for *Andraste* to guide your life, Lorcan of Garrigill. You surely will have need of her help since the gods show here that your future will not be an easy one."

Lorcan's awkward gulp was probably heard by the druids since it echoed so loudly inside his head.

Irala continued, but his tone became increasingly less solemn and more optimistic. "The gods make no mistakes."

The Chief Druid then pointed to a particular part of the bulbous entrails that lay before him.

"This first chamber has mostly sorted the plugs of food into small lumps to allow them to slip through into the second chamber. Apart from this blockage here..." Irala broke off to point to a particular darkened, knotty lump. "This swelling is not a good future sign for you, but what do you see here? In this second pouch which adjoins the first one?"

Lorcan had no idea what Irala referred to. He shook his head and looked imploringly at Maran, whose expression gave away nothing.

Irala continued, "This second chamber is free of disease, and the evenness of it tells me it works efficiently, probably more than the first chamber, though they are closely interlinked."

Lorcan was confused even more.

Irala's tone warmed. "You are your father's second-born son, are you not?"

Lorcan nodded, "Aye, I am."

Irala bent forward to point to the exposed second chamber. "Tully of Garrigill chose his second son for the task of negotiating. It is a skill that needs tortuous thinking and sifting out of information to be successful. Many critical decisions can remain hidden till sufficient learning teases forth the straightforward paths, the ones that will lead to successful outcomes for all of your Brigante tribespeople."

Maran seemed to be in agreement, so Lorcan managed a strained nod before Irala continued.

"This unblemished part tells me that you, Lorcan of Garrigill, will become the principal spokesperson of the Brigantes – and sooner rather than later. These little remnants, scattered around here, show that your life will be endangered many times when your path crosses with our Roman enemies. But the signs indicate that you will prevail, and your continued sound arbitration will bring balance to your fellow Brigantes. As you can see in this smooth area here."

Irala turned to Maran. "What do you wish to add?"

Lorcan felt the full effect of Maran's solemn focus. "The indications in the entrails point to troubled times ahead, Lorcan. Situations where your decisions will be questioned, even doubted, but you must maintain this steady course that the gods have set you upon."

Lorcan stared at the mangled carcass, unable to see anything apart from bloody entrails, yet was acutely aware of the responsibility that was being placed upon him.

"And then there is this!" Irala again flashed the original sacrificial knife to withdraw the no-longer pulsating heart. Changing to the two flat blades the Chief Druid held the heart over the carcass, directly in front of Lorcan.

Lorcan could see none of Irala's facial expression, but the eyes behind the mask had warmed considerably, to the point they almost twinkled.

"The condition of these opening and closing flaps tell me that your life-blood will flow on in a firstborn son who will surpass even your success, Lorcan of Garrigill." Irala paused when Lorcan's astonished intake of breath interrupted him. "This particular son will suffer many hardships, but will become a Brigante warrior that all Brigantes will be proud of. He will be a leader who will guide his fellow tribesmen in the resistance of our Roman invaders, many times."

Lorcan had difficulty in absorbing the information. Such a son? However, any momentary elation was wiped away when he realised that Irala had paused and was doing some further poking at the entrails, lifting the heart with the flat spoons to set it on its side.

A change of tone indicated what was to come would be less encouraging.

Irala waited till he had Lorcan's full attention on him. "Your firstborn son will never cause you any disquiet, envy or greed, but wariness must sit on your shoulder. There will come a time when a highly powerful and influential man will desire to claim your firstborn as his own son."

Lorcan knew his staring was inane, but could do nothing else. The implications Irala spoke of were too hard to comprehend. "How? How will I know how to prevent this?"

Irala's gaze blazed. "The gods will not leave you bereft."

Lorcan felt his whole insides erupt. The prophecy described meant he would leave the Sacred Groves a hale and hearty man with an incredible task ahead of him.

And perhaps, one day, he might find the mother of his prophesied son? He might even – if the gods favoured him sufficiently – come to love the mother?

His heart lightened, though he was much less sure of that last conclusion.

Nara

Small Mercies
Tarras

Small gifts kept arriving. Always anonymously.

A cloth-wrapped bundle of already milled oats was set inside her door when she was out wood-gathering on the second day of her new life. It was not much, yet just enough for baking flatbread for a few meals, so long as she kept the grain dry.

A medium-sized cauldron was also mysteriously dumped round the back of her dwelling on her second day. The top rim of the iron was worn and breaking up, but the bottom of the metal pot was still intact. The oatmeal she made in it seemed like a gift from the goddess *Brighid*, though she knew that there really was someone at Tarras who was thinking of her welfare.

She left the hillfort early every day to forage for nuts and herbs that were winter-hardy. She hunted down small animals, though her success in that was hard-won. For some unfathomable reason her spear skills were getting poorer by the day, which she put down to a lack of concentration. She refused to think about the trembles that still beset her aim.

Collection of firewood was a constant chore, even on the days when the wind howled and the rain pelted her cheeks. However, the roughly-bound frame that she had made for bearing the wood pile was worth the time it had taken her to fashion it. Now she was able to pull along larger branches that she could split into logs.

The outer guards changed regularly, as did the ones at the inner gates, though most let her in and out with only minimal interaction. When that did occur it remained unpleasant,. Their talk was brash because the men continued to be confused about her solitary residence and total self-reliance.

Direct hostility came from some of the tribespeople whom she encountered as she moved around Tarras. Their frequent snide low comments were wounding –about being a failure in the tribe, and of being worthless to the goddesses. All of the goddesses.

Others attempted to completely ignore her, or they walked in the opposite direction when she came near them. They did not acknowledge her greetings at all, even though she persisted in being cordial to them.

Many of those that she had tended to before her downfall – if that is what it could be called – looked as though they wanted to reply to her inquiries over their health, yet they shied away and maintained silence. All the while those particular people looked around them to see who might be watching them.

Callan's influence was all-persuasive.

Nara put on a brave face every day and refused to creep into a shell, though at night her solitary state almost destroyed her.

Close to a se'nnight into her sentence – for that is what it seemed to her to be – she approached the communal water source within Tarras, her water skin in her hand. A couple of women stood talking at the well. Their wooden buckets stood at their feet, ready to be filled from the natural spring that constantly pooled from below a smooth stone slab, of the reddish variety of rock that was commonly found around Tarras.

Only one of them was a woman she had spoken to in the past. Their conversation stopped abruptly and the familiar woman immediately moved aside, an instinctive gesture giving Nara the former respect that would have been due to her.

"What are you doing?" the second woman hissed. "Let her wait. She has no business here amongst us."

Nara held her breath.

To her surprise, and immense relief, the first woman held her ground. "Princess Nara may well be shunned around here. Nevertheless, nobody in Tarras Hillfort should be condemned to die of thirst."

Seemingly unhappy with the answer given, Nara watched the second woman stride off, her bucket still only half-filled.

"*Diùbhadh!*" The woman's comment was tossed over her shoulder at Nara.

Nara was stunned. She felt the initial heat drain from her cheeks, an icy chill replacing it. No one had ever called her scum before.

"Pay her no heed," said the one who had come to her defence. "She is far too keen to believe everything she hears in this hillfort."

Struck dumb Nara watched the woman point to her water skin.

"Is that the only thing you have to collect water in?"

Nara nodded, immensely glad to share a few amiable words with another person at Tarras who was not calling her unfounded and sickening names. It had been so long since she had spoken that her face felt frozen.

"Aye, but do not concern yourself. I will come and collect my water at a time when I will not be seen."

The woman picked up her bucket that had been filled before Nara arrived and set off along the path, but something prompted the woman to turn back towards her.

"What they are doing to you is not right. Chief Callan makes his declarations daily, yet the people remain confused. You were never really one of us before, and yet we are now told that we will have to accept you as exactly

197

that. You wear the clothes of a man, yet you are now a woman of the tribe. The men are confused over how to treat you, and wonder what the clothes conceal."

Nara was stunned, unable to decide how to respond.

The woman shook her head before she again wheeled away and headed along the path, her final words lingering.

"You should know, though, that the women at Tarras are even more confused by the reactions of their men. They watch their men's gazes tracking you wherever you go."

Nara heard the last words, but had no sight of the woman's lips, or her facial expressions. Only her retreating back. The words persisted in Nara's head, and gave her more than a moment's hesitation before she filled her water skin.

It seemed too much of a coincidence when, the following day, a very ancient wooden bucket was left at the door of her roundhouse. She found it after she came back from her daily foraging, the gift much more public than the previous ones. The carved carrying handles were long since worn away, though a pair of reed ropes would soon sort out that problem. She would only know how much it leaked on filling it, but even small cracks or holes could be given some form of repair.

An unaccustomed small smile broke free. The next time she encountered the woman, whose name she now remembered, she would give thanks.

"In the meantime, *Brighid*, goddess of my dwelling, I give thanks to you. Your benevolent influence spreads to some of your subjects who are not daunted by Callan's cruelty."

As the light of *Arianrhod's* full silver orb of that first night waxed and waned into a second one, Nara was still no further forward with her quest. However, one thing she did understand better was the mood of some of the people at Tarras. Gifts of food continued to arrive, which Nara welcomed heartily. Since it seemed well-known that she went out to hunt for herself – and that she regularly foraged to add to her stocks of herbs, nuts and early-season fruits – the gifts she was given were generally of oats, or emmer wheat stalks, and sometimes already-cooked flatbread. The arrival of a circular quern, the topmost stone with a hole for milling grains, was a donation that made tears rise and fall, even though after the first few days, she had vowed that would never happen again.

Someone must have been watching her sitting outside her doorway, painstakingly attempting to bore a hole in a reasonably flat stone that she had found and dragged back to her dwelling. With her limited tool supply it was a very long arduous labour, and now her problem had just been solved.

When she walked towards the inner gate one morning, well into the second moon of her return, her progress was halted by one of the elders who had spoken to her on that first day.

"Princess Nara. I am glad to intercept you."

Some of the confidence that had returned to her wavered a little at his words, but more so by his grave tones. Nonetheless, acknowledging his status in the tribe, she gave him a cordial greeting and waited to hear his purpose.

"Though you may not believe it, we have been attempting to speak to Callan on your behalf. Not everyone at Tarras shuns you. Is that correct?" the elder asked.

Nara reluctantly agreed, wondering if the anonymous help would now cease, her priestess training forbidding her from mouthing untruths.

The man continued, "It has come to me that you have been asking regularly at the horse pens if you can ride the filly, Eachna. The one that belongs to the priestesses horse stocks. Sadly, I have no positive news on that for you, nor about your other inquiry regarding practising your warrior training skills."

Nara's disgusted huffs reached the man.

"You have the right to be feeling this way, Princess Nara. And what I have to say will probably make you even more disgruntled."

"Can anything you say be much worse than it has been?" Nara was blunt and fixed the man's gaze.

"You are not dead, Nara."

She had to concede that was true. "Aye, but I live a much poorer life than before. If I cannot practise my horse or sword skills, am I allowed to tend some of the sick? I believe the herb-woman is sorely tasked just now."

The elder was the one now to give some deep sighs. "Your father has not specifically forbidden this, yet you must have seen that most of the women of Tarras are not happy with your presence near their dwellings."

Nara knew that was correct, but hated to acknowledge it. "Many of those very women were once delighted to have me tend to their illnesses, and to those of their family. Why must that be so different now?"

Compassion oozed from the old man. "Princess, you have become an ordinary woman of the tribe. That means they regard you as no different from the female neighbour who regularly mates with the man they name as their hearth-husband."

Nara felt her cheeks go from normal to stone cold.

"How can they think I will bed all of their men?" Even as the words were uttered, Nara acknowledged that it was the normal reaction of most of the tribeswomen. If they took a liking to a man, and he showed willingness, mating was as natural and regular as that. Some men of the tribe would not be led astray by beckoning eyes, and stayed faithful to their one woman. However, they were in the minority.

Nara realised her thoughts had strayed. The elder remained patiently waiting by her side.

"The women see me as a threat?" Her words croaked out. "Even though I have never in seasons and seasons long gone given them any reason for doubt?

200

The elder cleared his throat before he looked into the distance, his words sending Nara an even greater chill.

"Your father made it perfectly clear that you are not a priestess acolyte, Nara, and that you are no longer bound by the vows of chastity to the goddess. He declared that any man who might want you can have you. He also made it clear that your duty as an ordinary tribeswoman is to bear children to fill Tarras. But fear of retribution from the goddess still lingers, and makes the men continue to be hesitant."

"But not one single man of the tribe has even looked me in the eye and talked to me about anything, never mind about bedding me."

Nara's attention instantly shifted away from the elder, accepting that her statement was not quite true. She drew her focus back to him, though her tones were still antagonistic. "Apart from a couple of the warriors, who already know that I would never ever choose to take them as my lover."

"That may be so, Princess Nara. But everyone at Tarras gradually becomes accustomed to your continued presence here, even if they are not friendly. Time changes all and better days will come to you." The old man sounded quite certain.

"I did not know you for a seer," Nara quipped.

"That I am not. It is the nature of people to forget, even though many may not forgive so easily. Take care in the coming days as we approach the Beltane Festival rites. You know well – even if you have never experienced it personally – how our tribesmen act before our spring festival of rebirth."

An afterthought seemed to occur to the old man before he turned away from her to leave. "The answer to your question about using your healing skills is that if any tribeswoman is prepared to let you help, you will not be doing anything wrong. But do not let your hopes get high, since it is unlikely. Unless, of course, Callan declares that your period of being ignored is over. He is testing your resilience every new dawn, Nara. And even if he is not impressed by your ability to keep going, then many of the rest of us are. You will have what we all consider normal life, and perhaps a much better than normal family – someday."

Nara felt the heat rise to her cheeks, due to more than embarrassment. Did this elder have some idea of her quest? Could Swatrega, the High Priestess, have mentioned anything about it to the elders? Shaking her head, she decided that could not have happened. What she had to do was a secret between her and the goddess.

Nara continued on to the inner gate, looking directly with unblinkered eyes at the women and men who lingered outside their roundhouses, working at this or that task. Some women were definitely inclined to still scurry away inside their dwelling. Others did present definite hostility, if their man took any notice of her.

Nara realised that the elder was correct.

As the nights passed into new days, the attitude of the bulk of the men at Tarras subtly changed. When she greeted them cordially, their response was a hesitant reply. Some of them even stared at her body, though that was swiftly superseded by a tacit withdrawal when she stared back. When she gained any form of verbal reply, she felt that was progress.

None of them, however, drew her to think of them as a potential lover.

It was late in the day when she lugged the carcass of a small doe behind her. Passing unchallenged through the inner gate, her pull on the thick reed rope was a careful one. She had spent a long time fashioning the twine during the long lonely evenings spent in the roundhouse, which was no longer so dilapidated and empty as when she had first stepped into it. The multitude of routine chores were exhausting, but she had to admit that of late she had been sleeping much less fitfully.

She put that down to her regular obeisance to her favourite goddess *Rhianna* and to her becoming more used to her situation. That did not mean she wanted her lone existence to continue for longer, far from it, but as the elder had said some days before, she was not dead at the order of Callan of Tarras.

She took her accustomed circuitous route back to her roundhouse, which led her well off the pathways that went to her father's roundhouse. She had never seen him at all since the awful confrontation on her first day back at Tarras. And she was perfectly happy never to see him again.

"Princess Nara." The deep voice that came to her from the side of one of the roundhouses was one that she knew well. "How do you fare?"

She relaxed the tension on the rope at her shoulder, and waited for the man to appear on the pathway. "I am well Cearnach, but I thought you had also spurned me. It is so long since we have sparred with swords. I miss our sessions."

"I do, too. Please be aware that I regret the position I have found myself in. I am hidebound by your father's dictates."

Nara's smile was small as she stared at the admirable warrior who stood before her. During her earlier life she had always appreciated his strength, his patience with the younger warriors, and the sharing of his skills with her. Nevertheless, she had not really looked at the fine man that he was. If she did not already know the depth of his character and devotion to Iola, then he would be a good choice of a man to mate with. She liked Cearnach very well, but nothing inside her urged her to take him as a lover. It was dispiriting to find that no sparks beset her when she looked at him, just as it was with every other man who had actually looked at her.

"It does me no good to dwell on what was good before and was not properly appreciated, Cearnach." The smile she gave him was rueful.

Before any reply could be formed, Iola stepped out of the nearby roundhouse. Her young son in tow, she came to join them. Nara knew it was not the dwelling they usually lived in, so they must have been visiting.

Her immediate reaction was to reassure the woman she used to think of as her only friend.

"We are only exchanging a few words," Nara explained.

Iola did not berate her. Neither did she drag Cearnach away and out of her presence, as other women had blatantly done. Iola's smile was a genuine one...and a brave one, since it was so openly seen.

"I despair of how the people of Tarras have been treating you, Nara. They have such short recall of how you have assisted the families at Tarras for many long seasons."

Nara watched in some surprise as Iola reached forward to pat her arm, a familiarity that would not have happened when she was an acolyte.

"You are to be admired for how you have dealt with the treatment meted out to you," Iola declared. "Know that Cearnach and I will always stand by you."

Nara felt foolish and so grateful at the same instant. "*Tapadh leat*," she said. "You are the ones who have been leaving the gifts for me? I should have known it and thanked you sooner."

"Aye. We left you sustenance and other items during those earliest days of your return."

Nara felt muddled. "But the gifts have continued to arrive."

Iola laughed. "Of course, they have. We were not the only ones leaving them for you."

"But that does not make sense..."

Cearnach interrupted. "More than a moon ago, your father sent me out to do more surveillance on the southern coast of Tarras Territory. Since I was already away, Iola went off with our little lad to be with her family whose farm is on our border with the Votadini." Nara watched Cearnach's focus shift to his woman, an unmistakeable glint of happiness brightening his expression. "We only returned today, though we arrived home from different directions."

Nara was the one to grin when she spoke to Iola. "You went to give them your news?" Her glance at Iola's middle was instinctive, to see if there was any evidence of the babe Iola was bearing.

Iola let go of her son's hand and stretched her dress across her still-flat stomach. "Nay, there is not much evidence of it yet. But I am healthy this time, Nara."

Nara's chin dipped, momentarily squashing her beaming smile. "Then may the goddess *Arianrhod* be praised."

Their discussion resumed, about Callan's treatment of Nara.

Iola was insistent. "Should you have succumbed to a natural decline, Nara, also know that we would have defied Callan's orders and would have assisted you more."

Cearnach put his arm around his hearth-wife, a loving and proud claim, though he addressed Nara. "We are both heartily proud of what we have heard about you. You have managed to cope so well this past moon on your own."

Iola agreed, adding even more. "We hear that the attitude of the tribesmen is still resistant, but it is changing. Soon, you will not be so alone." Iola giggled at her declaration, but snuggled even further into Cearnach's embrace. "However, you are well aware that this man in my clutches, is already too occupied to take on another woman."

Nara own giggles were genuine.

She watched Cearnach's head swivel towards her.

"Iola has spoken! However, I will always look upon you as a younger sister, if that sits better with you?"

Nara's laugh was hearty. He had no need to elaborate his meaning.

205

"Nicely put! I believe you, and will be delighted to be classed as such."

There was a lightness in Nara's step during the following couple of days as she went about the business of keeping herself fed and sheltered. She continued to ask if she could ride Eachna, and was repeatedly told that the orders had not changed. Her request to have sword practice with Cearnach was also denied, time after time, but Nara was determined to be persistent.

If her father could be so obstinate, then so could she.

Lorcan

Lorcan knew something was afoot as soon as the farmer threw down the tool he was using and trotted towards him. He and Maran had just skirted an outlying roundhouse that lay a short distance from the defences of the Hillfort of Garrigill.

"I heard earlier that warriors of Rigg of Raeden have been causing trouble!" the man shouted.

The farmer's grin was not out of the ordinary, since Lorcan knew that particular person was inclined to spread gossip.

"Raeden is a Selgovae hillfort, is it not?" Maran asked.

Lorcan nodded. "Aye, it lies just beyond the high hills of our northern territorial border."

When he got up close, the farmer added, "Your brother, Arian, left after dawn with some warriors to confront Rigg. He will soon sort out those Selgovae thieves."

Petty feuds with their Selgovae neighbours had been common enough, but though the farmer liked to pass on rumours, he was rarely in possession of all of the circumstances. This incident was no different, since the farmer could add nothing more, though in typical form, the prying man was keen to find out about Lorcan's reasons for journeying home with the druid.

Not inclined to give the man any information at all, he bid the farmer a courteous enough farewell.

"Have there been other recent disagreements between Tully and Rigg of Raeden?" Maran probed when out of earshot.

Lorcan was careful with his reply. "I have not heard of anything for many seasons. Though, it may be that there have been incidents but none of them important enough for me to learn about during my time spent at home. Visits have been quite rare, of late."

From the expression on Maran's face Lorcan could tell that the druid had some concerns.

"All tribes of the north need to be in accord with each other while this Roman threat of domination looms over everyone. And that includes the Selgovae and all of the others beyond the high hills." Maran's words were indisputable. "The Roman legions were relentless many seasons ago when they decided to subdue the tribes of southern Britannia. None of us are safe if it is in the Roman mind to conquer the north."

"Father? Are you within?"

Lorcan still needed to dip his head to make haste through the wattled entrance tunnel into Tully's roundhouse, even though it was much higher than normal.

"Aye, where else should I be, my son?" Tully's manner was as terse as usual.

Lorcan was used to the tone, but was distressed by the severe pain that was evident in Tully's response.

"The druid, Maran, accompanies me."

Tully's manner continued to be pithy. "You are welcome, as always, Maran, but it seems that my son should remember his manners and allow your entry to reflect your status!"

Lorcan moved aside to allow Maran to approach his father.

"No offence has been taken." Maran reassured the Chief of Garrigill. "We heard there was trouble with the

Selgovae? Lorcan is dutifully concerned, as he should be. What news is there?"

Tully's eyes reflected dismissal. "Ach! It is just another of those petty, trivial raids undertaken by our warring neighbours. One of our outlying farmers sent word that three of his horses had been spirited away during the night. The trail led over the hills to Selgovae territory. Arian has gone to sort it out."

Lorcan swallowed a deep heartache as his father hobbled from the sleeping-stall door jamb that he had been propping himself up on.

"Take a seat, Maran." Tully pointed to the far end of the fireside where he usually sat.

It took even longer for Tully to reach his usual stool than during Lorcan's previous visit home – so painful to watch the hunched-over frame that had once stood tall and erect.

"Carn!" When seated, Tully issued orders, his hollering usual. "Where are you? Come and tend to Lorcan and our guest!"

Though Carn was not in the roundhouse, Lorcan felt no need to find her himself since he knew that the young lad who was playing outside, not far from the entrance tunnel, was tasked to fetch Carn when she was required.

As expected, once he was seated next to Tully, the questions began. Tully was hungry for every detail, wanting to hear about everything that happened during the time Lorcan had spent away from home. Maran was favoured by having fewer inquiries sent his way, since the druid had visited Garrigill relatively recently.

"The Sacred Groves?" Tully whispered, in a tone that was most unlike himself.

Lorcan watched in concern as his father's chest heaved alarmingly for a few moments, Tully's curled old fingers sliding up to massage it.

"But…" Tully continued, "You are here before me and seem…normal?"

The whole episode had to be explained, Lorcan reliving some of his terror when deep in the Sacred Groves. Though subtle headshakes, and flickers in Maran's eyes, made him watchful about how much he could relate of Chief Druid Irala's commanding presence and of the inner sanctuary. Some things, it seemed, were not for sharing – not even with Tully.

When it came time to reveal the prediction of his future, he tripped over the incredulity that still lingered inside him. Suppressing prideful feelings were almost impossible, but he knew that Tully always hated a braggart. As word followed word, he found that his father looked only to Maran for confirmation.

"Chief Druid Irala truly prophesises this future for my son Lorcan?" Tully asked Maran, his expression proud, yet disbelieving.

Lorcan knew his father was not denying the divination, but was stunned that his offspring should be so favoured by the gods.

"The gods have indeed spoken." Maran's head dipped a little, and there was a twinkle in his gaze when it moved from Tully to Lorcan, and then to the young woman who had just entered the roundhouse and stepped along to stand beside the chief.

"You called me?" Carn's question was respectful after the slight lifting of Tully's chin, which indicated she could speak.

"Go and find us all some good food, and not that hound's piddle that you usually feed me, Carn. We have reason to celebrate my son Lorcan's future!" Tully ordered, adding almost as an afterthought, "And send for Brennus and Gabrond to join us now, though it is still early in the day."

Carn – not a slave servant but a young woman of distant kin who saw to his daily needs – was not cowed by Tully's tone. "I should bring the best food, but not a feast?" Her eyebrows questioned as much as the words spoken.

"Exactly that. Now get on with it!" Tully's weak hand-wafting was as dismissive as his gruff words.

Lorcan suppressed the urge to grin at Carn's raised-browed and rolling-eyed expression after she turned away from Tully to execute his orders.

Her mouthed words were for him alone as she passed by, "But I will also bring him some of that nourishing broth that keeps him going."

Lorcan knew fine well from his last visit that Tully could no longer stomach much more than the thin soup she referred to.

Unless a feast was expected to be held in the chief's roundhouse, the cooking of food was done elsewhere and brought when requested. Lorcan's belly grumbled in anticipation of what would soon appear, since Carn was efficient at her tasks.

He listened as Maran kept up an almost one-sided conversation with Tully, about the forthcoming Beltane festival at the king's hillfort, and the one that would be held at Garrigill.

"I will not be able to return again so soon to celebrate Beltane with you, Tully, but I will make sure you have someone suitable to lead the festival rites," Maran declared.

Tully's response was brief, but without the curtness that everyone else supposedly benefitted from.

Lorcan thought the druid looked genuinely regretful. But, since he had nothing useful to add, he was happy to let them discuss it further while a file of tribeswomen entered and left the room in quick succession.

A steaming pot was suspended from the carved iron supports that hung permanently above the burning logs at Tully's end of the hearth, a stretch of the floor that took up the central section of the room, and was bordered by flat stones. The whole fire-stretch was only ever set aflame if there was a large gathering, or if severe weather conditions made the large dwelling unbearably cold. The smell wafting

Lorcan's way indicated a herb-laden broth was contained in the cauldron. Thick or thin – it appealed greatly.

Jugs of small-bere and wooden beakers were set down next to Tully. A large wooden platter, of roasted pig ribs, black-charred bird wings and still-sizzling juicy meat portions, was placed on one of the hot stones at the fire's edge.

Lorcan licked his lips in expectation of when Tully would stop the questioning and would declare they eat. Though, realistically, he knew that was not likely to happen till his brothers were alongside.

A sound at the doorway made him sigh with pleasure. He might not have to wait too long after all.

"What is this news about your future that father claims we must share?"

The speaker, after coming in via the low the roundhouse entryway, was stretching up to a formidable height that none at Garrigill could match. The huge blond-haired man was Tully's fourth son.

Lorcan laughed. "*Ciamar a tha thu,* Brennus? News travels well inside the ramparts of Garrigill."

Brennus padded towards him. "I am well enough, brother."

Lorcan looked at the damp marks that soaked his brother's tunic from neck to hem. "You look as though you have met your match! Who is the warrior who makes the sweat drip from you?"

The playful cuff at his ear was typical.

"Ha! It was five of them, at the same time. Their swords all flew into the air before they knew what was happening," Brennus quipped.

"Sit down, Brennus, and cease your boasting." Tully growled. "Where is Gabrond?"

Brennus answered though Lorcan felt the beam come his way, Tully's grumbling making no difference to his brother's mood.

"Gabrond has been summoned. He is doing the job you allocated to him and is presently checking over Lorcan's horse."

"That should not take him as long as this," Tully groused again.

"How so, father?" This time the grin was for Tully. "That beast, Dubh Srànnal, has the shortest temper and the snappiest nature in the whole of this hillfort…bar one that I could name."

Lorcan appreciated his father's glares, knowing them to be overdramatised. Brennus' good humour was only surpassed by Gabrond's, the third-born brother.

Brennus' allocated task at Garrigill was as overseer of the training of the youngest warriors in combat skills, even though he was still only nineteen summers old. Tully had ensured that all of his sons were battle-trained and excelled at weaponry skills, but Brennus, as tribal champion, was unmatched in sword skills. It was also fortuitous that Brennus had the best temperament for teaching the younger members of the tribe. He commanded their respect by good example and with a degree of humour, rather than by fear.

Brennus edged towards the sleeping-stall that was permanently allocated to him, next to the one that Lorcan's usually used.

"Have I time to pull on a clean tunic?"

Tully's roundhouse was a sizeable one and large enough to accommodate a number of guests, in addition to the two sons who were in the room.

"Aye, but be quick about it." Tully gestured with a mere flick of one finger. "The smell from you will curdle that watery fare that Carn feeds me. And if Gabrond does not get here quickly enough, the rumbling of Lorcan's stomach will knock down the timber supports in here." Tully paused, his breathing causing him to gasp and draw painful breaths, yet it did not stop him from summoning enough strength to yell even further, "Carn!"

213

"I am here, father. Conserve your breath." The newcomer, whose hair was equally as dark as Lorcan's, covered the floor area quickly. "There is no need to call Carn."

"Aye, there is." Tully remonstrated. "It is her place to serve our food."

Gabrond was bid to sit on the far side of Maran, while Brennus was waved down next to Lorcan, as befit their place in the tribal hierarchy. Once Tully was satisfied all were settled, and after Carn had entered the room carrying fresh-baked bread, his intonation to *Brigid* – goddess of the hearth – held none of his usual gruffness.

After Maran and Tully had been given a wooden bowlful of broth, it was Lorcan's turn to receive his.

"*Tapadh leat*, Carn," he said, also accepting a roughly torn off piece of flatbread.

Tully ate his soup much more slowly than the others, but since they moved on to devour the roast meats it was not too obvious.

Gabrond grinned on hearing that Lorcan was prophesied to become a great Brigante spokesperson. "How is that news to us, father? Lorcan has always been the best talker. He was always the most successful at squirming his way out of trouble when we were growing up."

Lorcan watched Gabrond smirk even more at his father's expression. Undaunted by the scowls, Gabrond continued, "And that is why you decided he should be our tribal emissary."

"Watch your manner, Gabrond!" Tully chided. "Respect is given where it is due."

Lorcan felt the warmth in Gabrond's smile as the wooden beaker was raised towards him. "I have long known your expertise, Lorcan. And though I may jest, you also know the strength of my admiration for you. You are doing a task that few of us would be good at, and in truth, few of us want. You bear the need to be away from Garrigill so well when the rest of us have the comfort of our own hearth to warm us at night."

Lorcan felt the nudge at his elbow. Brennus had also raised his beaker and was saluting him. "Gabrond's words are mine, too, my brother. I know you will not fail us, nor the whole of Brigantia."

The small-bere went down with slurps of appreciation, Lorcan glad to see that Tully was smiling when his pains ebbed. He was sure that his father had never favoured one brother over the other, and never would. They had never been allowed to be hateful to each other, and, as far was he was concerned, none had never had any need to be jealous of the other. Tully's love for his sons was shared equally, as had his mother's been when she was alive. Once into adulthood, Lorcan had realised that his father had also been very astute at recognising each son's capabilities and special skills.

A short time later Gabrond's laughter knew no bounds. "You will have a son who will become an even greater Brigante leader than yourself?"

Lorcan could see that Maran enjoyed the brotherly banter that rang around the room. The druid had mellowed sufficiently to be smiling when he confirmed it.

"The gods have willed it will be so."

Gabrond's doubt was a funny thing for Lorcan to see across the fireside. "Aye, indeed. The gods are never wrong, but who could surpass my brother Lorcan?"

Brennus joined in, with more elbow nudging to gain Lorcan's attention. "You have never yet claimed to me that you have sired a son. It seems as though you have a very interesting future ahead of you."

Gabrond guffawed. "Siring the bairn will indeed be a fine time for you, Lorcan. But your usual disdain to take a hearth-wife, and your sour temper regarding that, have ensured that few women at Garrigill favour you to warm their beds these days!"

215

"That is not true!" Lorcan protested. Feeling Maran's inquiring gaze upon him, he repeated it. "I am as popular as the next man!"

Yet, he had to acknowledge that part of what Gabrond said was true.

Nara

A New Future Beckons
Beyond Tarras

There was a subtle difference around Tarras that Nara sensed, though could not put her finger on, when she made her way around the settlement to fill her bucket the next morning.

The atmosphere between little clusters of warriors, when she passed them by, was secretive. They paused their conversations till she went beyond them. If their wary, almost fearful attitude towards her had changed she might have thought they were talking about her, but in her gut she felt that was not true. The warriors seemed tense about something else.

"Where is Cearnach?" Nara asked.

She had taken a route back to her roundhouse that led her past the one inhabited by Iola and Cearnach.

Iola stood just outside the door twisting a cloth between her fists, wringing out the excess water into a small bucket. After straightening up, she pushed back the stray blonde wisps that had loosened from her braids and smiled at Nara. "I had a feeling you would be coming here. There is little that escapes your interest, even given the disgusting treatment you are still experiencing at Tarras."

"So there is something afoot around the settlement?"

"Aye. Cearnach has gone to attend a warrior council with the elders." Iola's tone was matter-of-fact, yet Nara sensed some disquiet behind her eyes.

"But that is wonderful," she said. Her smile was encouraging, though it was to no avail since Iola still looked concerned. "It surely must mean that Callan values him more and more every new day?"

"That is true. The chief does value him much more, and has elevated Cearnach's standing among the elders." There was a weak tweaking at Iola's lips that carried her happiness at that news, but Nara could see that it was overshadowed by something else.

Nara lifted the bucket when she saw Iola was about to empty out the muddy water. She cast it aside, a resulting arc of water attracting the hens that pecked around close to the dwelling.

"Then what causes your concern?" she asked, trailing inside the dwelling after Iola.

"It is not what happens at Tarras that troubles me, but more about the places that Callan has been sending Cearnach to. They are dangerous."

"Dangerous?" Nara was startled by the word used. Iola was not inclined to exaggerate about anything. Neighbouring tribes were not always friendly, and local skirmishes sometimes happened. She had not heard of any recent happenings, but then how would she since hardly anyone had been talking to her?

"I fear for Cearnach's safety."

"'Did he say why they were dangerous?" Nara knew very little about the tribes who lived beyond the territorial borders of the Selgovae.

"Nay. It is not neighbouring tribespeople, and Cearnach is not unduly worried himself," Iola clarified. "The rumours of Roman vessels making landfall closer to the shores of our firth are even more frequent."

"Romans disembarking so far north? Surely they have not?" Nara could scarcely credit it. What she had heard at the nemeton of the priestesses was that the treaties the Brigante tribal groups had made with the Roman Emperor, many seasons ago, continued to halt any expansion of Roman Empire boundaries.

Iola's tutting drew back her attention.

"I am probably worrying about nothing," Iola said. "It is just…what if Callan sends him again, and Cearnach is near the shoreline when Roman ships do land on our Selgovae territory?"

Nara did her best to console Iola, though she had no sway over her father at all, and could see no way of influencing Callan's choice of scout.

Nara trudged back to her roundhouse and used the water to prepare new daub to repair some of the cracks in the circular roundhouse walls. She had packed the worst of the leaks in the conical roof with dried grasses as best she could, though she knew it was not the best season to repair the thatching properly. Late summer would be better for drying off long rye stalks, after the heads had been removed for grain storage.

That night, Nara carefully turned the two small birds she had spitted across her meagre fire to slowly roast, and then rose to pour a wooden beaker of her own-made small-bere. The grains for it had been gifted in a wooden tub, suitable for producing a small quantity of the drink, and what she had mashed together was sufficient to last her a good few nights.

It had been a challenge to make the fermented drink that she had often seen others making with ease. So much so that after she had prepared it, she had ignored it for many nights, unsure of how long to leave it.

She raised her beaker to her roof beams and thanked her ally.

"If it was you who left the grain, Iola, I salute you. I also give eternal thanks to you, *Brighid*, for blessing my hearth."

The first sip of her own brew was sadly distasteful. Persisting, she attempted another, and the more sips she took made it almost palatable.

"Well," she declared to her empty room, her smiles increasing as a delicious warmth flooded her empty belly. "It makes a change from life-giving water."

Nara was feeling less than her best when someone called out her name at her doorway, early the following morning.

She was not asleep, yet she struggled up from her bed of mosses and brackens that was still laid low on the floor, to go out to speak to whoever visited her.

It was the elder that she was more familiar with.

"Callan wishes to see you, Princess Nara."

The words hit her like a blow from a fist to her nose.

"My father? Now? What has changed his mind?" Her question was incredulous.

"That I cannot say, though know that we have asked day after day that you be treated in a way more suitable to your status. Callan has much to occupy him just now; however, he requests your presence."

Grinding her knuckles at her eyes, to remove the stickiness that had collected there overnight, she blinked to make sure she did not imagine the man at her door. Taking a deep breath, she smoothed down the hair at her temples that had escaped her disordered braids into a semblance of neatness. She pushed back the long auburn lengths behind her ears before she nodded her agreement and followed the elder.

Just as she reached the entrance tunnel of her father's large roundhouse, she heard her name called again. Though this time she immediately recognised the speaker and turned around to face him.

Cearnach had run to catch up with her, and from the sounds of his gasps he had seen her from quite a way back.

"Callan summons you, too?" Cearnach could not mask the surprise from his question.

Nara smiled. "Your presence will make this visit so much easier, for me, for sure. Whatever Callan's demands might be of me."

The elder interrupted. "Stand back. Princess Nara should enter first."

Cearnach gestured her to proceed through the well-maintained wicker-sided tunnel. The light brown twinkle at his eye was only for her, as though declaring that he needed no elder telling him to remember her tribal status.

Inside the roundhouse Nara halted at the doorway. She lifted her chin and faced her father, who sat in his usual place at the far end of the firestones. Though it cost her dearly, she held her tongue and waited for him to speak.

Callan took his time, while the elder entered the room behind her and walked up towards him. On the elder's heels, Cearnach came in, but remained alongside her.

A hushed conversation took place between the chief and his elder, too low for Nara to hear properly.

Callan than deigned to direct his words her way. "I am told you have been very resourceful since your return to Tarras. You have been out of the hillfort every day, though you have always come back."

Nara almost laughed. Was her father attempting to converse nicely?

"Did you expect me to run away?" She refused to soften her tone.

"I did not!" Callan's words became more shrill.

Nara decided there was nothing to lose. "Did you expect me to beg you for help?"

Her father's harrumphing reached all the way down the long fireside.

She found she could not leave it at that. "Do you expect me to beg right now?" It was with great difficulty that she maintained her dignity.

Callan's arm waving was imperious. "Come closer. We do not need the whole of Tarras to hear us."

Nara padded forward, wariness sitting on her shoulder since that was not at all normal for Callan. He generally wanted everyone to hear what he had to say.

"That will be far enough." Callan's upraised palm was a deterrent to coming any closer, though the man took his time to speak.

She still stood well short of him and idly wondered if her father was worried she was about launch an attack on him. On thinking about it, she decided that the idea had merit, but taking the old man's life in such a way would not give her sufficient satisfaction. Slow and painful would be better retribution. But they were unworthy thoughts – she was sure the goddess *Dôn* would not approve.

"They tell me you have continued to be been persistent in asking to train with that highly-valued warrior behind you."

To say she was surprised at the way the conversation was turning did not do it justice.

"I would like to do weapon training again with Cearnach, but I hear that you have many tasks for him outside of the hillfort." She maintained his stare, actually finding it easier than she expected. Her blood was roiling inside her, but her father did not need to know that. "Perhaps Cearnach is too busy to help me sharpen my sword skills?"

The jut of Callan's jaw and the lip-curl told her just how much he was reining in his temper.

The elder leaned closer to the chief and whispered. "The horse."

Callan's cheeks tightened as if it was difficult for him to speak. "I remember. I am coming to that."

She watched her father turn to face his elder, his expression more reconciled than aggressive towards the old man at his side, though his next terse words belied it. "You may go, your duty is done for now."

As the elder stepped past her to leave the room, Nara noted the small smile of satisfaction on his face.

"I am hearing that you have pestered the horse handlers every day about riding the nemeton filly." Callan's word drew her attention back to him.

Again, Nara almost laughed. Her father's comments were succinct, wrenched out of him, whereas he generally like to bluster.

"Aye. I have missed riding her."

Callan snorted, and peered down the room. Without turning round, Nara guessed the elder had just gone through the entrance tunnel. Callan impatiently waved his arm at her, a very wide gesture of dismissal. "Move right back near the door. I need to talk to Cearnach."

Her father broke eye contact with her to look directly at Cearnach, who stepped up the room and took her place closer to the chief.

Standing back down near the door, Nara was quite amused that Callan had actually had her so close to his presence for even a few moments of discourse.

"I need to send you on another errand outside the hillfort. Are you willing to have this…" Callan's words hesitated, dripping with disdain. "…so-called daughter of mine accompany you?"

It was obvious to Nara that Callan had omitted the word failed, or something of that nature. The man's expression was wreathed with his usual contempt for her.

Cearnach, she was pleased to see, did not hesitate.

"I will be honoured to ride out with Princess Nara any time you wish."

Callan's head nodded, a sneer curling his lips. "Then you are a more magnanimous warrior than most others around here."

Nara stood there waiting, once again put aside as Callan described what he wanted Cearnach to do.

"You want me to take the big chestnut stallion?" Cearnach asked.

"Aye, that one." Callan said. "It is a Roman horse, a much taller and sleeker breed than our own."

Nara barely listened as Callan went on to brag to Cearnach about which chief from the south had sent him the

223

horse. There was no brevity in his expansive boasting when talking to his warrior.

Nara watched Cearnach's nod of agreement, though she could not see his facial expressions.

"And you believe that Rigg of Raeden Hillfort has a mare that may be of a similar breed?" she heard Cearnach ask.

Nara's thoughts drifted. Was Callan actually going to let her ride away from the hillfort, on Eachna, to do something useful for the tribe? An unaccustomed thrill started deep inside her, and was very difficult to control. She felt her lips widening. But even though she was partly obscured by Cearnach's bulk, she refused to show Callan her pleasure.

"Aye. I know it could be dangerous." Callan was answering, but she only half-listened. "If Roman ships have landed on any part of my coastline, or even further south on the opposite side of the firth on Carvetii sands, their marauding Roman soldiers could be anywhere now."

"Is sending Princess Nara not too dangerous?" Cearnach's question was circumspect.

Callan's nasty laugh jolted Nara from her wanderings.

"Nay, not at all." Her father's smile was dismissive.

To her surprise, Callan beckoned Cearnach to lean in even closer, his words becoming more indistinct. Her father was not whispering, far from it, but was secretive. Though she was not intended to hear the next words, she did.

"At the first signs of Roman trouble, you will abandon her and get yourself to safety," Callan ordered. "Do not put your life at risk. I need you for many more tasks."

"But…" Cearnach got no further, his words cut off by Callan's aggressive tones.

"If she dies it will make no difference to me – her life is entirely expendable. The task I send you on is not an important one, but it will appease the elders who constantly harass me to do something more about her status."

Nara felt the silence in the room deafening.

Cearnach risked Callan's wrath.

"I can do the task myself without taking Princess Nara." Cearnach said.

"Nay you will not. The elders breathe down my neck all day long. They force me to call her a princess of the tribe, so she must learn to make negotiations as one. I am told she knows enough about horses to drive a good bargain with Rigg. The mating of the stallion and his mare will benefit us all."

Nara began to breathe normally again. Had her father just said that she would be going as an emissary for him?

Even if expendable?

Callan was almost done, his last words again for Cearnach. "While you are at Raeden you can find out any new information on what is happening over Rigg's border in Brigante territory. Find out if those *Cèigan Ròmanach* turds are advancing forwards into Brigantia. For myself, I do not care if the Roman shite wipe out every Brigante, but I do care if they are encroaching on my territory!"

Any further words were unimportant to Nara as Callan droned on; nevertheless, they floated into her ears unwanted. Like the wispy loosened feathers of a flapping white owl floating to the ground in a deepening dusk, the words hovered then drifted slowly away.

Her father hated her, yet he also hated almost everyone else as well. She thought, not for the first time, that to live such a bitter life was no life at all.

"The elders will have their way. I would have sent her alone, however, they insist she must have a warrior guard with her. It has to be you, Cearnach, since I know you can be trusted not to strangle her along the way before you get to Raeden." Callan's hateful words rambled on. "Most warriors at Tarras cannot tolerate her anywhere near them – and her haughty attitude withers their desire before it can even kindle. Maybe some less discerning warrior from Raeden will make her want to stay there with him. Then I will never have to be reminded of her, or of her traitorous mother. And the elders will no longer pester me about her every single day."

"I do not think..." Cearnach got no further. Callan's forbidding palm was pushed irritably towards the warrior's face.

A tense silence drew back her attention. It was clear to her that Cearnach was unable to defend her without encountering Callan's wrath heaped upon him. Nothing was going to make a difference to Callan's opinions, so Cearnach was right not to waste his breath. Though she appreciated that he had tried.

Yet again, Callan's arm waved in the direction of the doorway. First at Cearnach, then belatedly at her, as if he had completely forgotten she was still in the room.

Which he probably had.

"Get out. Both of you. Make preparations to leave at daybreak."

Nara turned on her heel and strode out of Callan's roundhouse, her beaming grin so wide it was almost a painful one. Callan could not see it!

She was being given leave to ride out, away from the stifling confines of Tarras Hillfort, for a while.

After a few paces she stopped and waited for Cearnach, who did not look anything like as elated as she felt.

Cearnach's thunderous expression was forbidding, his striding towards her as tense as a taut piece of rope. His words seethed.

"Before you say anything, Nara, my anger is not directed at you. How that man can be so cruel is well beyond me." His voice level dipped. "I will be delighted to go on this...errand with you, but you have my word that I will never abandon you if trouble looms."

Nara was too excited to be bothered with Callan's hateful attitude. Most of her father's words she tucked away and refused to dwell on.

"Please be happy for me, Cearnach. I have been stifled for so long. I am so desperate to get out of Tarras for a reason that is not purely for my own survival. All of my skills have been lacking of late, including the minor joy of riding a horse!"

She did not mention that she was a failure at finding a way of fulfilling Swatrega's prophecy, and that the Beltane Festival time was only a half-moon away.

Cearnach's smile was small, but there was a tiny twinkle of amusement lurking. "Do you now realise that it falls to you to tell my devoted Iola what we are set to do, come the new dawn?"

"Ah." Nara grimaced, though it was really a happy one. "Indeed. Then let us make plans."

On the way to Iola, Nara vowed many times to as many goddesses as she could that she would be a worthy emissary. And, more importantly, that she would really try hard at Raeden to find a suitable man for her quest. She had found nobody she could relate to at Tarras, but surely it would be different at Rigg's hillfort?

Suddenly she was terrified of the new changes.

She stopped so abruptly that Cearnach almost tripped over her, having been walking deferentially just behind her shoulder. Without being really aware of it, her palm covered her palpitating chest.

She had been so unsuccessful since her exit from the nemeton. How would she find the courage that she obviously lacked?

A terrifying new beginning loomed.

How could she do justice to the prophecy that the goddess *Dôn* had laid out for her?

How would she find the warrior who would sire her foretold son?

.

Lorcan

The Prophecy Unravels
Hillfort of Garrigill

Though Maran left just after dawn the following morning,
to fulfil more of his own responsibilities, the druid's
farewell had included a recommendation that Lorcan should
remain at Garrigill till after the Beltane Festival. It was an
instruction that Lorcan was more than happy to adhere to.
He looked forward to remaining among his family for a
while.

He found it was a joy to relax during the following
couple of days. Just being a part of the vibrant and thriving
hillfort of Garrigill bolstered his feelings, and made him feel
more prepared, and more confident, about carrying on with
the task set him by King Venutius.

Accompanying Brennus down to the young warriors'
training field was a pleasure. Sparring with the fledgling
ones was good exercise for him, though Brennus did tend to
hold the upper hand when it came time for the pair of them
to demonstrate.

Gabrond, as overseer of the horse stocks and chief horse
trainer of the younger members of the tribe, was delighted
to spend time showing him the newest horses in the
communal Garrigill herd. Lorcan was glad to see that
Gabrond was never too busy to ensure that the Garrigill
chariots were in prime condition, and that his brother had
not lost his spearman skills. Though it would have been
normal for a prince of the tribe, as Gabrond was, to drive

the two-person chariot, it was good to see that Gabrond still preferred to leave that task to Seamus, who was a better driver than any of Tully's sons.

"That bay fell over there might be a good replacement, if you want a change from Dubh Srànnal." Gabrond pointed to a spirited colt. "He is fully trained but needs firm handling."

"Did you find anything wrong with Dubh Srànnal?" Lorcan asked.

A huge grin split Gabrond's face. "You mean apart from him being a naturally instinctive and wary horse? And, of course, apart from his rider's exploits making him fearful for his continued existence?"

Gabrond ducked the slap that Lorcan sent across his brother's shoulder.

"Nay," Gabrond explained, the mirth receding. "I found nothing beyond the fact that Dubh Srànnal is a creature that likes routine. I cannot find anything physically wrong with him, but it may just be that your constant travelling meant there were too many times that he was irregularly watered, and his feed was perhaps insufficient for his needs. Leave Dubh Srànnal at Garrigill and choose another horse for your next wanderings."

Lorcan considered the suggestion. A horse at Garrigill was generally assigned to a particular warrior, however, no one at Garrigill personally owned any of the stock. Dubh Srànnal sometimes annoyed him with his agitations, but if the horse needed more stable conditions to thrive perhaps it was time to use a different one?

"Tell me more about that colt." Lorcan indicated the one Gabrond had mentioned and walked towards it.

While he was looking over the colt, Lorcan decided that it was perhaps time for him to consider making other changes to his routine.

Contrary to Gabrond's jest about women not favouring him, he was easily swayed later on that evening when he allowed himself to be lured into indulging in a brief coupling with a woman who had been a previous lover. Though not unpleasant an experience, the next morning it meant nothing to him beyond being a brief relaxation and a shedding of his seed.

On the fourth night after Lorcan had returned to Garrigill, nobody seated at the fireside expected the sudden eruption into the room,

Carn's expression was anguished, her fingers covering her mouth. She was clearly horrified.

"I...it is Arian." Unable to say more, Carn burst into floods of tears.

Tully was on alert instantly. "What is amiss, woman? Where is Arian?"

Carn stepped aside as the inert body of Tully's firstborn son was carried through the roundhouse entryway. The two strong bearers laid Arian down, their heads bowed.

Lorcan sped around to the doorway, but did not need anyone to tell him that Arian, whom he had always held in high esteem, was long gone to the otherworld.

Tully's wails were stifled, but the sounds of them cut Lorcan in two.

"How could this happen?" Tully demanded, struggling to rise to see his lifeless son.

One of the bearers lifted his head and dared to give Tully even more awful information. "They were ambushed. Arian and the other five warriors were all slain. Cleuch, the outlying farmer, says it was men from Raeden."

"All of them dead?" Tully's slump back down onto his stool almost keeled him over.

The euphoria over Lorcan's own glowing future was immediately gone – and like a burn in spate, tumbling and frothing over a low riverbed, he felt the deepest fury roil in.

"What makes Cleuch believe they were from Raeden?" he asked.

The second bearer cleared his throat. "Cleuch is waiting outside, though he fears retribution for being the cause of the incident."

From hidden depths, Lorcan watched Tully somehow managing to find the strength to roar. "Cleuch! Do not skulk outside my door. Enter now!"

"Let me question him, father." Lorcan's palm at Tully's shoulder was for support, but was also to urge his father to calm down and to steady him on his stool. The turmoil still churned inside him, but he forced a stillness to his expression while Cleuch was bundled inside.

On Tully's nod, he bid the man to come closer. "Fear not. We will not have your blood stain my father's hearth. Tell us what you know." He was not yet convinced of that, but felt compelled to reassure the quaking farmer.

Cleuch began, his voice fearful. "Arian came some nights ago to find out what had happened to my missing horses."

"Aye, we know that bit. I sent him." Tully had recovered his breath but not any patience. "After that. Tell me about after that!"

"I had sent my lad to track the hoofprints. When Arian arrived at my roundhouse, my Colm had followed the hoof tracks along the riverside and then near the foothills of the fells. The first dwellings to the north – along that path – are those at the Selgovae fort of Raeden, so Arian and his warriors went off to investigate further along the trail. He was preparing to confront Chief Rigg, if that was necessary."

"Was that when my brother was killed?" Lorcan asked.

"Nay!" Cleuch had gathered more of himself together. "Arian and his warriors brought back my three colts the next afternoon."

"Had the beasts just ambled off by themselves?" Lorcan wondered if the man was such a poor farmer that his stock could escape so easily.

"Nay, they had not. The horse tracks led Arian all the way to Raeden, but Rigg claimed no knowledge of any thievery. Arian said the Selgovae chief was furious and immediately ordered a search to find out who was responsible. Rigg, Arian said, had no intention of breaking the peace between his hillfort and Garrigill." Cleuch moved from foot to foot, clearly still uncomfortable in the telling of the now rambling story.

"And I suppose the search took some time?" Lorcan prompted.

"Aye. Dusk was already falling, but Arian said Rigg was most accommodating. Rigg's men found the horses fairly quickly. Arian told me he watched the young warriors who were responsible being punished. It was after that when he, Arian that is, decided to stay the night at Raeden when Rigg issued an invitation. Since the matter had been severely dealt with, Arian agreed."

"Did those traitorous Selgovae murder my son around the fireside?" Tully squeaked, his throat so strained.

"Nay. That is not what happened," Cleuch said.

"Make me understand this," Lorcan urged. "My brother brought back your colts?" He paused till Cleuch's nod confirmed it. "This was after a night spent at Raeden?" Lorcan waited for another nod. "Then how in the name of the god *Taranis* is Arian dead?"

Cleuch looked to Tully before he answered. "Arian brought back my horses the next day, before the golden light of the god *Bel* was overhead. Since the matter was resolved, Arian said he was in no haste to return to you here at Garrigill, and that they would all spend a further night with me. He told me that he wanted to be sure the horses would not be snatched again, but…I do not think that was the real reason."

Lorcan watched the exasperation grow on his father's expression, since what was being said was unlike Arian's usual conduct.

"And then?" Tully prompted.

That Cleuch was visibly sweating and wiping his forehead was making Lorcan's frustration greater.

Cleuch took a deep breath before he continued. "While we were eating, your warriors boasted about Arian's seduction of one of the young women, the previous night, at Rigg's hillfort."

"Well, that is neither here nor there!"

Tully's interruption gave Cleuch time to swipe his hand across his upper lip hair. "She is a princess of Raeden, one of Rigg's daughters."

Lorcan watched his father scowl, the downturned lips meaning Tully harboured a great aversion to the ongoings mentioned.

"I may not like that he lay with this Selgovae princess, but Arian's tribal status was as good as hers. All of my sons are named princes when occasion requires their rank to be recognised. This princess must have made Arian know she desired him," Tully reasoned.

Cleuch made an awkward clearing of his throat. "One of your warriors jested that Arian was very taken with her, though another said the opposite: that Arian had given the woman no choice and had been overly persuasive."

Tully's frustration mounted even further. "None of this explains why my son and his warriors are dead!"

Lorcan forced himself to keep his tone even. The story was too convoluted. "Are you saying that the sons of Rigg came to your roundhouse to challenge Arian? Because of his dallying with this Selgovae princess?"

"Aye, it was because of the Selgovae woman, but they did not battle on my land!" Cleuch protested.

Lorcan glared at Cleuch to make him continue.

"When he had finished eating, Arian left my roundhouse to check the horses – so he said – but when he did not return after a while, your warriors went to see what was happening. My horses were there but not your son."

Lorcan paced around the farmer. He slid his hand up to his neck to wrest free the thin torc that was almost strangling him. "Go on," he prompted again, as he slid the metal through his cupped palm.

Cleuch looked at the floor rushes, unable to meet his gaze. "Arian had arranged to meet the woman again that afternoon, though none of your warriors knew of this tryst when they left my roundhouse to find him."

"And how do YOU know all of this?" Lorcan was losing patience, even more than Tully.

"When none of them returned that night, I knew something must have happened. Come today's dawn we left to search. My son and I found Arian and the others on the foothills of the fens that separate Raeden from my farmland."

"Just inside Selgovae Raeden territory?" Lorcan asked.

"Aye. One of your men was still alive. Arian had met the Selgovae woman at the far end of the gulley near the Maiden Way, on the track that skirts around those foothills. It was after he had bid her farewell that they were ambushed. They were almost back out of the gorge when the Raeden warrior band attacked them."

"Fetch the warrior here! I will speak with him!" Lorcan demanded.

Cleuch shook his head. "He did not survive the journey back here."

Lorcan stopped directly in front of Cleuch, his teeth clenched so hard he feared he would not be heard properly.

"Did this man give you any more information?"

Cleuch nodded. "The woman's brothers claimed she had been forced to mate with Arian, but that cannot have been true. And they were angry about the punishment meted out to the young firebrands who had stolen my horses. The blood on the ground, I am sure, was only from our warriors. The attack must have come as a great surprise and they must also have been vastly outnumbered."

A rage such as he had never felt before descended on Lorcan. His brother had been slain over a Selgovae princess? A woman he was now sure had not been resisting his older brother? A woman who had probably had some knowledge of the attack, and had done nothing to stop it?

She was a treacherous, deceitful and insincere Selgovae princess!

In the name of all the gods, how could this happen? The gods had promised him a glorious future, yet they had just claimed the life of his older brother?

As Lorcan paced around the roundhouse, he vowed that his work for King Venutius would have to wait a while longer. Retribution against the Selgovae must come first.

The death of his brother must be avenged.

He eventually lifted his head in front of his father and declared,

"I vow I will claim a life for a life!"

~~~

Dear reader, you have had the opportunity to meet Lorcan and Nara, though they have not yet met each other. You'll find that their mutual story begins at the beginning of *The Beltane Choice*, Book 1 of the Celtic Fervour Series.

Please read on to the end of this book to read an excerpt from the beginning of *The Beltane Choice*.

Glossary

Throughout this Prequel novel, I have used *italics* for the names of gods and goddesses, and Gaelic phrases.

In Lorcan's story:

Roman Emperors mentioned during the Year of the four Emperors AD 69
Nero, Galba, Otho, Vitellius, Vespasian

Roman Governors of Britain
Bolanus 69-71
Cerialis 71-74

Commander Legio XX
Agricola

Roman legions/ units mentioned
Ala Augusta Gallorum (cavalry)
Legio IX
Legio XX
Legio II Augustus

Gods
Ambisagrus (am-bi-sag-rus as in bus) –weather
Bel (bell) – sun
Cernunnos (ker-nun-oss) – forest god/woods
Ialonus (eye-ah-lone-us) – local god of the meadows (Cumbria)
Manaan (man-ay as in hay-an) – sea
Taranis (tah-ran-eesh) – thunder
Goddesses
Andraste (an-drast-eh) – war goddess
Belisima (bel -iss-im-a) – ford/river goddess
Brighid (bride-ee) – hearth

Cerridwen (ker-id-wen)– night dark
Epona – horses
Suala – river goddess/spring/ waterfall

Lorcan's Horse
Dubh Srànnal – [black snorter]

Festivals
Imbolc (im-balk)– 1st Feb
Beltane (bel-tay-n)– 1st May
Lughnasadh (loo-na-sa-t)– 1st Aug
Samhain (sew-vah-n) – 31st Oct/1st Nov

Gaelic used:
coileach-fraoich – heather birds, grouse
Cèigan Ròmanach! – Roman turds!
Ciamar a tha thu? – How are you?
Diùbhadh! – scum!
Dè thu a dèanamh?– What are you doing?
Tapadh leat – Thank you

Tribes
Brigantes
Carvetii
Cornovii
Dobunni
Ordovices
Parisii
Setantii

Locations in Lorcan's Story
Blennerhasset – Roman camp/fort
Brigantia – Territory of the Brigante Federation of Tribes
Garrigill – Lorcan's tribal hillfort
Londinium – Roman fortress
Mona – island home of the druids (Anglesey)

River Swale – mentioned and important in Book 1
Stanwick – site of settlement thought to have been the headquarters of either Queen Cartimandua, or King Venutius, or both
Viroconium Cornoviorum – site of a Roman Fortress at Wroxeter

In Nara's Story:

Gods
Ambisagrus ((am-bi-sag-rus as in bus) – weather god
Bel (bell) – sun god
Taranis (tah-ran-eesh) – sky/ thunder god
Goddesses
Arianrhod (ar-ee-an-rh-i*d*) – fertility goddess and daughter of *Dôn*
Brighid (bride-ee) – all-powerful goddess
Cailleach (kale-yee-a-ch) – old hag of winter, crone of winter and guardian of the Otherworld
Dôn (daw-en) – main goddess of the nemeton on the Islet of the Priestesses
Rhianna (ree-an-ah) – goddess of the hearth

Festivals
Imbolc (im-balk) – 1st Feb
Beltane (bell-tay-n) – 1st May
Lughnasadh (loo-nah-sa-t) – 1st Aug
Samhain (sew-vah-n) – 31st Oct/1st Nov

Gaelic used:
Cèigan Ròmanach! – Roman turds!
Ciamar a tha thu? – How are you?
Diùbhadh! – scum*!*
Tapadh leat – Thank you

Tribes
Brigante
Carvetii
Novantae
Selgovae
Votadini

Locations in Nara's Story

Islet of the Priestesses of the goddess *Dôn*
Hillfort of Tarras
Outlying farm on Selgovae/Novantae border

Historical Context

Providing an accurate historical context for late first century Roman Britain isn't an easy task. Prime Sources are extremely scant, and the one that is generally regarded as the best is the writing of the Roman writer, Publius Cornelius Tacitus. What I tend to rely on as a deeply-interested 'hobby-historian', is a combination of the 'facts' as described by Tacitus and corroboration that is provided from archaeological interpretations. It's extremely useful that there have been many new advances in archaeological excavation techniques during the last couple of decades.

What follows mainly mirrors what is written by Tacitus in his works named the *Annales*, *Historaie* and in his writing *De Vita et Moribus Iulii Agricolae*, the latter being an almost eulogy on the life of Tacitus' father-in-law – Iulius Agricola – who was given the credit for much of the early Roman occupation of northern Britain.

After Emperor Claudius invaded Britannia in AD (CE) 43, the Ancient Roman focus was on subduing the southernmost Britannic tribes, and absorbing them into the Roman Empire. Their method of setting up Client Kingdoms, where possible, was continued which meant swathes of land were largely administered by the local ruler, who complied with Roman laws and was directly answerable to the Roman Administration in Britannia. Many of these Client Rulers encouraged the development of Roman culture and customs, and compelled their subjects to adopt Roman habits into their daily lives. In turn for paying taxes to Rome, in goods and in man power for the armies, the ruler was given assurance of help from Rome's armies should they be involved in confrontation with a rival local tribe. It's likely that some tribes were also given an additional sweetener, perhaps in the form of a direct bribe.

Queen Cartimandua of the Brigantes Federation is mentioned as becoming wealthier during the two decades following the invasion of Emperor Claudius, perhaps due to inducements in the form of gold, silver or some other precious commodity like iron. So long as the Client tribe (as in the case of Cartimandua) instigated no major aggression against Rome, it is thought that they continued to, more or less, carry on with their normal daily traditions and lifestyles.

Queen Cartimandua of the Brigantes Federation became a Client Queen of Rome in approximately AD 50. During the period from AD 50 to the late AD 60s, Cartimandua's dealings with Rome meant her Brigante territory did not seem to suffer the large-scale invasion, and often destruction, that befell many other resisting tribes. So, it can be said that, in a way, her dealings with Rome brought a sense of security to her people for many years.

However, this situation came to an end when her relationship with her consort, King Venutius, broke down. When Cartimandua divorced Venutius (and declared a marriage with Vellocatus, Venutius' standard bearer) civil war ensued across Brigantia, though Cartimandua still appears to have had the official backing of Rome.

Following the death of Emperor Nero in AD 68, by suicide or assisted suicide, civil war also ensued across the Roman Empire. Consensus amongst the Senate, and the ruling elite in Rome, about the next ruler could not be found. Within the legions, including those stationed in Britannia, there was volatile disagreement over who should step into the role of Emperor of Rome. The Year of the Four Emperors (AD 68/69) saw a quick succession of short-term military rule of the Roman Empire – first Galba, Otho, and then Vitellius who lasted eight months. Next to be proclaimed emperor was Vespasian in AD 69, who ruled for the next decade. The turmoil caused by the series of men to become the Roman Emperor in AD 68/69 sent ripples within the Roman Army in Britannia, and this unrest, in part, possibly enabled King Venutius to rise up and confront Cartimandua's loyal warriors. It's believed that many of the Brigantes fighting alongside Venutius, rebelling against Roman domination, were lost in skirmishes and battles fought against Cartimandua, who was still, perhaps nominally, backed by Roman troops. The Roman troops may not have entered the battle alongside Cartimandua, but it may be that they organised her withdrawal from the battlefield. Such details are unclear.

In AD 69, Cartimandua disappears from the scant records. It's not known whether she died during a conflict with Venutius; or if she fled to Rome after being rescued by the Roman Governor Bolanus, as is alluded to by the Roman writer, Tacitus. Perhaps some other scenario occurred regarding Cartimandua, and will be revealed in the future.

King Venutius appears to have taken up the reins of rule in Brigantia in approximately AD 69, and must then have had the task of ensuring he had the allegiance of all of the Brigantes. The 'Brigantes' are thought to have been a Federation of individual tribes inhabiting the land mass in northern England that is now referred to as Yorkshire, Cumbria and Northumberland.

Vettius Bolanus became the Roman Governor of Britannia in AD 69, followed by Quintus Petillius Cerialis in AD 71, and Sextus Julius Frontinus c. AD 73/74. It's not clear yet which of those governors were responsible for invading and initially settling troops on parts of Brigantia – even on a temporary basis. Cerialis was nominally given credit for some campaign successes in northern Britannia, but the most recent archaeological records appear to indicate that Bolanus may have had more incursions in the north than he has formerly been credited with. It now also seems that those early incursions of Bolanus may have included the territory that is now southern Scotland.

It is into this historical backdrop that Lorcan of Garrigill – a Brigante, and Nara of Tarras – of the Selgovae find themselves in **Before Beltane**.

Author's Note

Though I always make a conscious effort to make my settings as credible as possible, it has to be said that this is my fictional interpretation of what life may have been like amongst the tribes of northern Late Iron Age Britain.

The explanations which follow are relevant to this edition of **Before Beltane**, which is a Prequel to the Celtic Fervour Series, but they are also relevant to the books throughout the series.

As mentioned in the Historical Context, there are very few written sources to research for first century AD (CE) northern Roman Britain, and what I've found to date can only be used in a broad context. I believe there will always be ongoing views of the work of Cornelius Tacitus, the map maker Ptolemy, and fellow Roman writers of those early centuries AD—as in how much of the writing is hyped up propaganda, and how much can be considered to be realistic.

During the writing of my *Celtic Fervour Series*, I've continued to research Iron Age Roman Britain. I've acquired new knowledge over the years about the circumstances of late first century northern Roman Britain, and some of my earlier conceptions (I wrote *The Beltane Choice* in 2011) have become modified slightly as I write this note in 2022.

Why would this be so?
Archaeology is an organic process. My reliance on particular archaeological findings has to be judiciously used since they, too, are an interpretation of what might have been. Some archaeological interpretations of the 1970s are slightly different from the current beliefs in 2022, often due

to more sophisticated scientific analysis being used, which can alter dates estimated from earlier excavations. In terms of the Ancient Roman campaigns of northern Roman Britain, it may become a new question about which Governor of Britannia was in place, or which General commanded the armies during the slightly 'altered' time of occupation.

Thus, interpretations of what happened when, in northern Roman Britain are constantly fluid. I find that this variability is one of the most fascinating aspects of writing about a time and place that is essentially in a pre-historic context. Keeping up with the newest findings about the conquest of northern Roman Britain is a time-consuming passion.

The decision to use the word 'CELTIC' in the title of my series has been made with great deliberation. During the past few years, I've avoided arguments with people who believe that all of the Iron Age tribes of Britannia should be named Britons – and that the word Celts should only be used for the Iron Age tribes of Central Europe. The use of the word Celt to describe the cultural aspects of a broad range of people is something still being debated in the halls of academia, and exhibitions have been mounted to try to display an answer to 'Who Were the Celts?'

Archaeological interpretations can demonstrate that the tribes of northern Britannia had similar patterns of living to other groups of people loosely named Celtic, for example as in evidence of roundhouse dwelling. Other findings of horse 'helmet' decoration, or the remains of a carnyx found in northern Scotland indicate a (possible) similar culture to other parts of Europe. Therefore, I've used the word Celt loosely, mainly to distinguish between an indigenous Iron Age tribal character and an Ancient Roman in my novels.

And when used in dialogue, indigenous Iron Age Briton is so much more long-winded, than Celt!

Another aspect I deliberated over is my use of the Ancient Roman names for the tribes of Britannia. The indigenous tribes left no definitive record of what they termed themselves. I could have invented new tribal names for my fiction, but by using those as given down to us by the map maker, Claudius Ptolemaeus (making maps approximately AD 120-150) my hope is that it's easier for my readers to imagine the geography involved in the tribal territories that I've described.

I've also deliberately chosen contemporary place names in northern England, and in Scotland, because I like the cadences of them, and because they lie close to places thought to be Iron Age settlements. Whorl was deliberately chosen as the battle site at the end of Book 1, *The Beltane Choice,* because the topography of the hilly area at Whorlton would have been suitable for battle chariots, and for ranked layers of Celtic warriors on the slope above the plain. It's also relatively close to Stanwick which is thought to have been a settlement of either King Venutius of the Brigantes, or of Queen Cartimandua.

Character names are also chosen with due care because I take great delight in finding a name that fits my characters, and are ones which I hope also give a sense of relevance and authenticity. Again, as a response to a reader asking for a way to pronounce the character names, I've added a phonetic-style addition in the Characters section at the beginning of the book. My own knowledge of Scottish Gaelic is very scant, and my knowledge of Old Welsh is non-existent. It was only when I was well-into the writing of the series that I discovered the most recent etymological theories point to the language used in northern Britain, during the era I write about, as being a common Celtic language thought to have resembled Old Welsh more than the current form of Scots Gaelic. (P versus Q but I won't get into those intricacies here) By the time I made this discovery, I had already been adding some Scots Gaelic to give a flavour of the era, and I deemed it too late to change it to old Welsh. Please forgive any inconsistency regarding this use. As I would say in the current Scots language – 'Yer aye learnin'– and I am definitely always learning something new every day!

The first edition of Book 1, *The Beltane Choice,* which was published in 2012 had no maps with locations or tribal names. It was as a result of a comment made in a customer review in 2012, that maps were made for the subsequent books. This newest **Before Beltane** Prequel addition to the Celtic Fervour Series has relevant maps added to make it easier for the reader to envisage the geographical areas my characters inhabit.

I'm completely fascinated by the Roman Iron Age Britain era and hope you will be, too, as you meet Lorcan and Nara in **Before Beltane**.

About the Author

Nancy Jardine's passion for all aspects of history continues, the Ancient Roman invasion of northern Britain having become a deep study. Those barbarians (according to the Romans) who lived beyond the Roman Empire's boundaries left secrets that have still to be unravelled. Thankfully, there are hundreds of archaeological projects being undertaken and it's so welcome that the findings are shared with the general public very quickly. Since she became a devotee of the academia.org site Nancy now has far more academic archaeological papers to read than she can cope with! It's worth mentioning here that there are so many theories about what Roman Britain was like but…we don't really know and that's part of the fun, and the slog to find out.

When not researching, or engaged in various writing and marketing tasks, Nancy is a fair-weather gardener. The 'castle' country of Aberdeenshire, Scotland, is a fabulous place to live—there are thousands of years of history on the doorstep which she delights in. This can be through physical visits, when possible, and also via the internet.

A member of an Aberdeenshire Crafters group, she takes the opportunity to sign and sell paperback versions of her novels at various local venues. She relishes the meetings with new readers and with customers who have become regular buyers of her work. This direct contact is also a fabulous way to gain bookings for the author presentations she gives to various groups across Aberdeenshire. Some smaller groups prefer to learn about her novels, though many larger groups book her for professional presentations on Roman Scotland.

An ex-primary teacher her pen is now used differently.

Since retiring in 2011, she now has ten novels published. Six are in her historical Celtic Fervour Series; one is a historical 'teen' time travel; and three are contemporary mysteries – two of which have ancestral based plots. Some historical short stories await a permanent publishing home. She's currently 'sort-of' taking a break from writing about the Roman Scotland era and is working on a family saga which begins in Victorian Scotland, though short story additions to the Celtic Fervour Series are on the planning chart.

Nancy is a member of the Historical Novel Society; The Romantic Novelists Association; The Scottish Association of Writers, The Federation of Writers Scotland and the Alliance of Independent Authors. A quick 'google' search will take you to many other places she is associated with via the internet.

Nominations

After Whorl: Bran Reborn, Book 2 of the Celtic Fervour Series, was accepted for THE WALTER SCOTT PRIZE FOR HISTORICAL FICTION 2014.

The Taexali Game, a time travel novel set in Roman 'Aberdeenshire' AD 210 achieved Second Place for Best Self-Published Book in the SCOTTISH ASSOCIATION OF WRITERS – Barbara Hammond Competition 2017. It achieved an *indieBRAG* Medallion status, January 2018.

Topaz Eyes, an ancestral based mystery thriller, was a Finalist for THE PEOPLE'S BOOK PRIZE FICTION 2014

Books in the *Celtic Fervour Series* have Discovered Diamond Status and other noteworthy Book Club awards.

Novels by Nancy Jardine

Historical Fiction
Celtic Fervour Series
Book 0 A Prequel **Before Beltane**
Book 1 *The Beltane Choice*
Book 2 *After Whorl: Bran Reborn*
Book 3 *After Whorl: Donning Double Cloaks*
Book 4 *Agricola's Bane*
Book 5 *Beathan The Brigante*
Contemporary Novels
Ancestral/ family tree based Mystery/Thrillers:
Monogamy Twist
Topaz Eyes
Romantic Comedy Mystery
Take Me Now
Time Travel Historical Adventure
Set in Roman Scotland AD 210, *The Taexali Game* is suitable
from an early teens through adult readership.

Reader appreciation of the Celtic Fervour Series:

*"I can't wait to dive in and continue with this captivating tale of
life during the Roman occupation."*
 Book 1 *The Beltane Choice*

'Ms Jardine is an accomplished writer ... a most satisfying read!'
Book 2 *After Whorl Bran Reborn*

*"If you enjoy Historical Fiction or you're curious about the
genre, I highly recommend this series."*
Book 3 *After Whorl: Donning Double Cloaks*

*"The descriptions are wonderful as usual, letting you really
immerse yourself in the story and imagine what it was like being
there."* Book 4 *Agricola's Bane*

*"This book was an enjoyable read as they all were. I enjoyed the
whole series."* Book 5 *Beathan The Brigante*

Ocelot Press

Ocelot Press

Thank you for reading this Ocelot Press book. If you enjoyed it, we'd greatly appreciate it if you could take a moment to write a short review on the website where you bought the book e.g. Amazon, and/or on Goodreads, You can email the author and/ or recommend the book to a friend. Sharing your thoughts helps other readers to choose good books, and authors to keep writing.

You might like to try books by other Ocelot Press authors. We cover a range of genres, with a focus on historical fiction (including historical mystery and paranormal), romance and fantasy. To find out more, please don't hesitate to connect with us on:

Website: https://ocelotpress.wordpress.com
Email: ocelotpress@gmail.com
Twitter: @OcelotPress
Facebook: https://www.facebook.com/OcelotPress/

The 'mutual' story of Nara and Lorcan continues in *The Beltane Choice*, Book 1 of the *Celtic Fervour Series*.

It begins like this...

AD 71, Ford of Sequanna – Selgovae territory

Nettle-sharp tears of frustration reduced Nara's vision. She pressed her hand under her ribs to dull the pain and ploughed her way through the pitted undergrowth. Wrenching aside jagged gorse bushes dotted with yellow blossoms, the thorns scraped blood-red lines on her arms.

"You have my spear and my blade, but you will not have my life."

Gruelling breaths were snatched between curses. A glance over her shoulder caught the beast smashing on behind, scattering leaves and pinging twigs and branches. The folds of its hairy flesh quivered, its trotters pounding the earth, thudding minor tremors.

She scanned around for refuge. In the past, she had felled a boar, though never such a hefty beast, and this one exuded such vigour it would pursue her till she dropped if she could not climb out of its reach. The slight beech up ahead must suffice since the trees in the bush-strewn thicket were limited, all thin-limbed.

At the bole of the tree she wheeled round, a glint behind the bobbing animal snaring her attention. Her spear lay there on the ground, torn out of the boar's hide in its relentless drive through the spiny broom. Only paces away, yet how to reach it? The trickle of blood seeping from the animal's wound made her cringe, her long knife still embedded in the beast's flank. She had no hope of using that blade a second time, and fingering the hilt of the small knife tucked in her waist pouch was futile. Though sharp enough, it was useless against the tough flesh of the beast lumbering closer.

"Your tusks will not be my future."

Her hiss was stubborn. She may have been expunged from the *nemeton*, the island home of the priestesses where she'd lived for many years and now discarded like a broken loom, but there was still a life for her.

"Nara of Tarras entreats you, *Rhianna*. I put myself in your hands."

Startled by her outburst, the boar skittered to a halt, giving her time to use the flat of her foot. A mighty leap made, she grabbed the lowest branch, her legs swinging upwards as the frenzied boar thudded against the bark. Knees encircling the bough, she edged her way along to the trunk, her juddering thigh muscles clamping around it. Climbing higher, she selected the strongest join of bole and branch where she rested astride, hugging it tight. Exultant relief followed, her heartbeats ceased their frantic pump, and her breathing settled despite the boar continuing to hurtle its mass against the base.

"Sweet goddess, *Rhianna*, I thank you." Her words whiffed against bark. Safety was not assured but her bodyguard, Cearnach, would no doubt come to her aid before the animal uprooted the tree.

A smirk broke free in spite of her predicament. Life had changed drastically these last two moons, but the changes did not all have to be bad. Perhaps a handsome stranger would rescue her from the fearsome creature of the forest? Her grin widened. It was due time something exciting happened.

"Cearnach? Where are you?"

Impatience mounted, the pummelling below continued, her repeated cry ringing out over the copse while the beast yowled and squealed, its energy infinite. Small disturbed creatures scurried off, the fluttering and cheeping bird cry alerting the forest floor to danger.

"Woman! Be ready."

***

Printed in Great Britain
by Amazon

23892215R00149